Deep in the night,  again, the large presence an amalgamation of earth itself—fire, water, air, son. They strolled along a beach together. No, they did not stroll; they floated, skimming the water where the foam-inflected sea met the sand, a moonless night enveloping them in a forever darkness. Pauline exceeded the confines of her body as the boundaries defining day and night, space and time, fell away.

Come home, he said.

My home is with Grey.

Your forever home is with me.

Chaitanya hummed, low and deep, the warm notes filling her in places she didn't realize were empty.

In the morning light, as her eyes flickered open, Pauline was briefly disoriented, her dreams bleeding into her waking life. Who is she—was she—with?

I am torn asunder.

Grey climbed on top of her and even as he grew hard, she could not stop thinking of Chaitanya.

Praise for *The Nighthawkers*...

"A swashbuckling adventure with fantasy, love, and, at its heart, a search for peace and truth. Absorbing and fascinating."

—Leonie Mack, Author of *Italy Ever After*

The Nighthawkers

by

Amy L. Bernstein

The Nighthawkers

Cover Art by *The Wild Rose Press, Inc.*

The Wild Rose Press, Inc.
PO Box 708
Adams Basin, NY 14410-0708
Visit us at www.thewildrosepress.com

Publishing History
First Edition, 2022
Trade Paperback ISBN 978-1-5092-4227-6
Digital ISBN 978-1-5092-4228-3

Published in the United States of America

Dedication

This story is dedicated to everyone who dreams of crashing through the gates of limitation, to emerge into the land of the all-powerful self.

PART 1: EARTHBOUND

Chapter 1

An all too familiar feeling stole over Pauline Marsh. Seated onstage in full view of her Carthage University peers, she went all weak, a useless pile of wet noodles.

The *pulse*. Again.

Damn! I wish this thing came with trigger warnings—or left me the hell alone!

The first stage of the *pulse* descended as it had for the last dozen years, beginning when Pauline was eleven. First, a light fluttering, like moth wings, beat against the inside of her belly. She stared into the stage lights, hoping that burning eyes would distract from the onslaught headed her way. Blinded by the glare, Pauline nevertheless knew exactly what to expect. Footsteps rang across the stage from the podium. Dean India Nojes, the living legend who'd run Carthage's graduate archaeology program with an iron fist for decades, came toward her, bedecked in a black cap and gown draped with tassels, cradling a gaudy green-and-gold statue.

The moths beat rapidly as stage two of the *pulse* began its assault. Tingly, prickly skin followed by waves of electric shocks shivered along Pauline's arms and legs. The hair at the nape of her neck stood on end. She swallowed hard to control panting breaths as bolts of lightning charged up to shoot out the top of her head.

Keep it together, Marsh. The torture will end soon enough. It always does. At least the rest of them have no clue.

With every muscle clenched in an effort to keep still, Pauline peered through narrowed eyes as the dean, a fuzzy two feet away, began her speech. "It is my great honor to announce that this year's recipient of our university's most prestigious award, the Boniface Prize for outstanding scholarship in the field of archaeology, goes to..."

In stage three, Pauline bit her tongue. The hardwood floor fell away beneath her as she floated up toward the auditorium's rafters, untethered, on the verge of departing the only world she'd ever known and becoming something else. Reality and illusion collided, as Pauline looked down on the tops of heads while, at the same time, she hadn't moved an inch. The dean continued speaking.

"Pauline Marsh!"

Tepid applause. The dean held out the statue, waiting for Pauline to grasp it. She hesitated, then took it. What choice did she have? Pauline forced her gaze upon the audience of her peers—at eye level now. Scores of bored faces, most turned down toward the phones in their laps.

"In all my years at Carthage," the dean continued, "I have never met a graduate student with such an exceptionally gifted grasp of the art, science, and history of archaeology as Pauline. She is also only the second student ever, after yours truly, to achieve and maintain a 4.2 average in each and every semester of our program. Truly a remarkable achievement, and Carthage is fortunate to now claim her as an esteemed alumna. Congratulations, Pauline."

When Pauline received the e-mail a week earlier informing her that she was the recipient of Carthage's most coveted academic prize, her first impulse was to delete the message and pretend she never got it. She flirted with leaving campus early to avoid the ceremony entirely, or better yet, asking the dean to give it to someone else, a student who'd actually busted their butt, studied constantly, and pulled all-nighters.

Pauline knew full well she hadn't done any of that. And they were giving her the damn award, anyway. Thank God her foster parents weren't around to make a fuss—not that they'd come even if she begged them. Which she wouldn't, ever.

As the heavy statue plopped into Pauline's lap, she didn't crack even a polite smile, for the *pulse* was still having its way. A brown, filmy haze masked her vision. A rush of images filled her mind's eye so that all she saw were split-second flashes of seemingly random objects—axes, snuff boxes, buttons, wooden shafts, and countless more. So many images flying by, none of them having anything to do with her. And yet, the objects weren't unfamiliar.

Nothing about the *pulse* made sense. Not now, not ever. Pauline was resigned to enduring it. But only after years spent trying to find a cure. Because one thing was for damn sure: She had no one else to do it for her. At thirteen, she experimented with holding her breath until she nearly passed out. The phases of the *pulse* arrived undeterred. At fifteen, she tried drinking gallons of water to flush out the damn thing, like a nasty virus. Throughout high school and college, she tried lucid dreaming, praying to secular gods, calling upon an exorcist. Well, she didn't get that far with the exorcist. No point dragging somebody into a mess she couldn't explain to herself, let alone a stranger eager to cast out demons. If demons were involved.

The ceremony dragged on. Dean Nojes handed out other, lesser awards to students who must have worked a thousand times harder than she and wanted the recognition a whole lot more. Pauline's only friend on campus, Bette French, sat next to her, smiling modestly as the dean handed her a certificate on fake parchment paper, rolled up and tied with a green bow. Cheesy, just like the statue. She'd never say that to Bette who tried—and failed—to hide her pleasure at being recognized for her thesis on ethical practices in contemporary archaeology. Bette took that shit seriously—way too seriously. Pauline knew for a fact the world was teeming with artifacts, millions of them, and in the fullness of time, if an ancient wheel or an arrow happened to go astray, to fall into private hands outside of proper channels, well, there was plenty of time for the artifact to find its way into more deserving hands. As to why she felt this way and how she'd formed this opinion? Add it to the pile of unanswered questions.

The effects of the *pulse* receded just as the awards ceremony ended. Drained, craving some form of release that never arrived, Pauline frowned, drew a deep breath, and cursed her wretched body for playing nasty tricks again and again. As the students clambered to their feet, Dean Nojes raised her deep alto to be heard above the noise. "I'll see you all back at the compound," she yelled. "Remember: it's a party *and* a requirement. You skip out, and I'll know it—and there will be consequences."

"What a tyrant," Bette said as she and Pauline left the stage. "Absolute power corrupts absolutely. And she's had way too much power for too long."

"But we're not gonna slip the noose, are we?" Pauline asked, knowing the answer.

"Not if we actually intend to graduate. Aren't you drooling for that piece of paper with the gold star and your name on it?"

"Suitable for hanging," Pauline said with a cynical laugh. She gripped the Boniface statue in her right hand, an odd mash-up of a winged angel and a wolf, daring the thing to slip and crash to the ground. She'd never told Bette about the *pulse.* She'd never told anyone. The whole point was to act like a normal person, not a freak.

The pair left the low-slung brick building on the Carthage campus, in a tidy suburb north of Baltimore, and began the short walk in the chilly April afternoon to the dean's house a few blocks away. Other students heading the same way streamed through the residential neighborhood in clumps. No one joined Pauline and Bette, a mismatched-looking pair—dark-haired Pauline in a wrinkled, second-hand cotton dress and scuffed black boots, and Bette with slicked-back short blonde hair, a black leather skirt, and fishnets. Pauline knew she was an object of suspicion among her peers. She was quite sure they whispered about her behind her back. Nothing new about that. Bette, at least, didn't seem to care if Pauline was persona non grata on campus. At a minimum, Pauline figured that if Bette wasn't her enemy, then by default, she was a friend.

"That's an impressive piece of crap you got there,"

Bette said, seizing the Boniface statue from Pauline's loose grip.

"Crap is right. Is this what my life is gonna add up to—a hunk of glass and marble?"

"Show it off on your coffee table, smack in the middle."

"Where it gathers dust, which I'm too lazy to wipe off. No thanks. Besides, I don't have a coffee table." She had a bed, a mini-fridge, and second-hand clothing. Not much else.

"On the mantel, then," Bette said, heaving the statue like a barbell.

"What is the point of a mantel, anyway?"

"A doorstop, maybe. Or no, when somebody breaks into your house. Crack 'em over the head." She swung the heavy ornament with both hands.

"No house and not a thing worth stealing, anyway," Pauline said as the dean's house came into view. "All that blood on the floor, for nothing."

Bette laughed and handed the statue back to her. "I bet someday you'll wake up and find you've become a little more ordinary, like the rest of us. You know, a house, a spouse, a kid or two."

"Who says?"

"You wanna stay weird?" More of a statement than a question.

"I am who I am, Bette, take it or leave it."

"I can see the class notes a decade from now. 'Pauline Marsh, MA Archaeology '22, still weird.' "

"*You're* weird. Chipping away at rocks under a hot sun—that's way too normal for you."

"I keep telling you, Marsh, not everybody in our field is swishing a soft brush and peering at bone

6

fragments under a microscope. There are so many bad guys infiltrating honest digs."

"Infiltrating? Ooh, that *does* sound bad."

"Seriously," Bette said, getting worked up. "They sneak stuff out that doesn't belong to them. They sell stolen artifacts because they're greedy bastards. And they just piss the hell out of me, y'know? Somebody has to go out there and stop them in their tracks. Nobody's paying enough attention!"

Bette pretty much had one speed—indignation. Pauline was used to it by now.

Students streamed into the dean's ranch house—all seventy-two members of the graduating class. A look of angry resignation was the expression Pauline caught on most faces. They'd all known this day was coming since their first week at Carthage two years ago. At orientation, they'd been informed—perhaps warned is the better word, Pauline thought—that Dean Nojes threw a party at her house for all graduating Masters' candidates, and attendance was mandatory. Miss it, and the dean would withhold final credits, without which a student could not graduate and officially call herself an archaeologist. As for what supposedly went on at this party and why it was so important, nobody was willing to say. It's as if the dean's party induced some form of amnesia. It was common knowledge that this event had been a Carthage tradition for years, yet the details remained a blank. The standing joke—not all that funny, but repeated ad nauseum—was that Dean Nojes's graduation party was like Las Vegas: whatever happened there, stayed there.

"You comin'?" Bette asked. Pauline had paused a few yards from the front door.

"I'll catch up," she said. She decided on the spot that the dean's blue hydrangea bush was an excellent place to hide, or perhaps, mislay, the Boniface statue. She stuffed the useless paperweight deep into the bush and when she looked up, the dean was peering at her from the doorway. *Shit.*

Dean Nojes resembled a modern-day Gertrude Stein, short and round, dressed in a loose, gauzy blouse and a billowing full-length skirt. Even her hair reminded Pauline of late-stage Stein—close-cropped, gray, with bangs. But unlike Stein, her arms were loaded with bangles that clinked every time she moved. In her seminars, the sound of all those bracelets knocking together as she wielded a laser pointer drove everyone crazy. Pauline wasn't the only student convinced the dean did it on purpose. To keep them awake, perhaps.

Nojes smiled and patted Pauline's shoulder as she entered the house. Before she could slip past her, the dean stood on tiptoes to whisper in Pauline's ear. "I wonder what's in store."

"Excuse me?" She wasn't sure she heard her clearly above the students talking, laughing, and drinking beer in the dean's living room—taking full advantage of whatever was on offer. But the dean merely smiled again and waved the next batch of students into her house, which was filling up fast. *I wonder what's in store.* What did that mean? Or had she misheard? Maybe the dean said, *I wonder what's by the door.* Had she seen her ditch the statue, after all? Was she insulted? Would she hold up her diploma? *And do I care?*

What the hell, she thought. *I'll manage.* She

squeezed past the dean as quickly as she could and made a beeline for the long sideboard loaded with beer, wine, and baskets of pretzels and chips.

"What's wrong now?" Bette asked, handing her a beer.

"Nothing," Pauline replied. "Nojes said something to me on the way in. I just—"

"You're her pet. You know that, right? I don't care, personally. We're done here. This place is already in my rearview mirror. But you're this year's flavor. At least you don't humble-brag, which is why I can stand to put up with you." Bette held her bottle out so they could clink them. "What should we drink to?" Pauline shrugged. "Oh, c'mon. You just won the biggest award this place has to offer, the one they only give out, what, like every five years? And you can't think of a single reason to celebrate? I take it back—what I said about you not humble-bragging. This is borderline obnoxious, Marsh."

"I don't have a job. I don't know where I'm going to live. I don't have any money. Maybe I can sell the angel-wolf statue online, or something."

"Poor little you," Bette said, tugging on one of her enormous hoop earrings. "So, Sad Eyes, let's toast to *me*. Off to Hell Gap, Wyoming. Where I guarantee you I will *not* spend all my time digging for Paleoindian spear tips. They've had a rash of thefts out there."

"I expect to see you on the gram with your pickaxe buried deep in the skull of some artifact-stealing loser," Pauline said as they concluded their toast. "Our very own Jessica Jones of the pit crew."

"Something ridiculously amazing will fall out of the sky for you," Bette said, sounding a tiny bit jealous.

"I mean, you make everything look so easy. I don't know why you're worried."

"Did I say I was worried?" Bette wandered off to mingle as Pauline called after her. "I'm not worried!"

Alone, nursing a beer, Pauline watched her fellow budding archaeologists laughing, talking, flirting in clusters. Quick furtive glances came her way. *They're talking about me. So obvious.* She met and held their gazes, forcing them to look away first. Among them was Sue Rios, heading to Princeton for a PhD. Not about to get her hands dirty. Gayle Connaught, off to a museum job in Saskatchewan. Also dirt-averse. And Dan Finland, who everyone knew had landed a six-figure job with a giant oil company. He made a deal with the fossil-fuels devil.

The trio headed toward Pauline. *To rattle me? No chance.*

"So, congrats and all," Sue Rios said with a little toss of her head. "Can I ask you something, Pauline?"

"Sure." She swigged her beer, the four of them standing in a tight group while scores of students milled around the dean's overcrowded living room. "What do you want to know?" *Like I'd ever tell you one real thing about me.*

"What I want to know—what *we* want to know, actually," Sue said, looking at Gayle and Dan, "is why you seem to know absolutely everything about archaeology. Like, *everything.* All the chemistry, all the cultures, all the important digs everywhere in the world. The whole friggin' discipline."

"From the first day, even," Dan said, frowning. "I never saw you open a textbook."

"I never saw you in the library," Gayle added.

"What's your deal? Your secret sauce?"

"And then you graduate with, what did Dean Nojes say?" Sue said. "Like, a 4.2 GPA. Better than perfect. How the hell did you do that?"

Pauline smiled—a fake-sweet sort of smile.

"Have I been a puzzle all this time?" she asked. "Like, a hard sudoku puzzle where you can't fill in the grid?" *The kid nobody trusts.*

"Well, yeah, sorta," Sue said, a bit sheepishly. Gayle and Dan nodded.

"I studied," Pauline said. "You just didn't catch me at it. It's not like we were hanging out. What can I tell you? Archaeology and I—we're sympatico. I don't think you'd be asking me these questions if we'd studied, say, astrophysics." Half-lies, half-truths. She knew they couldn't tell the difference.

"It just seems weird, is all," Gayle said. "I don't mean *you're* weird." *Oh yes you do.* "I mean, it's like you're a walking encyclopedia. I guess that's what seems weird."

"Do you have a photographic memory, Pauline?" Dan asked. The interrogation was getting more ridiculous with each question.

"I don't know, Dan," Pauline said. "Never thought about it. We only know what's in our own heads, right?"

An Egyptian necklace of tin-glazed earthenware with bright carnelian beads.

An awl made of deer bone.

A ring of braided horsehair.

Smooth stones etched with map markings.

"Did you cheat, Pauline?" Sue asked, her voice sharp. The others looked away. Sue tossed her head again, for no apparent reason, then squinted at Pauline. "Did you?"

"Well…if I did…" She enjoyed toying with them, a little. "If I cheated, why would I admit that to you, here, now, in the dean's house?"

"Well, I—" Sue stammered.

"What's your problem, Sue?" Pauline let an aggressive edge creep in. "Why do you care what I did or didn't do to get through the program? Did I take something away from you?"

"Well, uh, no, that's not—" Sue's face flushed.

"You got friends in high places?" Gayle asked. They were just fishing now. Pathetic.

"It's a reasonable question, Pauline," Dan said, his brow still furrowed. "Whether you cheated—and how you did it. Not like you'd tell us. But we all worked our fucking asses off, while you never seemed to make an effort. All those details poured out of you. So we're wondering, yeah."

"What do you wonder, Dan?" A deep voice had intruded on the conversation. On Pauline's left stood Grey Henley, vaguely familiar. She knew him by sight, usually surrounded by classmates hanging on his every word. There he was, suddenly by her side—and about to *take* her side, she guessed, whether she wanted him to or not. "Do you wonder why Pauline graduated with highest honors while you skated by and did just enough brown-nosing to land your cushy job with the biggest oil polluter in the world? Is that what you wonder, Dan? 'Cause I sure don't."

"Oh, come off it, Grey," Gayle said. "Dan deserves—"

"You wanna know how Pauline did what she did?"

Grey continued. *Okay. Let's see where this goes. At least he knows my name.* Grey took half a step toward Dan that bordered on menacing—or it would be, Pauline thought, if they weren't in the dean's house, drinking her beer, waiting for her to live up to the legend about this party. Grey took another half step forward, then held his ground, leaning slightly into Dan's personal space. Pauline watched his hands curl into fists and wondered if he was aware he was doing that. "Because she's a fucking genius," Grey said. "While the rest of us are morons who try hard. End of story."

"Fuck you too, buddy," Dan said. He turned and melted back in the crowd, Sue and Gayle following right behind him, but not before tossing Grey sweetly apologetic smiles.

"Did you get off on that?" Pauline asked Grey.

"Yeah. Did you?"

"Waste of breath."

"Nah," he said, lifting a beer to his lips. "It's good to take them down."

"I don't need you to." She tried to avoid a certain *tone.*

"I know, but they're—"

"They're assholes," she said. "Obviously. Always sucking up when it suits them and putting other people down—or trying to—to feel better about themselves. Sorry if I'm insulting your friends, but…"

Grey laughed. "But what do you *really* think of them? And they're not my friends."

"Anyway, who says all archaeologists are nice? Just ask Bette."

He smiled, and Pauline allowed herself to take him

in. All of him. *Handsome. My God. I've had two years to notice, and I failed.* Six feet, broad, muscular shoulders. The kind of guy who played rugby or some other rough-and-tumble spot. Curly dirty-blond hair with stubble to match. His only imperfection: a mole on the bridge of his nose, on the right. Which made him even more perfect, actually.

Not a chance, she figured. Nobody had ever been into her before. Why should that change now? Nobody goes for the circus freak. Even Bette kept her at arm's length.

"So what are your post-grad plans?" Pauline asked. May as well keep him talking a minute longer, if only for the sheer pleasure of the view. She braced herself for a detailed recital of his great new job, big archaeology dreams. Blah, blah, blah. Figured she'd look without really listening. But Grey merely shrugged and smiled. A crooked smile, one side of his mouth turned up slightly higher than the other. Another perfect imperfection that gave his handsome face a slightly goofy look. Handsome *and* approachable.

"I'm keeping my options open at the moment," he replied. "Waiting to see what turns up. Can I grab you another beer?"

This guy was at loose ends? That was a surprise. Good thing he didn't turn the tables on her, pump her for her five-year plan, or whatever. If he did, she'd parrot him—tell him she was keeping her options open, too. How else to explain that she hadn't lifted a finger all semester to look for a job, any job?

"Come on," Grey said. "Nojes is holding court outside. I'm curious."

"Me, too. What happens in Vegas stays in Vegas,

right?" *Oh, lame.*

"Yeah, right." He laughed, and she looked for the crooked smile.

I could be in some kinda trouble here.

Chapter 2

Pauline and Grey walked through the sliding glass doors of the dean's kitchen and into a grassy backyard. Tiny white lights were strung in the trees and along the patio railing, giving the cool spring evening a festive, expectant air. The entire class had moved outside, sitting on the grass or standing in clusters. They had unconsciously recreated the semicircular C-shape of the amphitheater where the dean delivered all her lectures.

Dean Nojes sat on a lawn chair at the open end of the C, her bangled arms gesturing energetically, making a familiar racket. Pauline looked around for Bette, thinking she might join her, but Bette was not in sight. Pauline posted herself apart from the crowd, as usual, expecting Grey to wander off to join his own circle of friends, whoever they were. But he remained close by. Pauline was both pleased and embarrassed. *Keep a lid on it, kid.*

Women came up to Grey, smiling, tossing their hair, but he didn't appear to give them any real encouragement. Pauline felt like a spy and forced herself to concentrate on what Dean Nojes was saying.

"If you want to stay high and dry, keep your hands soft, then go to law school," the dean said in her lecture-hall alto. "If you're looking for glory, play sports. But if you're ready for back-breaking labor, diarrhea, scorpions, or hypothermia, and long days filled with tedious, painstaking, repetitive labor...well, then, you've chosen the best profession in the world."

The dean paused to remove all her bangles and roll up the right sleeve of her blouse. She held out her bare forearm.

"My favorite scar," she said, sliding her fingers up a jagged pink scar running vertically from her wrist to just above her elbow. Several students gasped. Was this the thing—the hidden thing—this party was famous for?

Grey moved closer to Pauline and whispered, sending an unexpected shiver through her. "Is it me or is this just a little bit lame? Isn't she due to retire any day now?"

"Pure theater," she whispered back, slightly woozy. "Anything to grab center stage."

"You think this is just the warm-up act?"

"Gotta be. Otherwise, what's all the fuss?"

The dean kept her scarred arm outstretched, presumably so everybody could get a good look.

"An unexpected encounter with the Khmer Rouge," she said, matter-of-factly. "Cambodia. Nineteen seventy-eight. A band of sweaty men, armed to the teeth, found us on a night dig. They jumped from their Jeeps, blinded us with flashlights. Next thing I know, a machete comes straight down on me. I thought he'd sliced my arm off. Thought I was about to die. But nah. It wasn't that bad. A few nights in the local infirmary, where no one spoke English, and I was good as new."

Dean Nojes pulled her sleeve down, slid the bangles back onto her arm, and leaned back in the lawn chair with a satisfied grin. Her little performance seemed intended to burnish the lore every student already knew about her. Nojes had been awarded a MacArthur "genius" grant in her early thirties for her field research at the Carrick ringwork, one of Ireland's most important medieval monuments, dating from the Anglo-Norman invasion. Pauline had to admit that even more impressive were the stories about her being shot at, burned, and nearly drowned when she was doing her doctoral fieldwork in one of the most remote sections of the Amazon. They story they'd all heard repeated around campus was that it wasn't the Indigenous people who came after her, but corporate emissaries for a giant logging company.

If even half the stories about the dean were true, Pauline had to give her props for being a tough broad. A lot tougher than, say, Sue Rios or Dan Finland. And the dean got the last laugh—several of the artifacts she risked her life to recover were on display in museums around the world. Pauline could readily picture each of them. And she had publications up the wazoo, of course.

The dean reached into the folds of her voluminous skirt and pulled out a small object.

"It was all worth it," she said, "for this." She held up an elaborately carved Cambodian bronze dragon, about four inches long. The figure stood on all fours with a protruding snout covered in elaborate scrollwork, which was repeated across the beast's breast. A series of nubby scales arched around the head like a lion's mane. Time had dimmed the figure's original brassy color to dark brown tinged with dark green. Everyone leaned in for a closer look. Except Pauline. She didn't need to. Every carefully shaped detail on the small, ancient figure was familiar. She could turn it around in her mind and see it with crystal clarity. She may as well have stared at the thing every day of her life.

That was not all. Pauline didn't only know the dragon by sight. She heard fragments of its story too. The dragon spoke directly to her—in a voice only she could hear, as far as she knew, the words planted deep in an odd corner of her brain. *The girl held me in her palm, showing me off to her father. But he ignored her, and so she dashed me to the ground in frustration. Luckily, I'm too strong to break.*

The bronze dragon wasn't a fluke. Every single archaeological artifact she'd seen in photos, books, websites, museums, was intimately familiar. Dan, Sue, and Gayle were right to be suspicious. There *was* something going on. She *did* know things others did not. But as to where this knowledge sprang from and why it seemed to be hers alone?

A big, fat *nada* from the universe.

Moving farther away from the others, Pauline instinctively shielded them from her freakish imagination, which was built like a wild forest, a dark tangle, with no path in or out. As for family—the people who were supposed to care the most, love you unconditionally, warts and all—that was a bust. Her foster parents, Nora and Herb Heller, the only parents she ever knew, were worse than clueless. They didn't give a shit. Why sugar-coat it? The *frosters,* she called them. Cold, distant, no help at all. She pictured a black hole where her heart should be and a giant question mark standing in for an identity that made sense.

I'm out of whack. Plenty of parlor tricks—but no luck, no love, no discernible future. Oh, shut up. I'm boring. Stop feeling sorry for myself. Listen to the dean. Maybe you I still learn something.

"When I die," Dean Nojes said, holding up the bronze dragon, "this goes straight back to the cultural antiquities museum in Phnom Penh. Unless, somehow…" She paused and looked around, her gaze traveling among the students until she found Pauline. *Why is she looking at me?* "Unless someone comes to claim this lovely item sooner… I do believe in repatriation. But after a thousand years, a few decades spent privately caring for something as magnificent as this surely will not matter."

Exactly. She couldn't have said it better, though no one would listen if she had. A tug on her sleeve.

"She fucking stole it." Bette barely bothered to whisper. "Did you hear what she said? Am I wrong? And why are you hiding out in the shadows? What's your problem tonight, Marsh?"

"You could say she just borrowed it for a long time," Pauline said. "Like checking a book out of the library and then holding onto it for a couple years past the due date." She'd let Bette's other questions drop. Her friend had other bones to chew on.

"It's not like that at all!" Bette pushed an impatient hand through her short, blonde hair. "You don't really believe that, do you, Marsh?"

"Look at it this way, Bette. The dragon will never find its way back to the water-carrier who carved it to please her father because she's been dead for centuries."

"What are you even talking about? A water-carrier? Why would you say that?"

"Um, just a wild guess." *Oops.* "But anyway, the

dragon is safe. The dean's taking good care of it. It's not like she's using it to crack walnuts. At some point, it'll find its way back to a place where Cambodians and tourists can enjoy it. The dragon's just on a little detour."

"Wow." Bette shook her head and smacked her lips. "I've known you two years, and I'm just realizing you're a completely amoral person. At least, your morals are pretty squishy. Nojes has no business holding onto that artifact, and I'm going to report her. She's breaking the law, Marsh. She's a criminal. Period."

"Judge much?" Pauline asked. Bette, disgusted, turned away. "No, wait. Please." Pauline was too late. Bette headed toward a pack of students, and Pauline wondered if she'd just tanked their friendship. Her *only* friendship. Well, Bette was too damn rigid. Saw the world strictly in black and white. You're a good guy or a bad guy. No in-between. Who needed friends like that? But then Bette turned around and headed back to Pauline, who felt a surge of hope. Did she owe her an apology—or was it the other way around?

"Why would you make up shit like that?" Bette asked in an icy tone. "A female water-carrier? I get that you're smart, Marsh, but when you invent the history of an artifact you know zilch about, it's like spitting on your profession. Like archaeology's one big joke. Think about that before you go off somewhere to dig shit up and claim to know all about it."

Pauline sighed. "You're right, Bette. You're so right. I'm sorry."

Ah, too little, too late. Pauline watched Bette storm off again. Like the slogan says, what goes on in

Pauline's head, should stay in Pauline's head. Bette probably saw her just as Sue, Gayle, and Dan did: an obnoxious know-it-all who will say practically anything to show off her big brain. It wasn't true, of course. But it seemed Bette had made up her mind.

"All right, children!" Dean Nojes called out, rising slowly from her lawn chair. "It's time for the next chapter in our final evening together."

"Finally," Grey said, reappearing at Pauline's side. His breath lightly grazed her neck. "Let's get this show on the road."

"Will you miss the dean's lectures?" Grey's presence was rather delicious, but Pauline was also thinking about whether she wanted to win Bette back. "Of course, she's always the star of every lesson, isn't she?"

"No, really?" Grey's crooked smile banished all thoughts of Bette. His smile seemed like a rich dessert—or maybe, the itch of an addiction. Something you couldn't stand to give up once you had it. If you could get it in the first place. She assumed she had a little time to mull this over—"this" being Grey. The *pulse* had visited earlier that day and wouldn't reappear for weeks, maybe months. It was maddeningly unpredictable. Nothing like her period. Imagine saying *any* of this to Grey. Oh, God.

Dean Nojes disrupted her train of thought with a series of claps to regain the students' attention, now that they'd all reassembled in the living room. The dean stood in the center, holding court, as usual. There were too many of them to spread out. Grey's arm brushed Pauline's, communicating its heat through his shirt, her dress, as if they were skin-on-skin. Yet again, she forced herself to focus on the proceedings. Glancing around, she noticed the room was curiously devoid of any personality. The art on the walls looked store-bought, pale abstract paintings like you might see in a hotel room. No sign of artifacts, sculptures, figurines, or photos that would speak to the dean's adventures.

"Listen up!" the dean said, looking very Gertrude Stein-ish. She was by far the shortest person in the room, yet seemed to take up a lot of space, nonetheless. Pauline guessed that none of them had forgotten the dean's hold over them, still fully in force. "What happens here tonight will put a stamp on your future. Your whole life. The experience will stick with you to your dying day. Rituals, people. Rituals make the world go round."

Nojes once again sought out Pauline among all the students, or was she imagining this? No, this was the third time she'd felt the dean's eyes on her, just her, that very day. Why? Pauline shivered. Did Grey notice anything out of the ordinary? She turned to watch him and noted a wary, cynical expression, his eyes slightly narrowed.

"I'm going to call you in pairs," the dean said. Only two at a time? Soft groans rippled through the room. This would take forever. Several students inched toward the front door, no doubt wondering how to escape without forfeiting their diplomas. "Don't even think about it!" the dean bellowed.

Bette squeezed in next to Pauline. "She's a megalomaniac. And crazy. She can't keep us here. She has no right. If the Fire Department knew how many people were crowded in here right now, they'd impound her sorry ass." Bette practically danced on her toes with agitation. But Pauline was glad they were still on speaking terms. Or at least, Bette still saw fit to vent in Pauline's direction.

"Aren't you curious, though?" Pauline asked her on-again, off-again friend. "Don't you want to see what comes next? After such a big build-up?"

Grey chimed in unexpectedly. "Curiosity has nothing to do with this." His deep voice reminded Pauline of a coursing river. "She's extorting us. I guess the university gives her a pass on account of her reputation, which, you'll notice, she polishes herself every chance she gets."

"Maybe no one's ever had the balls to report her to the provost or whoever has power up the food chain here," Bette said. "But I will. I won't hesitate, when this is all over."

"Do what you gotta do," Grey said to Bette. "But I respect her. She's a manipulator, sure, but she's awfully clever about it. That's a real skill—knowing exactly how to get what you want before anybody realizes what you're doing."

"You think deceit is a skill?" Bette asked, her voice rising above the din. "Boy, you two are swimming in the same unethical swamp. Gack."

"I think you're both right," Pauline said. "It's not cut-and-dried, Bette. That's too easy. I don't mind being manipulated if there's a chance I'll be surprised. Something new under the sun! She mentioned rituals. I'm up for that. If it's not cheesy. Something real, though…" Pauline broke off, her thoughts wandering toward a haze of objects floating in her mind's eye.

"Rituals?" Bette said scornfully. "That's the dean's bullshit. Archaeology only works because there are rules in place—guardrails—about what we do and how we do it. It's science, not Burning Man."

Grey and Pauline chimed in together. "Rules are meant to be broken."

They looked at one another and laughed. Pauline blushed—for the first time in a very long time. She focused on the sound of his deep laughter, which bore traces of mocking self-awareness. Bette simply rolled her eyes.

"Freiburg and Sullivan," Dean Nojes called, consulting a printed list. Everyone watched the first pair of students work their way from opposite ends of the room toward the dean, who stood next to a door presumably leading into another room. She made them dump their cell phones into a basket by the door, then gestured for them to enter, pulling the door closed behind her. Pauline figured they all wondered whether these two students had some special connection, or was the dean calling pairs in at random? Was there a method to her madness?

The living room fell silent, leaving everyone ample time to speculate in silence. The dean's cryptic question, *I wonder what's in store?* came back to Pauline. What *was* in store? Surely it couldn't be sexual. The dean could never get away with that, after all these years. Maybe a pop quiz? If so, Pauline would ace it. She smiled, thinking how pissed off that would make Sue, Gayle, and Dan—and just about everybody else.

"This is so stupid." Pauline recognized Sue Rios's simpering voice from across the room. "Next, she'll have us playing pin-the-tail-on-the-donkey." The students tittered.

"This is probably illegal, you know," Bette said loudly to the room. "A violation of all the codes this school is supposed to follow. Who does she think she is, holding us here against our will? I'm gonna file charges. Who's with me?" Murmurs and whispers, but no audible response. "Bunch of sheep!"

Barely five minutes later, the door opened, and Cynthia Freiburg and Carl Sullivan emerged. Pauline stood on tiptoes to get a good look at them. The pair didn't meet anyone's gaze. They appeared pale and drained and quickly put distance between them. Pauline caught a brief glimpse of Carl's face. His eyes were blank pools. A shiver ran through her—not of fear, but anticipation. Whatever happened in that room must not have been pleasant. Nobody would get that upset over a pop quiz, surely. Something was unfolding here, something far beyond anyone's imagination—including, perhaps, hers.

Cynthia and Carl scooped up their cell phones and made their way through the crowd toward the front door, shaking their heads.

"What happened?" Gayle Connaught called out before the guinea pigs bolted from the house. They ignored her.

"Will she let you graduate, at least?" Dan Finland asked.

"Will you testify against her?" Bette shouted.

Pauline believed she was overdue for some kind of shift, or turn, in her life. Maybe this was it, though she tried not to get her hopes up.

"You were right, Pauline," Grey said, once more by her side. "This will be an adventure. Good luck."

"You too. Whatever happens in there…"

"I'm up for it." His smile raised her core temperature at least a degree. "Why not?"

"Same," she said.

Grey pressed an index finger to the back of her hand, the simple gesture sending a fresh shockwave through her system. The feeling was nothing at all like the *pulse*. It felt earthy and grounded. Was he flirting? *Why me, when he can have any woman in this room?* Perhaps he already had. Perhaps she was fresh meat. Ugh.

The dean reappeared, list in hand. "Harvin and Loren," she called. Dawn Harvin and Bruce Loren threaded their way toward the door, looking terrified. The pattern was the same. Dump the cell phones, enter the room with the dean, and emerge five minutes later, looking shaken to the core. This time, no one said a word. They all simply watched the pair leave as quickly as possible.

Only Pauline and Grey were smiling.

Everyone stopped drinking. Most turned to their phones, aiming for nonchalance, but fooling no one. Waves of dread swirled around the room. Pauline put a hand on her heart, which beat steady and calm. She wished she could do the same to Grey. He wasn't on his phone, at least. He watched the proceedings, as she did.

"Off with their heads!" A lame attempt at gallows humor from across the room.

Somebody else voiced the opening tune of Chopin's funeral march. "Dum, dum, de-dum…"

Bette stood nearby, quietly fuming. She tapped furiously on her phone. Pauline imagined she was sending irate texts to the president of Carthage and anyone else she could think of. She didn't want to ask, in case her questions triggered a fresh lecture on squishy ethics.

Grow up! Pauline wanted to shake them all by the shoulder. *You think this is hard? Well, it's not!*

Grey turned to her. "I'm taking bets on who faints first. My money is on Finland." His smile was mischievous. A man of a thousand smiles. Pauline laughed, and everyone glared as if she'd unwrapped a cough drop in the middle of a death scene.

"Marsh and Henley," the dean called. *Whoa. What?* Pauline took a deep breath and looked at Grey, who was looking right back at her. Is this what luck felt like? She'd had so little of it in her life, she wasn't sure. Maybe. A day ago, if she'd been asked to choose a partner to go with her into that room, she'd have chosen Bette, by default. But now Grey Henley was the only person she wanted to share this experience with, even though she'd have walked right past the guy if she'd passed him on the street a scant four hours earlier.

To Pauline's amazement, Grey took her hand as they headed toward the door. An unfamiliar emotion flooded her. Happiness? If so, a little went a long way. Heady stuff.

The windowless room was dim and gray, as if lit by shadows. An odd smell lingered faintly. Fear or flop sweat, left behind by classmates? Unlike the living room walls, every inch of the room was adorned with tribal masks and shelves loaded with figurines from all over the world. In each corner, a statue or sculpture filled the niche. Pauline didn't need long to catalog the artifacts all around her. She could identify every object and where it came from. Edo. Yoruba. Igbo. Burkina Faso. Inuit. Aztec. Yunnan. Guizhou. Venice. Papua.

Dominican Republic.

The masks grimaced, leered, and smiled, their faces painted bright red, yellow, green, black, brown, white. Some were framed with halos of coarse straw or feathers.

Yes, Pauline had lied outright to Sue, Gayle, and Dan. Told them she'd studied when she hadn't. She'd enrolled in the Masters' program at Carthage University not to learn but to obtain a credential others would recognize—to secure a veneer of normalcy and respectability. Her degree offered legal entrée to digs and excavations around the world. She'd wanted to acquire the formal vocabulary of the discipline to complement her own innate store of knowledge. The credential was a cover. If Bette knew this, perhaps she wouldn't be so hard on her. Or maybe the opposite was true. Bette would cut her off, permanently.

Grey, on the other hand…what went through his handsome head?

These thoughts flashed through her mind within the first few seconds of entering the room. She barely had time to glance at Grey before the dean issued instructions in a clipped, no-nonsense voice.

"Face each other," she commanded. "Closer. Still closer. Now clasp hands." The gesture felt incredibly intimate, as if she were standing naked in front of him. She took advantage of the inches between them to observe the flecks of silver laced in his dirty-blond hair, the loose curl resting on his forehead, and the silver that glinted in his neatly trimmed stubble. Light tendrils of chest hair rose from the neckline of his black T-shirt. She could just discern the contours of his strong pectoral muscles. She risked tipping her head back slightly to look straight into his blue eyes, flecked with shards of gray. He returned her gaze without hesitation, a slight smile playing around his lips.

"Keep your hands together," the dean said. "And do not move. Do not separate. Do not speak. Remain absolutely still until I tell you otherwise." Dean Nojes swiftly blindfolded Pauline, who assumed the same was done to Grey. She heard the dean step away, followed by the sound of a match being struck. In seconds, a strange, pungent odor filled her nostrils. Sage, loam, ground acorns, oil of oregano, and oak bark tannin. She could identify the smoke's components but had no clue as to its purpose. Then she and Grey coughed violently for several seconds as the smoke penetrated their lungs. The coughing stopped abruptly, and Pauline's lungs cleared. She heard Grey take a clearing breath, and she did the same. Perhaps her body had absorbed it. Perhaps the smoke had gotten into her bloodstream. That didn't make sense, but a familiar feeling came over her. Not the *pulse,* she pleaded. It's too soon. And not here, pressed up against this guy. He'll think something's wrong with me—that I'm frightened, weak, or crazy. None of which is true. Except, maybe, the crazy part.

But was this the *pulse*, after all? If so, she'd skipped to stage three, the out-of-body floating-above-the-earth stage. This had never happened before. The stages of the *pulse* had always unfolded in the same sequence.

She gripped Grey's hands even tighter, as if to keep her body from flying up and away. But clutching didn't help. She rose out of her body and, despite the blindfold, she could see perfectly well as she soared above the treetops, above the dean's house, rising higher and higher. She rose thousands of feet in the air, traveling not only through space but through time as well. Her body dissolved, and she existed in a realm of pure feeling, connected to all things that humans made or crafted to pray or protect, nurture or defend, share love or blood lust.

Seeing and feeling became one enormous sensation. She witnessed children spearing fish in a river. The dark, open mouth of a stone cave lit from within by a fire. Small animals carved in wood and ivory, neatly arrayed on a plinth. A joint of meat roasting over a spit. A henge of stone in which people danced wildly. A woman dying as she gave birth. Two men clubbing one another until both were bloody. She experienced their heat, cold, hunger, joy, pain, fear, anger.

And something else, besides. A presence, separate from her, yet somehow connected, accompanied Pauline on this journey. Not Grey—not someone she'd met in real life. This presence, a spiritual companion of sorts, emitted a faint hum, like a vibration rippling the surface of her skin. She couldn't see him—yes, it was masculine energy. All she knew for certain was she was not alone. But she'd always been alone. What could this mean?

As suddenly as Pauline departed her body, she just as suddenly slammed back into it, back to earth, back to the room in Dean Nojes's ranch house. Her perspective shifted radically, just long enough for her to silently berate the cosmos.

Why? Why did you bring me back, when I was no longer alone? When I finally belonged? When the world and I had joined as one?

While Pauline was still blindfolded and breathing hard, the dean whispered in her ear yet again. "You will have questions. Return when you are ready."

The dean removed her blindfold, then Grey's. He was breathing hard too. They looked down at their hands, clasped so tightly the knuckles were white.

"You may release your hands," Nojes said. They disentangled slowly, wordlessly. Grey looked pale, but his blue-gray eyes sparkled. The dean opened the door leading back into the living room. Surely, this episode had not lasted five minutes, but rather five hours, five days, five weeks, and all the other students would be long gone. But no. There they stood, watching Pauline and Grey intently, curious dread plastered on their faces.

But she fooled them, and so did he. They flipped the script, bursting out in laughter. They smiled and waved before heading out into the spring night air, triumphant and together.

Not so cheesy, after all.

Chapter 3

Laughing still, like carefree children, Pauline and Grey stood in chilly darkness on the sidewalk in front of Dean Nojes's house. His warm, strong body pulled her suddenly close, and they kissed as if compelled. *Ah.* So *this* is what she needed, what she craved, and what she'd been missing without realizing it. The kiss opened a longing in her, as if she were a tightly closed bud about to blossom in the sun's warmth after years languishing in darkness.

Desire rose in her, clamoring for attention as strongly as the *pulse* itself. Yet desire grounded her in the present, whereas the *pulse* threatened each time to take her away to something, or somewhere, unknown. In Grey's arms, securely tethered to solid flesh, she was a real person, not a freak with a tendency to come apart at the seams.

"I live nearby," she murmured, gripping his arm, barely able to catch her breath. A few entangled steps later, a streetlight cast a gleam on the Boniface statue she'd parked under the hydrangea bush. She ignored it, this symbol of recognition for gifts she did not wish to confront or acknowledge. Grey was the only gift she wanted. She pulled him close while guiding him to her barely furnished basement studio apartment near campus. They entered the gloomy room in silence. Eager to feel his flesh against hers, she threw off her coat, kicked off her boots, and began unbuttoning her cotton dress. Grey gently pushed her hand away and took over, opening the long row of buttons down her front, trailing his index finger along her exposed ribbon of flesh. He reached around inside the loosened dress, which slipped to the floor, and unclasped her bra.

Seconds later, Pauline stood naked before him, almost as if she'd conjured this moment when they stood with hands clasped in the dean's room. Naked before a man for the first time in her life. She understood then why she'd waited. It had all been for this moment. Grey kissed her shoulder and moved to her breasts, as her body caught fire and melted at the same time. She reached to undo his pants, tugging at his shirt, running her hands over the taut muscles sheathing his ribs and the pectorals she had glimpsed earlier, in the room that joined them a million years ago.

They fell onto her narrow maiden's bed, which had hosted no bodies but hers. She allowed instinct to guide her, drawing her legs up and open to receive his urgent thrusts. They shared a hunger to taste, touch, smell every inch of one another. As Pauline reached orgasm, the release she had longed for was hers at last. And she privately rejoiced in knowing, for sure, that she was an earth-dwelling creature like everyone else, composed of hot blood, hard bone, and primitive instinct.

I belong here on the ground, with everyone else— maybe even with him. Not a loner-freak, after all.

Afterward, Grey fell asleep, the crooked smile playing on his lips, his thigh draped across her groin. Pauline watched him sleep while stray thoughts drifted unbidden, insistent as always, far removed from the moist flesh and first flush of sexual satisfaction filling the small room.

Roman coins scattered at the bottom of a well.

A sheep's fleece worn as a cape during a winter gale, ice shards clinging to the dark beard of its wearer.

A delicate flute carved from the antler of a springbok.

She drifted off at last to a chorus of murmured voices, a sound so familiar she hardly noticed anymore. In the early morning hours, Grey stirred, and they had sex again, slowly, kisses sparking like fireflies on a summer night. As dawn filtered through the below-ground window, they began to talk.

"Why did she bring us in there together?" Pauline asked, running her hand along the hard stubble of his firm jaw. "Why us?"

"I like your hair, the color of dark chocolate," Grey said. "A deep forest sort of chocolate, like Brazil, and the way it stops right at the middle of your neck. So sharp and neat. Like you. And your bangs, how they fall into your eyes. You try to hide behind them, don't you?"

"Just overdue for a cut, lover boy. Can't find my scissors."

"But your best feature—do you know what it is?" She shook her head, wondering what he'd say next. Her mind? Breasts? Ass? "This dimple in your chin." He pushed his finger into the small divot. "Such a little mystery." He kissed the spot, then pulled away, propping his head on his arms, sculpting a perfect bicep. "Nojes likes playing head games. Carthage is the perfect place for someone like her to hide out, spin her webs, get away with all kinds of shit."

"Maybe she's a witch. A magician. An alchemist? Or maybe she belongs to a secret cult of sadists who play mind games with needy grad students."

Grey laughed, and she vowed to make him laugh again, and soon.

"Well," he said. "Where I come from, you more or less have to con people into getting what you want. There's no magic involved. Sorry."

She sat up, eyeing him closely. "Sounds like you come from dysfunction junction."

She won his laugh. "You could say that. But I'm different from all of them. Smarter. I won't repeat their mistakes."

"What mistakes? Whose?"

"Never mind," he said, putting his finger to her lips.

"Anyway, you're sexier than all of them put together."

"Hell, yeah," he said with a grin. "What about you? You from dysfunction junction also? Or one of those families you always see in cereal commercials. Laughing. Perfect. Not a care in the world."

"I fucking *hate* those commercials," she responded, more vehemently than she intended. "Fake people and their frozen smiles. It's a big come-on. I never knew my parents. Fostered until I was eighteen. Well, 'fostered' makes it sound like they cared, the Hellers. They fed me just enough. Kept a roof over my head. Couldn't get rid of me fast enough. I live off other people's money now—scholarships. Barely enough to get by. All the money's dried up, anyway."

"So I was right. You're a fucking genius. Living by your wits. People like Sue Rios can damn well kiss your feet."

"No thanks." They laughed, and she admired the way his eyes crinkled. "I'm not a genius, but what I am is flat stone-cold broke. If you're a trust-fund baby, then I'm a gold-digger, starting right this minute."

Grey laughed again, a rich bass rumble. Pauline knew that if forced to choose, she'd rather live with that sound than without.

"Sorry," he said. "Flat broke, like you. No bank. But not for long. I'll be a multimillionaire before I'm thirty."

"Oh, yeah? How?"

"You're gonna help me." He smiled again, but this time, it was different. He was dead serious, his eyes boring into hers. This sexy stranger. What was he thinking?

"Tell me what you saw last night," she said. "Your vision."

"I've decided to call you Penny. Not Pauline, which sounds like somebody's fussy old aunt. You're going to be my lucky penny. Because you know what I saw? Heaps and heaps of treasure. Gold coins and rare antiquities. We find them, you and I, and we dig them up. And they make us rich."

"But what else did you see? That's not all, right?"

"Don't you get it?" Grey stroked her arm. "You were there, in every frame. We go on adventures together, all over the world. Explore mountains, deserts, and deep caves. You said something about magic. I don't believe in magic, but I do believe in fate. At least, I do now. Dean Nojes brought us together for a reason. This is what we're supposed to do. This is why I haven't gone looking for a job. Because I'm not going to make a move without *you*. It all makes perfect sense now."

"You're serious? This is what you believe." Pauline couldn't untangle the mixed emotions prompted by his words. Excitement? Doubt? Dread? He swept the bangs out of her eyes. "You honestly think we belong together? And there's no one else? You don't have a girlfriend waiting for you across town this very minute?" He shook his head. "Well, then."

Pauline rose off the bed and went into the tiny bathroom to hide her tears. Can't let him see that. *Sentimental loser freak. Bad combination. Not girlfriend material.*

She returned from the bathroom, somewhat collected. Grey sat on the edge of the bed in his boxers.

"Hold me," Pauline said. The warmth of his strong arms had a calming effect. "Okay, I'm not flying apart."

"Flying apart?" He laughed. "You mean, falling apart?"

"No. Flying apart is a lot more uncomfortable. Trust me."

"I won't let you fly apart, Lucky Penny." He squeezed tighter. "And if you do, I'll glue you back together, 'kay? Like, uh, oh, I don't know, like Pueblo potsherds. Good as new. We're gonna do great things. You'll see."

"Deal."

She heard what she needed so desperately to hear. Time to take a chance. Time to let Grey Henley be her person, her place, her home. Loner-freak would rip off the bandage, and do it fast before she chickened out. She was in his vision, after all. So they were meant to be together, right? She wasn't eager to share her vision—in which he played no part at all. Maybe Grey was right. They were brought together by fate, or simple chance, a random pairing of names on a list of grad students compiled by an eccentric old archaeology professor. Perhaps that was all there was to it. She determined not to dwell on what Dean Nojes had whispered to her upon arrival and again when she was about to depart. And she refused to obsess over how and when to tell Grey about her "condition." Why tell him at all?

Well, that wasn't so hard, was it?

But Pauline wasn't finished asking the universe—and herself—for small favors. She wanted a chance to test a theory. Could she really give herself up to love, and be loved in return? Could the loner-freak who didn't know what made her tick find something approaching happiness?

Chapter 4

Pauline and her new lover spent nearly a week together in bed, living on bananas, pizza, and cheap red wine. Exploring every inch of their bodies, mapping favorite places to touch and be touched, Pauline's orgasms grew more explosive as she learned to concentrate on the delights of the flesh and trust her body not to betray her. For the first time since childhood, she banished thoughts of the *pulse* for days at a time. She silently thanked Grey for teaching her, without realizing it, how to live in the moment. She wondered how she could ever repay him for helping her step into a real life—one where she wasn't alone in her head all the time.

Maybe, she thought, it was time for Miss Sad Eyes to take a break. Maybe she could just be a *girl*, for once, and do all the gooey stuff that came with it.

I have a boyfriend! Huh!

What if she'd taken a job and had to jet off to some far-off desert? For once, Pauline was sure she was exactly where she was supposed to be.

On their fifth morning together, Pauline woke to find Grey's side of the bed cold. He sat a few feet away at the little table—the only table—that fit inside the tiny studio apartment. She admired how the muscles on his bare back rippled slowly each time he shifted in his chair. She didn't imagine ever growing tired of the way his shoulder bones formed slight hills on his strong, symmetrical frame.

Wrapping her naked body in the bedsheet, she joined him at the table.

"Hey, sleeping beauty," he said, bringing her a cup of coffee. She could get used to this—being serviced in every way possible. "I want to show you something." Spread across the table was a topographic map of all of Maryland plus the northern half of Virginia and the southern half of Pennsylvania. The map instantly began to move and shimmer, as all maps did when she looked at them. The flat swirls of topographic lines expanded and morphed into three-dimensional hills, gorges, ravines, meadows, saddles. With the barest glance, she was inundated with images of earth, rocks, soil layers, structures, buried objects. All these things came alive, rushing at her mind's eye like a speeding train barreling down the track. She couldn't *not* see them.

As a defense against the onslaught of information, she'd taught herself to visually skim a map, to avoid concentrating on a single focal point. That way, she couldn't as easily reveal what she instantly gleaned. Blurting out some obscure fact about a hillock or a grove of trees—or worse, the precise location of, say, an ancient spear—would spook people. No way she wanted to chance scaring Grey off. He made noises about her being a genius, but she felt certain he was half joking. If he knew how she was actually put together, that would be game over. Too weird. Too unpredictable.

Pauline's reserve was borne of experience. She'd been down that road before.

When she was ten, her fifth-grade teacher, Mrs.

Milsap, pulled down a huge Mercator world atlas from a roll hung above the chalkboard.

"Can anyone tell me where China is on the map?" Mrs. Milsap asked. Pauline assumed she was joking. Of course she knew where China was. Didn't everyone? When no one responded, she walked to the front of the room and put her hand on China. Mrs. Milsap repeated this exercise, asking students to find India, Argentina, Israel, New Zealand, and so forth. Pauline easily identified every country. After several solo trips to the front of the room, her classmates were giving her goofy faces. Oh. Not cool. She sat back down, confused and self-conscious. But there was so much to discuss!

"Mrs. Milsap?" she asked, her enthusiasm getting the better of her social intelligence. "Can I show everybody where the big hill fort is?"

"The what, Pauline?" Mrs. Milsap asked, clearly annoyed. Pauline winced at the memory, feeling sorry for the naïve young girl who believed that sharing was caring. Undaunted, she had walked up to the map and reached up to touch Dorset County in England.

"This is where Maiden Castle is," Pauline reported to the class, sealing her fate. "It's not really a castle. More like a big hill that the Romans built so they could look out and see when their enemies were coming. It's cool. There are a lot of hill forts, but this is one of the biggest. See how it's like circles inside circles? They found a bunch of Roman coins and pieces of a tile floor in all sorts of colors and patterns, like zigzags and stripes."

The whispers and snickers grew louder. Benjy rolled his eyes and muttered *borrinng* loudly enough to be heard. She thought Benjy liked her.

After that disastrous show-and-tell, nobody in school looked at Pauline the same way again. She was reclassified by her peers as an egghead and a brown-noser. No one had to tell her to her face that she was weird. She figured it out. Soon, invitations to sleepovers and birthday parties dwindled to nothing. She didn't report her unpopular status to her foster mom, Nora Heller, because she already knew how she'd respond. Something along the lines of, "Life is full of hard knocks, Pauline. You better get used to it." Nora and Herb Heller talked a lot about hard knocks.

The first time the *pulse* descended on her, toward the end of that unhappy fifth-grade year, Pauline was convinced she was dying. She lay on the floor in her bedroom, terrified, waiting for the room to stop spinning and for the grim reaper to leap after her. She'd seen pictures of the skeleton in a black cape, holding a curved blade. Surely he was coming for her. Her body was breaking down.

She had no one to turn to but the woman who was supposed to be her mother. She called out weakly, waiting for Nora to come to her aid, hoping her indifferent mother might, just this once, shower her with love and kindness. Nora came to the doorway, and Pauline tried to string sentences together, explaining how she felt. Butterflies. Floating. Something in her eyes. Nora listened without comment, then left the room. When she returned, she handed Pauline a box of tampons. Pauline had no clue what they were.

"Read the instructions," Nora said. "You'll get the hang of it. You're not dying. Not by a longshot."

No way, adult Pauline thought, she could ever share her *real* self with Grey. She turned away from the

43

map.

"Penny?" Grey said, tapping her shoulder. "Earth to Penny?"

"Nice map. What do you want to show me?"

He smoothed the map, while she concentrated on the light blond hairs on the back of his knuckles. "I'm convinced there is treasure waiting to be discovered somewhere on these lands," he said.

"Why do you think that?"

"Because, Pen, look. Here, for instance." Grey circled a spot on the map with his index finger. It was in northwest Baltimore County, roughly an hour from the Carthage campus. "The topo data clearly suggests there are some small mounds here, in an otherwise flat field. You know what that means."

Ah, how to play this? She didn't want to look dumb, but she couldn't get too far ahead of him, either. "Indigenous burial sites, middens, lost structures. The mounds could signal anything along those lines."

"That's what I think," he said. "But you're the genius, so now I'm sure it's true."

"Well, this genius isn't aware of any open digs in that area. Carthage doesn't have anybody up there, right? Or Maryland? Or Morgan? Wouldn't we know if there were an open pit that close to us?"

Grey refilled her coffee cup. "Well, what if…" He paused and smiled, but to himself, not at her. "What if we went and looked around on our own? Scouted some sites that look promising?"

"Where? On whose land?" She pulled the sheet tight around her shoulders.

"Private land, probably. Or state land. Not sure." He shrugged, like this little detail didn't matter. As if they could go anywhere they wanted, no questions asked.

"That's crazy," Pauline said softly. She imagined what Bette would say. Bette had already posted Instagram photos from the dusty Wyoming plains, in which she pointed at rows of Paleoindian artifacts arrayed on a plastic sheet. Pauline was ready to place bets that Bette wouldn't last long out there before switching to chasing grave-robbers, or any bad guys she could scare up. Pauline admired Bette's zeal for justice, though she doubted Bette would value the compliment, considering the source.

"Is it so crazy, though?" he asked, with a goofy squint.

"And then what? How would we even know where to look? We have no access to a satellite to make a 3D lidar image for us, so we can see what's down there. No drones or geospatial data. Without the benefit of ground-penetrating radar, and other info, we can't just head out somewhere and say, X marks the spot."

I'm not your fucking magical unicorn. Don't ask.

Grey rose from the table in silence and pulled on the same jeans and shirt he'd worn all week, since the night they met. He seemed in a hurry to go. Pauline jumped up, the sheet falling, exposing her breasts.

"I knew it!" she shouted. "I knew you'd leave. Zero chance you'd stay. So get on with it. Go ahead. Get out. Don't explain yourself. Just get it over with."

The sheet slipped to the floor, leaving her naked and exposed in front of him. Grey's eyes widened.

"Hey, hey, hey," he said softly, wrapping her in a bear hug. "Are you flying apart?"

Pauline nodded and buried her head on his

shoulder. *Don't cry.*

"Well, where do you keep the glue?" he said, chuckling. A laugh escaped her like a sob.

"I'm okay," she said, putting on a brave smile.

"I'm going out, yes, to pick up a few things. But I'm coming back, Penny. Do you believe me?"

"When I see you again, I'll believe you."

"Wow," he said. "Look, my vision was real. It's all gonna happen. Think about it. We can figure this out. I know we can." He slowly picked up his car keys. "This is me, leaving. Am I coming back?"

"Yes."

"Okay, good. Glad we worked that out."

The door opened, letting in a blast of air, and then he was gone.

From time to time, Nora Heller had locked Pauline out of the house when the girl's temper flared. Winter, summer. It didn't matter. She sat on the crumbling front stoop, hugging her arms for comfort, pretending that her *real* parents would pull up any minute in a brand-new minivan, to take her back to her *real* home, which would be much nicer than the Hellers'. A home where she'd be smothered with hugs and kisses and greeted with mugs of hot chocolate on cold winter mornings.

If Nora thought that banishing Pauline would curb her temper, she was wrong. Anger lived inside her like a banked fire, the embers glowing and ready to burst out like solar flares.

Grey didn't leave you. Maybe he did. No, he wouldn't. He's coming back, you'll see.

He had no idea the extent to which she'd already lied to him—was lying every minute they were together, if she was being totally honest. She didn't need laser beams shooting down from the sky to tell her what lay beneath the topsoil in Baltimore County. She wanted him to believe she was smart—without crossing the line into freak territory. The freak flag would have to stay under wraps. The only way to accomplish that was to avoid the truth.

She ran a hot shower and stood under the faucet until the water turned cold. *I want to be a girl who wants a boy who wants her just as much. That would be enough.* She threw on a pair of old sweats and a clean shirt, then remade the bed with clean sheets and took out the garbage. With each boring chore, she felt a little more like a fraud, pretending everything was normal—as if she were entitled to "normal," simply because she wanted it so much. She tossed the emptied plastic garbage pail under the sink and plopped into a chair, the air in her body suddenly expelled.

The small taste of life with someone else—an attentive lover—made it impossible for her to pretend that she could easily slip back into her sad-sack, loner life.

But what if he didn't come back, after all? What would she do?

Like a bat using echolocation to stay on course, Grey had fast become the wall she needed to bounce off of, to feel oriented, so she couldn't drift away to…where?

The door opened, startling her from her reverie. Grey held a bag of groceries in one hand and a bouquet of flowers in the other. She took the flowers from him, inhaling the perfume of red roses, yellow tulips, and white freesia.

"Grey." She drank him in from top to bottom as if

he'd been away for months. "I think I know what we should do."

"Like, where to go?"

"Yes," she said. "And maybe more."

"That's my Lucky Penny," he said. He took her in his arms and threw her onto the bed. By the time his cock was inside her, sending blooms of orgasm coursing through her, Pauline knew she would give him what he wanted. This was how she would repay him for rescuing her.

Chapter 5

"Stop here," she said. Grey pulled his battered blue 2002 hatchback alongside the edge of a long narrow ribbon of back-country road in Northern Baltimore County. It was just past midnight. They'd each chipped in for half a tank of gas, squeezing the most out of every last penny remaining to either of them. Pauline had already calculated she had just enough money left for one month's rent. The area where they'd stopped was dotted with a mix of small family-owned farms and country mansions. The car's headlights illuminated open fields. This was their first outing since hooking up, and Pauline's first time in Grey's old beater of a car, which hiccupped ominously several times on the drive out.

"Here?" he asked. "Are you sure?"

"Pretty sure. Check the map." She handed him the topographic map that had plagued Pauline earlier with its loud and insistent array of images and objects. Naturally, the map was only for his benefit. He flicked on the car's dim overhead light and ran his fingers over the swirling lines. "If I'm right, we want to head straight back toward that fence in the far north corner of the field." She pointed in the general direction, toward the far reaches of the headlights. Grey again consulted the map.

"It looks promising on paper," he said. "But the

map only takes us so far, right?"

They exited the car, and he pulled out a couple of beat-up garden shovels and hand trowels from the rear. They lacked brushes for the delicate work, but Pauline figured they'd make do, for the time being. She didn't ask when or where he got the tools. Had he been planning something like this for weeks or months? Shivering in the damp night air, Pauline wished she'd brought a fleece. They walked across the field, their boots crunching the dry remnants of last summer's corn stalks. Grey waved a flashlight in an arcing motion to light their way, the shovels resting on his shoulder. Pauline carried the trowels.

"Over there, Grey." She pointed. "Maybe a quarter mile east of us. Probably the farmhouse. The landowners, I mean. I don't think there's any way they can see us from there, do you?"

"I'm not a genius, Pen, but I know some shit, too. The word *trespass*, for example. It just means to pass across. It's not a big deal. We're not hurting anybody, are we?"

"Did I say it was a big deal?"

"I don't want you getting all, you know, squealy."

"I'm *not* squealy." She laid a free hand on his arm. "Do you trust me, Grey?"

"Do you trust *me*?"

"That's settled, then," she said.

They walked in silence for several minutes, the tools clanging. Finally, the flashlight revealed a modest, grass-covered mound rising about thirty-six inches above the otherwise flat terrain. The mound itself was roughly four feet in diameter. Out here, at the fenced edge of an open field, the mound was a blip, not something anyone would notice unless they knew what they were looking for.

"This it?" Grey asked. "Are we in the right place?"

"These are the exact coordinates." She dropped the trowels.

Grey wasted no time. He began digging a pit just inside the mound's circumference. Pauline followed suit, digging on the opposite rim of the mound. She knew Grey was smart enough to have a general idea—an expectation, at least—of what might lie beneath the mound. Pauline hoped he didn't let his imagination run too wild. She counseled herself to let him take the lead, offering advice only when asked. She didn't want to risk jumping several steps ahead of his own path toward discovery. Part of her strategy involved digging more slowly than he.

The ground was soft but dense as clay from heavy spring rains. Just as they'd been taught, and as they'd practiced in field research, Grey dug a rectangular hole into the side of the mound, roughly a foot wide and eighteen inches deep. Pauline stopped digging so she could hold the flashlight over the trench, enabling them to peer at the layers of soil—not unlike cutting into a layer cake with a variety of flavorings and frostings. They were practicing the art of *stratigraphy,* a method archaeologists use to look back in time based on the *strata,* or layers of soil, revealed by the dig. Some layers, such as sediment, subsoil, and bedrock (much deeper down), are considered sterile because they don't reflect human habitat. Other layers, however, may offer clues to human activity, such as compost (decomposed food and waste), burned wood, bones and bone fragments, and artifacts, ranging from, say, an

Indigenous arrow spear tip to a piece of colonial dinnerware, depending on where the dig takes place.

Pauline guessed that Grey secretly hoped to find something as spectacular as Dean Nojes's bronze dragon.

"What are we looking at?" Grey asked.

"You first."

"I'm not the one they gave the Boniface to, genius." He picked up a small stick and pointed to the back wall of the trench. "But I'd say these top six inches or so, nothing but ordinary mud."

"I agree," she said, hoping he'd continue. "No real activity in the top strata."

"But then, about ten inches down, it gets interesting, right?" He scraped the stick horizontally where the soil changed color and texture. The older, darker layer beneath the mud line was noticeable under the flashlight. "I'm thinking, maybe a burn layer here."

"Cooking or hearth fires, potentially."

"You told me the Susquehannock people settled out here."

"Long before Captain John Smith and all the other white marauders," she said. "The Susquehannock and the Lenape dominated the region, all the way from southern New York to the Chesapeake. Of course, I only know this because I took an elective on Indigenous Maryland." He'd buy that.

"Lucky me, with my Lucky Penny. We should keep digging. How's your trench coming?"

"I'm not as far along as you. Smaller muscles."

"Then why don't you keep holding the flashlight, and I'll keep digging here."

Her plan was unfolding flawlessly. She held the

flashlight steady, peering over Grey's shoulder as he carefully excavated another few inches, keeping the trench neatly rectangular. Once the trench was about two feet deep, the strata changed again. Fat splinters of charred wood and fragments of baked clay were packed into the walls.

"Wow," Grey said, breathing hard. "This is looking really good. I think we're gonna strike paydirt, Penny, I really do." He reached for the trowel to begin the more delicate work of excavating possible artifacts.

Oh, but maybe the plan was working *too* well. They were making progress much too fast. She didn't want him to find what she knew he would find—not yet—because how would she keep him by her side after that? Yet how could she stop him when he was so excited?

You want him to leave? By all means, go the pathetic-clingy route. That'll do the trick.

An idea sprang to mind. She would take a page from the legend of Scheherazade. As the story went, Scheherazade was a brilliant young Persian woman who read widely and knew every legend, fairy tale, and dynastic battle associated with Persia. Despite the reputation of Persia's ruling sultan, Shahryar, for marrying and then beheading a new virgin bride every day, Scheherazade volunteered to marry him. She then held the sultan spellbound for 1,001 nights, as she regaled him with tale after tale—leaving him wanting more of her stories at the end of each night. At last, the sultan fell in love with Scheherazade, thus sparing her life. She was the opposite of pathetic or clingy.

"Grey, wait," she said. "Let's do this right. Let's not rush. The site's not going anywhere, is it? We need better tools. Brushes, small picks, bags, and labels. You know the drill."

Grey rocked back on his heels. A sheen of sweat coated his forehead despite the chilly night. "You're right. You're damn near always right. Have you ever been wrong—about anything?" He smiled up at her, his face half in shadow.

They threw loose brush and dried grass clippings onto the area they'd disturbed. The mound was not on land under cultivation, so there was no reason for anyone, including the property owners, to traipse back there any time soon.

"So, it's official," Pauline said on the ride back to her apartment. "We're nighthawkers now."

"One hundred percent illegal antiquity hunters, operating under cover of darkness. Yup." Grey was gleeful as a little boy catching tadpoles. "Do you care?"

"I thought I would, but I don't. What we're doing feels like a victimless crime. I don't think Dean Nojes's Cambodian dragon really wanted to stay hidden underground forever, do you?"

Pauline's private reason for earning an archaeology degree—to gain sanctioned entry into the profession— seemed irrelevant now. With Grey by her side, the rules other people followed appeared quaint. He'd changed her. Bette would never speak to her again if she knew what they were up to, but Bette was out of the picture. Let her chase after nighthawkers and grave robbers in Wyoming, if it suited her, as long as the Pauline and Grey went undetected and unmolested on their chosen turf.

A stirring, a *sshwwr*, a rustle, like voices whispering from miles away, intruded on Pauline's train of thought. Vivid images crowded her vision.

A family dressed in deerskins huddled around a campfire, the youngest poking the fire with the femur bone of a fox.

A trio of women washing clothes in the river, sharing gossip.

She tried hard to ignore the part of her brain working overtime, concentrating instead on her lover's voice as they drove along dark country roads.

"There's no one else I wanted with me in the dean's room," he said. "And that was *my* turn to be right. But I do have a question."

"Which is?" *Please do not ask me any "how" questions.*

"Based on your extensive research, do you really believe there's anything of value, *real* value, in that mound? Anything we might be able to sell to the right sort of people?"

"I strongly suspect there is." She didn't know who "the right sort of people" were, but she had no doubt about what lay beneath centuries of soil. *Shhh. Go away. Stop whispering.* Grey took her hand and kissed it.

"That's a small down payment," he said. "Call it a finder's fee, to be redeemed in, say, an hour."

Pauline wondered if Scheherazade felt this excited the first night she earned the sultan's reprieve.

Chapter 6

Pauline slammed the apartment door behind them and, with dirt still packed under their fingernails, they kicked off mud-caked boots, stripped off filthy clothes, and devoured one another's bodies like a pair thirsting in the desert. Grey took her from behind, and she arched her back in an agony of pleasure. Not long after that, they went down on one another, bodies twisted together, juices filling the tiny apartment with a musky perfume. Sometime around four a.m., they drifted off in the narrow bed, holding hands. Pauline drifted toward sleep with a smile. A first, for sure. *So this is happiness.*

They woke in the early afternoon, stinky and ravenous, devouring half a cold pizza and a couple of overripe bananas before squeezing together in a hot shower, where they soaped one another until the gray water swirling down the drain turned clear.

"Why did you become an archaeologist?" she asked, as Grey, looking trim in boxers, brewed the last of their coffee. *He's like a book I've begun reading, with several chapters still to go. I don't want to reach the last page.*

"Can you see me sitting in an over-air-conditioned office all day, staring at a computer screen?"

"You're a man of action."

"Right."

"But why archaeology?" Still hoping for a straight

answer.

"I told you right after we met that I intend to make a lot of money fast, and I told you how I plan to do it. I thought I was clear about that."

"So, for you, archaeology is just a means to an end."

"It's a beautiful science, full of mystery. Beats the hell out of grinding it out on Wall Street. But when you put it that way, yes, you're right—again. I don't plan on digging for the glory of some university, just so they can stick a unique artifact I risked my life to find behind a wall of glass. Or a museum, either, where billionaire trustees walk around drinking champagne and patting themselves on the back for their latest acquisition. I refuse to be just another sap who rolls over for all these high-and-mighty *institutions*. They can keep their prestige. I'll take cash, thank you." He paused to gulp his coffee. "You're not having doubts, are you, my Lucky Penny?"

"No."

She summoned the most carefree smile she could muster. No second-guessing. Grey would never know that she could easily achieve his dream without him—at least the first part, which involved finding artifacts. But why would she, having only recently concluded that knowledge is no substitute for human connection—and sex? Scheherazade came up with a plan to prolong her life. While she might not be in danger of losing her head, like Scheherazade, protecting newfound love seemed every bit as important.

That afternoon, the two of them reached an understanding. After Pauline paid the rent one last time, they'd have a grand total of $250 in their checking accounts, combined. Neither had any savings, and neither raised the idea of borrowing from relatives or friends. Pauline didn't have any, and Grey didn't say, either way. He agreed to bring his clothes over to her place, assuring her his roommates would be fine without him. He seemed determined to look ahead. And so would she.

"Our fortunes are about to change, don't you worry," Grey said a few hours later, as they trolled the aisles at the hardware store, shopping for the cheapest version of the materials needed to continue their dig. "Tonight's the night, right, Pen? You're gonna help me find it—whatever you think is down there."

She had realized there was no chance of stretching this adventure for more than two nights, let alone 1,001. Once again, just after midnight, the nighthawkers set off across the farm field under a nearly full moon that cast a silvery light intermittently blocked by fast-moving clouds. The night was chilly and humid, and they expected to dig in the rain. Dean Nojes would be proud.

Once they reached the mound and cleared the debris, Grey got to work like a man possessed. Pauline calculated she needed to offer more direct guidance to help him along, since she couldn't possibly hold him back.

"You might want to start another trench, over here," she offered, climbing onto the mound and stomping on a fresh section of earth.

"Why?" He sounded irritated. "We agreed last night that the trench I've already started is leading us to artifacts. You said yourself—the scorched wood, the clay fragments. You said they were promising."

"Right, but most of the material is lodged toward the center of the mound, don't you think? If you start fresh a little farther uphill, you might find artifacts sooner."

"Are you sure about this?"

"About as sure as anyone could be, under the circumstances."

Grey sighed. "I guess that's as good as I'm gonna get. You take over the first trench, and I'll start the new one."

They traded places on the mound, but Pauline spent more time watching him than deepening the original trench. She already knew the fragmentary artifacts in the first pit wouldn't deliver what Grey hoped and expected to find. Before long, the moon disappeared, and a steady rain began to fall.

"Cover that pit!" Grey yelled. She threw a ground cloth over the first open pit, while he hunched over the new pit, digging furiously, trying to block the rain from falling into the small but widening chasm.

"Watch your margins," she cautioned. Grey shoveled so fast, the edges of the pit grew sloppy, and the rain didn't help. They both knew an artifact's market value depended not only on provenance—where it literally came from—but also its age, condition, and context. If Grey dug carelessly, he risked destroying crucial clues that contributed to the object's mystique— or else breaking the very thing he was after. "Slow down before you crush something important."

His shoveling settled into a slower, steadier rhythm as the rain intensified. Pauline stood a few feet from him on the mound, monitoring his progress. After an hour, the second pit was twice the size of the first.

"Stop," she commanded, picking up a slim-handled pickaxe. "Do you want me to take over?" It was time to begin the more refined work of pecking gently into the oldest exposed layer. Grey, breathing hard, rain dripping off his chin, nodded and threw down the shovel.

The muddy trench was just wide enough for Pauline to crouch on her knees and scrape away at the exposed four-hundred-year-old strata. Grey kneeled above her on the wet grass at the edge of the trench. She felt his eyes on her, greedy with anticipation. After half an hour poking and prodding the black mixture of soil and other organic material, she exposed a portion of an object clearly made by human hands.

A rush of voices pummeled her, all talking at once until a single voice, that of an old woman, emerged above the rest. The woman spoke an ancient tongue that Pauline had no trouble understanding.

"Grind the willow bark in the bowl, faster, faster. Mix in the berries. Without the medicine, my granddaughter will die."

Pauline could see the bowl, feel the cool, roughened clay. An object of immense beauty. The bowl and the woman were fully alive—but only to her.

"Hand me a brush," she said, struggling to keep a quaver out of her voice. Grey must have sensed that he, and this excavation, had her full attention. She gently wiped away a layer of wet soil from the object, which jutted out from the trench wall like a curved rump. "Bring the light closer, please." Grey focused the flashlight on the six inches surrounding the object. After more brushwork, they could both see what Pauline already knew. The object they'd liberated from its soil coffin was buff-colored, made of fired clay, with parallel hashmarks scored across its surface, as if the tines of a fork had been drawn across the clay while still wet.

"What is it?" Grey asked.

"Be patient. Like Nojes always told us."

"She's one of *them*."

"One of whom?" She kept her eyes on her work, concentrating on Grey's voice alone.

"You know, in bed with all the rich people who expect people like us to do all the dirty work so they can brag to their friends about how cultured they are."

"Nojes isn't like that. Besides, I thought you couldn't wait to get rich."

"That's right. But I'm different."

"Oh, really?" She laughed to cover the sounds pinging in her skull. "Okay, here we go." She switched now to a tool resembling a dental pick, sharp and narrow, to loosen the object without causing structural damage. She pried a piece from the wall and laid it on her palm.

"And?" Grey leaned in for a closer look.

"The bottom of a vessel, for sure. We'll know more if we can find the rest."

"Oh, we'll find the rest. It's here. It's got to be."

"So now who's sure?" She looked up at him.

"Just keep going. You're doing great."

"Yes, boss."

Using the pickaxe to systematically explore the horizontal layer surrounding the first fragment, Pauline visualized the remaining pieces, well aware that even she could make a mistake and damage a delicate portion of the artifact during the removal process.

Another half hour passed before she succeeded in extracting two large fragments that clearly belonged with the first piece—same buff-colored clay, same proportions and curvature with the hashmarks on the surface. She brushed off the newest pieces—the rain helping to remove the surface dirt—and lay all three pieces on the ground near the open pit. Together, they crouched near the ground, staring at the pieces illuminated by the flashlight's circle, rain pelting their heads. Grey gently picked up the pieces and aligned the cracks so the fragments formed a nearly completed vessel, roughly the shape of a curvy coffee mug, about six inches in diameter.

"Wow." Grey whistled softly. "Look at the collar. And the faces. My God." He cupped the pieces in both hands, holding them together with gentle pressure. He turned his hands so they could examine the vessel from different angles. Around the rim, the sculptor had added a collar—basically, a thicker layer of clay sculpted to resemble fat, square teeth separated by vertical lines. A decorative embellishment that suggested a purely artistic intention. The maker had chosen to turn a utilitarian object into a work of art.

The bowl holds the paste that will salve the girl's wounds. She will recover.

"The artisans at that time crushed fresh-water mussel shells to help strengthen the clay," Pauline said. "Probably dredged from the Susquehanna River, not too far from here."

"Uh-huh. But it's the faces that make it. They're the jackpot." Grey lightly fingered one of two tiny faces protruding slightly on opposite sides of the vessel's rim. The faces were wedge-shaped, with broad noses, slitted eyes, and on top of each head, a row of "teeth" that mimicked the shape of the collar. It was, they both knew, a stunning piece.

Perform for him. It's what he wants. Maybe even what he needs. Tell, without showing. Share, without revealing. That's how this works.

"If I had to guess, I'd say this is a classic piece of Washington Boro Stage pottery. Made by the Indigenous Susquehannock people who lived here, right here where we're standing, between four hundred and six hundred years ago."

Grey laughed. "If you had to guess. You *are* a fucking genius, Penny Pauline Marsh. And this is just the start. For both of us."

Pauline took hold of the fragments and examined them under the light. Tears ran down her cheeks.

"Are you crying?" Grey put a hand on her shoulder.

"No. Well, yes. But only because it's so beautiful. Perfect. Holy." And because the bowl helped to save the girl's life.

"Whoa. Put your nighthawking archaeologist hat back on, please, Pen. Holy? That's—"

"Yeah. Stupid."

A thousand prayers sent up from my lips, a thousand lips wetting my rim. I was honored to serve, said the bowl.

A few more tears escaped before she willed herself to stop them. How could she possibly explain the pride and dignity and raw human hope baked into the clay of this small, broken face pot? She couldn't. Ever. And the question that nagged at her constantly: *Why does it speak to me, and only me?*

"You're not caving, are you, Penny? About nighthawking? You're not feeling guilty, or…or…"

"No, no, I'm fine with it, Grey. I love this…doing this…with *you.*"

"Are you gonna cry every time we dig a hole in the ground?" The crooked grin forced a smile from her.

"Well, I can't promise I *won't.*"

Grey nodded several times. "I guess, uh, you're a temperamental genius, then."

"I guess so."

Scheherazade lived another night and paid the necessary price—nighthawking laced with subterfuge—to ensure her escape from a life alone.

They hastily filled in the trenches, erasing signs of their presence as much as possible, and turned their backs on the site.

Shhh! Be still now, Pauline begged the voices in her head.

Chapter 7

By the time they drove away from the farm, a cold, gray dawn was lightening the sky. The vessel fragments were sealed in a plastic bag on Pauline's lap in the car. Grey, charged up, spent the whole ride back trying to guess how much the artifact they'd discovered was worth on the private antiquities market. Pauline cranked up the heat, shivering in wet clothes.

"I'm guessing, two hundred fifty thousand, maybe more," he said. "Of course, a lot depends on who puts it on the market, and how, and when. There are a lot of variables. What do you think?"

"Grey, I don't have a clue. I don't even know how to find out." No point in lying about *this*, at least. Confessing real ignorance, for a change, actually felt good.

Sure, her secret knowledge revolved around an inexplicable ability to visualize, recognize, and find ancient things, long buried things, the things once prized and long forgotten. But as to what these objects were worth to anyone, be it a collector, a museum, or a university, she couldn't begin to guess. She'd always believed these objects existed outside any economic equation and didn't perceive a rational relationship between a stunning artifact and its commercial value. But maybe only because she'd never had any reason to put two and two together. She'd never held onto an artifact for years like Nojes had, let alone thought about selling one solely to generate income. Nothing stopped her from heading down that path.

"That's okay," Grey said. "Because I know exactly what to do next. You have your area of expertise, Penny, and I have mine. That's why we're so perfect together."

"I'm not opposed to making money."

"Good, because you're going to. *We're* going to make a lot."

"I'm not sure I even know how to spend more than, like, twenty dollars at a time."

Grey laughed. "You'll figure it out in a hurry. You'll see. You'll feel different, too. Money does that."

"For somebody as broke as I am, you seem to know a lot about money."

Grey pulled up in front of the apartment and switched off the balky engine. He turned to her and combed his fingers through her wet hair. Her scalp tingled under his touch.

"Money is all I ever think about," he said. "Besides you."

After two nights in a row, the illicit excitement of their nighthawking finally drained away, leaving them both exhausted. Pauline laid the plastic bag containing the vessel fragments on the little table, expecting they'd examine it again later. Grimy and grit-eyed, the two fell into bed in their damp underwear and sank into sleep, arms thrown across one another. The heavy warmth of Grey's limb across Pauline's chest was reassuring—an acknowledgement, of sorts, that they were on the cusp of an adventure together.

But Pauline was unable to duplicate the happy

sleep of the night before. A shadowy presence, vaguely familiar, approached her within the folds of slumber. He reached for her, and she for him, as if they were a pair of powerfully attracting magnets. They met in a space that was dark yet also boundaryless. Pauline struggled to determine whether she was dreaming, semi-awake, or occupying a mysterious third state of consciousness. Or was she undergoing the *pulse* in her sleep? She had no answers.

The figure, hovering at the periphery of her interior vision, glided through space, and she glided close by his side, though she could not make him out clearly. He was all bulk and heat and a sensation she could not define, as if earth and air had mingled with flesh to create an altogether different type of being. The fragments of the Susquehannock face pot floated between them, assembling into a seamless, unblemished whole, until the pot appeared brand new. Darkness gave way to light, and Pauline, in her suspended state, saw through his eyes. Suddenly, they hovered above a slender yet muscled young man with long black hair, naked from the waist up, his skin nut-brown. The young man sat on a log, hunched over a lump of wet clay on a flat-topped rock. He held a pair of finely shaped knives, one broad and flat, the other pointed like the sharp pick Pauline had wielded during the dig, both implements carved from deer bone.

On closer inspection, the clay was not formless. It was the very pot she and Grey had excavated. The young man was pressing fresh clay against the rim of the cup.

"The collar!" Pauline wasn't sure if she'd exclaimed out loud or only in her head. "He's shaping the collar, with its beautiful dentil molding."

"And tomorrow, Tucquan will begin work on the faces." The shadowy figure's first words, deep and rich, reverberated like buried vibrations, felt rather than heard.

"He has a name," she said.

"Of course, Pauline." The voice was hypnotic and seductive.

"And you know mine."

"Just as you know his—our sculptor's name."

"Tucquan...it means...winding stream." The knowledge blossomed all at once. "He was born at a narrow bend in the river, and that's what inspired his parents."

The figure beside her drew closer until he and Pauline were one being, one shared consciousness. She feared she would explode, or disappear, or forget who she was. She was nowhere and everywhere, as in the vision at the dean's house. Some kind of code, like a set of instructions, pressed in upon her. Destiny. Responsibility. Stewardship.

And then he was gone, leaving behind a sharp residue of loss. And still, she was unsure whether she was awake or dreaming. Ah, but he hadn't left, had he? His strong bulk lay on top of her, rubbing his naked skin against hers with increasing urgency. He pulled off her panties. *Come out of the shadows and let me see you!* Her questions morphed into sexual hunger. Wet with urgency, a cock entered her, insistent and probing. She clawed his back, wondering how to hold onto this powerful presence.

She exploded into orgasm, snapping awake with a gasp to see Grey, more asleep than awake himself, cleaving to her. But no. This was not who…a blink of confusion before clarity returned…Of course he was. Grey was the only man she wanted. The real man she had.

What use are visions and dreams? None at all.

And yet, she could not shake an underlying sense that something, or someone, had been lost.

In the morning, Pauline, eyelids gritty, watched Grey yank on his jeans and pour his T-shirt over his perfectly sculpted torso. He darted around the little room, pocketing his wallet, grabbing his car keys. A vague sense of guilt stole over her, as if she'd cheated on him.

"I have some calls to make and some errands to run, babe," he said.

"You're leaving."

"Yes. And then what am I doing?"

"Coming back. You're coming back."

"With coffee and doughnuts. Okay?"

He turned away absentmindedly, his mind obviously on other things. *Good. In case I look guilty.* He picked up the bag containing the vessel fragments.

"Where are you taking that?" she asked.

"I'll explain when I get back. You trust me, right?"

"Until you give me a good reason not to. One day at a time, buddy."

So, clearly, he didn't want to sit around that morning and continue fantasizing about how much this artifact might be worth. Instead, he was all business. A new mood, a new side of Grey Henley. How many other sides were there?

"Listen," he said. "I need you to do us a favor while I'm out." His tone suggested he was telling, not asking. But she'd do his bidding. Scheherazade accommodated the sultan—as long as it was in her own best interest to do so. "Find us the next dig. Wherever you think we're likely to find something at least as good as this." He waved the plastic bag. "The map's rolled up on the counter. Look, I'm not expecting miracles, Penny. Just do your best." The crooked smile. "What I mean is, you do you."

"Grey," she called after him. He turned around in the doorway. "Aren't you forgetting something?" She walked over and reached up for a kiss. A peck, and he was gone like a shot.

Damn. What a drag, needing somebody. Not enough practice. *Not my fault.*

She was nine, roused by a racing heart from an awful nightmare—fanged monsters tearing off her arms and legs. She ran into her foster parents' bedroom, craving warmth and security despite a notion she'd be rebuffed. She climbed onto their bed and tried squeezing between them. Herb Heller woke up, snorting angrily.

"What? What are you—?" He grabbed her upper arm and pulled her out of the bed. "Back you go, missy, and don't ever do that again. Our bedroom is off-limits, understand? Drink some water and go back to sleep."

Back in her own bedroom, she turned on the lights and scooted all the way under the covers, telling herself that inside the cave of covers the monster could not possibly find her.

And she was right. And thinking she needed the Hellers to protect her was wrong.

She didn't need Grey to protect her, either. She just needed him, period. Maybe not even "needed," but "wanted." Even wanting came with risks.

Pauline would even the score: make sure he wanted her like she wanted him.

She spread the map on the table and allowed it to speak of buried treasures, to reveal the delicate craftworks forged by ancient hands like...just like...like who? A name was on the tip of her tongue. The faint image of a figure seated on a log, carving a lump of clay. What had she forgotten?

The hairs on the back of her neck rose. She was not alone in the one-room apartment. Something or someone was there, filling the small space with faint sense memories of places and people and the way objects feel when you hold them...bone awls, spear tips, earring clasps, coins, bowls...

Her head spun and next thing she knew, the *pulse* was upon her, beginning with the insistent flutter of wings in her belly. For the next several minutes, she would be erased, swept up in a tide from elsewhere that she was powerless to resist.

Chapter 8

Behind closed eyes, the void was bright and full of tantalizing promise, not the usual blackness that accompanied unconsciousness. She stirred, unsure of the day, the time, and the location. Ah, flat on her back on the bed. The *pulse* had dragged her away, as always.

She sat up, loose and disjointed, like a splintered puppet that needed mending. As her vision cleared, Grey was watching her closely, appraising her. His dispassionate gaze felt impersonal. Then he flashed the crooked grin, and he was *Grey* again, the man she l-l-l…really? Did she love him? Could she risk it?

Dizziness was the reward for trying to stand up too quickly. When was the last time she ate?

"Doughnuts," Grey said, pointing to the box on the table. "Just like you asked."

She pushed her way to the table and devoured a chocolate glazed, eating so quickly she nearly choked on crumbs.

"What did you find us?" he asked, using his thumb to gently wipe crusty sugar from her lips.

"Huh?" A grunt.

"Our next dig, Pen. The map. What do you think?"

The map sat unfurled on the table, exactly where she'd left it before the latest tussle with her condition.

"Working on it."

"Great. When do you think you'll know?"

"Are we in a rush?" Her voice rose as she snapped fully awake. "Are some other nighthawkers going to beat us to the next treasure? Is this like one of those competitions where teams race around the world on a massive scavenger hunt, driving each other crazy, hoping to beat everybody else to the ginormous jackpot at the end? Is that what our nighthawking means to you?"

"Am I driving you crazy, Penny? Am I? Please name one thing I've done that's driving you crazy. Because if we're talking crazy..." He cut himself off by cramming half a doughnut into his mouth.

"You think I'm crazy? Say it. Go on. Say it."

"You're a genius," he snapped. "It goes with the territory." He finished a doughnut.

"I'm not a trained seal. I don't leap out of the water whenever you dangle a fish."

"I don't know what you're talking about." He grabbed another doughnut, gulping it down with coffee.

"I didn't find the next dig yet, okay? But I will. I don't need you to push me."

"Look." He moved his chair closer and took her hands. "What we're doing, it's a business. The start of one, anyway. I'm giving it everything I've got. Whatever it takes. I have no choice. I've got nothing, Penny. Not even a pot to piss in. I can't live like that. I won't. This has to work."

"I get it, I really do."

"You *will* get it when I show you something. Close your eyes."

She obeyed. Maybe he'd glued the face pot back together. That seemed unlikely. He fanned a stack of paper an inch from her face, then pried open her palms and placed a thick wad across them. New maps, perhaps, neatly folded? That would make sense.

"Okay, now open," he said. A stack of crisp hundred-dollar bills lay in her grasp, more money than she'd ever seen or held at one time. She looked up in surprise. "I didn't rob a bank, if that's what you're thinking."

"Then what? This is…"

"Not even half of it. There's a lot more. A hundred and twenty-thousand dollars in total, to be exact." He held up an even larger wad of bills. "I sold the face pot, Pen. Of course, the end buyer will pay way more for it than our cut. But believe me, our cut is fair."

"The end buyer?"

"Our buyer is the middleman. He knows all the angles. He's got buyers lined up waiting for shit like this. We're gonna ride the gravy train, honey, to where the streets are paved with gold."

"But who…" Too many questions to frame even one.

"I know it's a lot to process, and I promise I will explain everything. But right now, I want you to get dressed. We're going on a little adventure to celebrate."

"Grey." She remained motionless.

"What, babe?"

"I'm confused. I don't understand what's happening. What about the next dig?"

Grey took her in his arms, and they waltzed around the tiny room. "I believe in you, Lucky Penny. I know you'll come through. For me. For us. Tell me you want this as much as I do." She nodded, the heat of his body warming her as they twirled. His kisses tasted of sugar. "Right?" His blue-gray eyes trained on hers, an inch away, were impossible to say no to.

****

The day unfolded like a waking dream composed of unpredictable sequences. Never mind Scheherazade. This was Cinderella territory. Wishes granted, and all that. Where money equaled magic. Pauline recommended stashing most of the cash in the bank, but Grey was having none of it. Instead, he stuffed most of the cash into the inner zipper compartment of a ratty-looking backpack. Pauline suspected that, like her, he hadn't had the luxury of buying new stuff and used his possessions until they fell apart. And so what if they lost the money or were robbed on the street? Easy come, easy go. That was nothing, compared to the thought of losing Grey.

Still, she'd earned her cut, and on their way to the car, she held out a hand.

"Grease my palm, baby." He handed her a fat wad of bills pulled from his wallet and his back pocket. No point counting it. Whatever she had now was more than she'd ever had before. The idea that she wouldn't run out of money the next day, or in a week's time, was new and strange, and still hard to believe.

"Feels good, right?" he said, clicking his seatbelt. "Makes you feel powerful. Like you can do anything."

"I don't know about that. But you know what? I think I'm ready to find out."

"That's my girl."

As they pulled onto the beltway, Pauline tuned the radio to a classic rock station and began bouncing to the thumping beat of a Queen song. The day felt loose and free, like anything could happen. She didn't care where they were going. Nonetheless, she gave Grey a quizzical look when he pulled off at an auto dealership in Timonium.

"First things first," he said. "We're ditching these old wheels."

Two hours later, they left the lot in a deep blue luxury convertible, sleek and sexy, which set them back more than fifty thousand dollars in hard cash. Grey didn't bat an eye, but the sum nearly took Pauline's breath away. She got over it. He chose the model. She chose the color.

Back out on I-95, putting the purring new motor through its paces, Grey instructed her to book a hotel in New York City for two nights. Nothing under a thousand a night, he said. She pulled out her phone.

"The Halifax," she reported, shouting to be heard in the open vehicle. "New York's hottest new hotel adjacent to the High Line. All suites are impeccably furnished by the Italian interior designer Arnoldo Silvestri and fully automated. Complimentary champagne and caviar await you, which you may enjoy while sitting on your balcony, gazing out over the Hudson River."

"Perfect!" Grey bounced his hands on the leather-wrapped steering wheel. "I've never had caviar, have you?"

"First time for everything." She laughed into the wind.

The hours flew by as if they were under a spell. By six o'clock, they were standing in the lobby of the Halifax Hotel in Manhattan, Grey having reluctantly handed over the fob to the new car to the hotel's parking valet. The lobby was stark and elegant, the floors all done in white oak, the furniture spare and cream-colored. A black cast iron stove in the center of the lobby, generating real heat, added a touch of warmth to the expansive lobby, which was roughly ten times the size of Pauline's apartment. A young woman dressed in form-fitting black asked if she could arrange to bring up their luggage.

Pauline turned to Grey, and they burst out laughing. "Luggage?" they said together. Empty-handed and under-dressed. But cash-rich. Absurd.

"We travel light," Grey told the woman, stifling more laughter.

"Very well, sir," she responded. She walked them to a private elevator that would bring them up to their suite, handing each of them a black-and-gold keycard. Even the keycard, cool and smooth in Pauline's hands, felt luxe. More instructions followed, including a heads-up about the private butler awaiting them in the suite, ready to do their bidding.

The elevator door closed. Pauline reached for Grey's hand.

"So it's true," she said. "Money talks."

"Oh, yes," Grey said. "Money never shuts up."

"Then I guess we'll be doing a lot of talking, won't we?" Pauline didn't remember ever smiling as much as she had that day, and the day was far from over.

"There's talking, and then there's *talking*." He pulled her to him, and his kiss reached down to her toes.

When the elevator released them, Pauline emitted a small gasp at the sight of the most spacious, well-appointed room she'd ever seen. Spare, elegant furnishings, like an image straight out of a magazine. White oak floors covered in part by large area rugs of abstract creams, blues, grays, and browns. Natural light streamed in through a picture window running the length of the room's west side, affording a view down onto the sinuous High Line and out across the Hudson River.

"Welcome to the Halifax." A rail-thin young man, dressed in form-fitting black, stepped forward to greet them. "I'm George. If there's anything you need during your stay, simply press here on your guest tablet"—he held up a small flat-screen device—"or the identical one in the bedroom. I understand you traveled light to be with us, and so I've already taken the liberty of preparing a list of several of the finest retailers, should you decide to refresh your wardrobes. That information is also on the tablets."

George expertly decanted a bottle of champagne awaiting them on a glass-topped coffee table, alongside a silver dish of shiny little black bubbles. So that was caviar?

"May I ask what we're celebrating today?" George asked, handing them each a filled flute.

Grey and Pauline exchanged looks.

"Luck," she said.

"Not luck." Grey shook his head. "She's being modest. Hard work."

"Very well," George said. They could've told him anything, told him they were thieves in the night, and he'd probably still say the same thing.

Moments later, George was gone. Grey slid open the glass door leading from the bedroom onto the balcony, which held a small redwood-slatted table and two matching chairs. Pauline inhaled the bracing evening air of spring, while the never-ending soundtrack of New York's streets floated up, muffled by distance. Arrayed before them, a beautiful tableau: the sun setting over the Hudson River, a glimpse of the Chrysler Building to the north, and the crenellated rows of stone, glass, steel, and brick that defined the city's two-plus centuries of building stock.

"To money," Grey toasted, raising his glass. "My favorite language."

"To us."

"Oh, that." Grey put his arm around her shoulder, its heavy warmth settling on her like a secure anchor.

****

"Do you suppose his real name is George? It sounds so...butlerish."

"Here, anything is possible," Grey replied. "He can be anyone. So can we."

"I believe that, Grey, when I'm with you. On my own...well..." She dropped the sentence. *Leave well enough alone. Don't spoil the mood—or a perfect evening.*

"The price of genius-hood, I guess. But no more doubts." He fingered the dimple on her chin. "Look where we are. We did this together, Penny. We're a team—an invincible one. When will you start believing me?"

"I believe you, absolutely, this very minute."

"Good." He put his glass down, then took hers and set it down as well. "But I think you still need some convincing."

He scooped her up without another word and carried her to the enormous bed, peeling away every layer of clothing, teasing every nerve of her body with fingers and tongue until the exquisite pain was almost too much to bear. She clawed at his crotch, wishing for union, which he delayed for minutes beyond reckoning. At last, he entered her, the screams filling the room seeming to emanate from someone else. Together, they flung their desire out into the New York night.

Afterwards, panting and sweaty, a jumble of brocade pillows thrown to the floor, Pauline looked at her lover, grinning like the Cheshire cat. *If only I could bottle this moment, but real life is nothing like archaeology. There's no mucking around in time at your leisure, no artifact to hold this exquisite moment forever—to turn it around in your hands. All one can do is make more moments like this. Just like this.*

****

Pauline sprang off the bed and retrieved the silver-plated dish of caviar and crackers. Using the elegant little mother-of-pearl spoons, they each piled glistening black fish egg beads onto thin wafers, feeding each other, sweeping crumbs off the sheets.

"Salty. Tangy," Pauline said. "It tastes like—"

"Sex."

"Yes!"

After a second bottle of champagne, Pauline was as fizzy as the bubbles. They put on plush hotel robes and glided back out onto the balcony, the lights of New York twinkling in every direction.

"Is this a dream, Grey? This morning, we had nothing. And now..." The city lights were a festive blur.

"What if this is reality, Penny, and everything that's come before, all the years we've both struggled along without money, what if *that* became the dream? More like a nightmare that fades when the sun comes up."

"I don't know."

"Why not? How could you not want all *this*, all the time?"

"It seems so…easy. Like we didn't earn it."

"Hah," he said, sounding bitter. "What you earn isn't the same as what you deserve. Just ask my mother."

She wanted a closer look at his face, but a shadow fell across it. "Tell me." Four weeks they'd been together, and already she couldn't imagine living without him. Yet who was he, really?

"She raised me alone." He bit off each word. "Always working three different jobs. We moved more times than I can count, trying to find a place we could afford without rats or cockroaches, where the hot water wouldn't quit on us."

Seizing the rare opening, Pauline asked him about his father, only to be told that he "wasn't available." The set to Grey's mouth told her she wouldn't get more—not immediately. Sharing wasn't necessarily fun. The Hellers, those damn *frosters*, had kept her minimally clothed and fed, more stingy with affection than even basic necessities. Not a great topic of conversation.

They'd both been dealt a raw deal, but here they were.

"Survivors in the lap of luxury," she said out loud, following her train of thought.

"Exactly," Grey said, his tone brighter. "That's us, Pen. That's who we need to be, you and I."

"You're right. Why not us?"

"Why shouldn't we get rich and enjoy life, and

travel, and stay in fancy hotels? We deserve it as much as, oh, Dan Finland."

"Way more than Dan Finland!"

They laughed until they couldn't breathe, then ordered steaks and pommes frites, which arrived under fancy domed lids, surrounded by white cloth napkins and impossibly heavy silverware. George served them.

"Thank you, George," Pauline said with exaggerated politeness. "You're the best. The greatest."

"We need a George," Grey said after George had left the suite.

"Somebody to wait on us, hand and foot."

"Or foot and hand."

After dinner, they raided the nicely stocked bar. Not a mini-bar with mini-bottles. That was for peons. A real bar with dimpled glasses, a full ice bucket (when did that happen?) and Scotch, bourbon, whatever they could desire. At some point, they wound up back on the bed, too drunk for sex.

"Gonna need more money," Pauline said, eyelids closing.

"Tons more." Grey laced his fingers with hers. "Best nighthawkers ever."

A last thought assailed her before she sank into a drunken sleep. From now on, everything would depend on her willingness to maximize her weird abilities. If only there were another way. But there wasn't, was there?

I have to be who I am, now more than ever.

Chapter 9

It was past two in the afternoon by the time the nighthawkers stirred, kissed, disentangled warm limbs, and took a long, lazy bath together in the huge whirlpool tub. They fiddled with all the jets, the near-scalding hot water a form of deep-cleanse, like wiping the slate clean. Pauline let Grey wash her hair, luxuriating once more in the feel of his fingers massaging her scalp. Her wet thighs hugged his sides as she pressed her feet against the tub's far wall, willing him to grow hard and enter her. Their lovemaking sent waves cascading over the rim of the tub. They didn't care.

They breakfasted in bathrobes on the balcony, basking in the sun.

"What's next?" Pauline squinted into the sun, ridiculously happy they'd have one more night in this fantasy world. She'd never felt so relaxed, almost liquid. If only she *could* bottle the moment—freeze time in its tracks.

"We're going to meet Chanel, Brioni, Fendi, and all their friends," Grey said.

"Who?"

"We're going shopping, babe. New threads for both of us. We gotta look the part."

"Look the part for what?" They'd surely be nighthawking again before long, which required only the grungiest clothes and boots. Grey smiled. She could press him, but wasn't ignorance delicious? The rare luxury of leaning into *now*, with no idea what the day might bring.

They agreed to split up for the next several hours to forage independently for clothing and other supplies. Grey confessed he didn't know his way around Manhattan, but laughed and shrugged, unfazed by the unfamiliar streets. Pauline couldn't tell him she didn't know what that felt like. She was never lost, anywhere. Her body functioned as a compass. But when it came to shopping, that was another story entirely. She tried to picture a new wardrobe and drew a blank. But help was on hand. George had thoughtfully loaded their tablets with long lists of retailers, which they both downloaded to their phones. They agreed to skip the sightseeing. The Empire State Building, the Statue of Liberty—too new, too far above ground to hold their interest.

Heading out into the city on her own, Pauline counted the wad of bills Grey had handed her the day before. *Holy shit. Six thousand dollars. All in one place.* All hers, somehow. They'd found a thing, and then the thing was transformed into money. That still didn't make a lot of sense, but the currency was real, even though it still seemed like board game money—part of a game she'd been roped into, to which she didn't quite know the rules. To Grey, the recent turn of events seemed to reflect the natural order of the universe. He hadn't turned a hair.

What's it feel like to spend a large sum of money all at once? May as well find out. George had recommended little boutiques scattered around Soho and the West Village. Pauline bought a fat soft pretzel from a street cart with the last of her personal funds and ate it as she walked south through Chelsea. The constant barrage of honking cars and taxis, and throngs of tourists speaking a variety of languages, helped to hold unwanted thoughts and images at bay. If only the bustling city—its vivid, noisy reality—was the *only* reality to worry about.

Pauline stepped inside the first boutique on George's list, on Spring Street, and was greeted by the calming scent of lavender. Or maybe not so calming. Looking around the racks of chic clothes, Pauline was Julia Roberts in *Pretty Woman*—an imposter. They'd probably kick her out any moment. But no. Maybe they smelled the money, after all. A woman about her own age, much better dressed, interrogated her, kindly but insistent. What style was she looking for? What effect did she want to achieve? Was she shopping for a special occasion? Pauline couldn't stammer out a complete sentence.

"Well, you are not so long in the limb, but neat and compact," said the woman in Italian-accented English. "Nice shoulders. Good breasts. I can work with you."

Pauline wore an over-stretched wool sweater over an ancient pair of skinny black jeans and second-hand preppie boots. Exactly what she'd arrived in at the hotel. She felt like a hopeless case. But then, so did Cinderella before she dressed for the ball. Why should girls in fairytales have all the fun?

The saleswoman was super put-together, in a form-fitting black one-piece outfit that Pauline learned was a jumpsuit, along with black stiletto boots and long dangling earrings.

"I like your look," Pauline told the woman,

meaning, I'll have what you're having. It felt like a shot in the dark, but what the hell. The saleswoman looked like the type who didn't take shit from anyone. Maybe looking a certain way on the outside could help her manage what went on, on the inside. Or maybe not. But this was the moment to at least try.

"Buffo!" The woman laughed, then promptly pushed Pauline into a dressing room and yanked the curtain closed. "I'm Francesca. I bring you everything to make a new woman." She handed Pauline one piece of clothing after another. Pauline, in turn, came out to parade a stream of outfits in front of the store's three-way mirror, while Francesca watched her closely. She tried on a deep V-neck leopard print ruched top, a zebra print scoop top, leopard slouch booties. Also a red leather moto jacket with a thick silver zipper, a body-hugging cut-out sheath dress, and a sleeveless mock-neck jumpsuit in deep navy silk. With each outfit she tried on, Pauline caught a glimpse of a new woman in the mirror—someone filled with new possibilities, ready to leave old dreams behind, just as Grey had said.

"I'll take it."

"Which?" Francesca asked.

"All of it." Pauline's stomach flipped at the extravagance. Nevertheless, she peeled off more than three thousand dollars from her wad as casually as possible. Francesca didn't bat an eye and wrapped everything in tissue paper. Easy come, easy go.

Exiting the store laden with chic black shopping bags, Pauline felt old layers falling away. She wouldn't call herself a freak now—or at least, that wasn't all there was to her, anymore. She smiled, thinking about the fashion show she'd put on for Grey later. She felt full, as if she'd just finished a big meal and needed time to digest. Enough for now.

Turning onto Thompson Street, her inner circuits sparked without warning. A presence nearby—felt rather than seen. Her insides hummed, resolving into some kind of harmonic chord that played on steadily. Then he came into full view, the stranger who had taken over her dreams. Her first good look at him, in real life, revealed a man more than a head taller than everyone surrounding him on the crowded sidewalk. Dressed all in black. A large head—bronzed skin, nearly glowing—with a strong jaw, deep black eyes, and black hair pulled into a ponytail. He came toward her with large strides, unjostled by other moving bodies.

A perfect day. Ruined now. Enraged, she ran across the street, shopping bags swinging wildly against her feet, pretending she could outrun him, outrun her true self. *What does he want? Whatever it is, I'm not giving it up.*

The stranger was undeterred, narrowing the distance between them. The closer he came, the louder the humming grew, filling her with its insistent thrum. She stopped running, seeing there was no point. The stranger stood inches from her, all other passersby fading away. A forcefield surrounded them, and her molecules rearranged themselves to suit him, somehow, to bring them into alignment.

A familiar stage of the *pulse* overtook her. She rose out of her body, released from gravity and the laws of physics. For an instant, she had a bird's-eye view of the streets of New York, able to look down and see near and far at the same time.

His deep voice emerged from the hum. *You are more*, he said.

Pauline shook her head in vigorous denial. *I don't want this. I don't want you.*

In a flash, he was gone, and relief mixed with unexpected sadness, as though she'd just lost something, or someone, dear to her.

An echo in her head, repeating: *You are more.*

She countered the echo with silent screams. *My life makes no goddamn sense. Only Grey makes sense. Stick to what you know for sure.*

Pauline stood on the sidewalk, her back against a rough brick wall—a solid surface to hold her up until her legs stopped shaking. But she couldn't walk away. Not yet. A swift-moving raft of images, voices, and information flooded her like a film running in full color.

The death of Charles Waters, a full-blooded Indian of Little Neck, the last of his race.

A Native American cemetery in Queens—miles from her present location—where the descendants of the Matinecock, Shinnecock, and Montauk peoples who once cultivated this land, were buried in the Christian tradition.

Charles Waters lived in a long house on a farm inherited from his mother, who inherited from her mother an axe with a wooden handle, a hand-hammered silver metal blade attached to it with sheep's catgut.

The cemetery was desecrated long ago, to make way for office buildings. The axe had been pushed ten feet deep into the airless, pitch-black soil, where it waited for a new era of utility that would never arrive.

Charles Waters wept with his ancestors, his bones scattered, his life, his family, his Indigenous lineage…all dispersed.

Focus. Breathe.

If Charles Waters were to appear this very instant, Pauline would know him intimately.

Why?

The string handles of the shopping bags cut into her fisted palms.

You are more.

Oh, no. *Crazy* would not drag her down, spoil this day, ruin a life already plagued by inexplicable forces for over half her life. Only last night, she had made peace with her secrets for Grey's sake. But this fresh intrusion wasn't fair. It was too much to ask.

Charles Waters be damned.

Pauline resolved to spend nearly every remaining dollar on beautiful clothing, shoes, and jewelry to go with her new life. The next few hours rushed by in a blur. Zigzagging between Grand Street and Canal Street, she sailed in and out of one boutique after another, snatching beautiful things off racks and counters, buying anything that appealed on the spot.

She worked hard at pretending to have fun, whipping around every few minutes to look over her shoulder, listening for unwanted voices, and dreading the return of the stranger and his claims on her—whatever they might be.

Late in the afternoon, with just enough money left to hail a taxi back to the hotel, she stuffed bags inside of bags—the spoils of a $6,000 shopping spree. Wouldn't Grey be delighted. She tried to froth up excitement, but her heart was no longer in it. Getting the feeling back, that feeling of liquid insouciance, would not be easy.

In the hotel lobby, Pauline struggled to keep hold of all her new wares while glancing back through the revolving doors to be sure she wasn't being stalked. She'd know, wouldn't she? Paranoia was pointless. She dropped a bag. A man arrived swiftly by her side to pick it up. An attentive valet, no doubt.

"I'm in 2806," she said, distracted.

"Yes, ma'am," came the reply. She turned in surprise. Not a valet, but Grey Henley, a devastatingly handsome, sophisticated businessman. His clothes and shoes were impeccable. His curly blond hair had been trimmed, making him look slightly older and more serious. He wore cologne—a musky, deeply masculine scent.

"Wow," is all she could manage.

"Fifth Avenue, babe. Nothing but the best."

Surely, she could will herself back to carefree lightness, for his sake, at least. Inside the private elevator, she reached over her packages to kiss Grey and inhale his aphrodisiac cologne.

"That's your ticket to the fashion show," she said. "Your only job is to let George know we need champagne. Lots of champagne."

"And oysters. You know, eating like the rich."

"Naturally."

The champagne arrived while Pauline organized outfits on the bed, pouring every ounce of thought into the new clothing. She'd instructed Grey to wait for her on the sofa. First up was the jumpsuit. She jutted her hips like a model, walking in a tight U on an invisible runway. That was followed by the red leather moto jacket worn over tight black leather pants and chunky black boots. Then, the white sheath dress with a tear-shaped cutout on the right shoulder. Last, by design, a black silk teddy, gartered stockings, and four-inch heels. Grey looked on, radiating confidence like a billionaire. When the teddy came down the runway, he scooped her up and threw her onto the sofa.

"Keep the heels on."

****

On her back, knees folded over the arm of the sofa, she eyed him greedily as he removed his new tie and suit jacket and slipped off his pants, revealing new boxers that drew attention to his taut abdomen. Sex on the couch was loud and noisy and full of urgent abandon.

Afterwards, they slurped ice cold salty oysters and drank champagne, she in the teddy and he in his boxers with the faint blue stripes.

"I wish…" Pauline began, full of too many wishes, and terrified none would come true.

"I know. Me too. We will."

Chapter 10

"You missed our turn."

Grey had been cheerful on the ride back to Baltimore. But he sailed past the exit to the beltway, which would have looped them around to Pauline's dingy apartment north of the city. She dreaded sleeping there, now that she'd had a taste of luxury living. That dark basement room was too small to contain them both any longer. Just as well she was done paying the rent.

"I wanted to tell you so bad, Pen, but secrets are much more fun. And I want to see the look on your face."

Grey steered the purring luxury convertible onto I-395, which arced around a curved ramp, depositing them downtown, near the Inner Harbor. He turned on Conway Street, then turned again, unexpectedly, and pulled into the garage of an ultra-modern high rise with glass panes reflecting the harbor's blue-gray water—the color of Grey's eyes.

"What's going on?" Parked beneath an unfamiliar skyscraper, she was grateful, at least, that she had dressed to impress, her tired jeans traded in for ivory linen pants, a white blouse with a collar that popped nicely, and a café-au-lait suede jacket. The woman who'd entered the Halifax Hotel two days before had been left behind. Good riddance. If only she could leave *other* things behind, as well.

"New digs," Grey said, exiting the car. "Hold on." He jogged around to the passenger side and opened the door for Pauline. He was also a fashion plate in a button-down shirt under a slim-fitting, black-ribbed cotton sweater and dark pants. "Follow me, gorgeous." She clasped his outstretched hand, trying to read his mind.

The building's lobby reminded Pauline of the Halifax, all cool colors and understated elegance, though perhaps the gold chandeliers dripping glass icicles were a bit much. Grey spoke briefly with a woman at the front desk who reminded Pauline of Francesca, the chic saleswoman who'd helped her spend thousands on a new wardrobe in New York. The woman handed Grey a set of keys, and he led her to the elevator bank where he pressed the button for the nineteenth floor.

"What do you mean, new digs?" she asked, still not putting the pieces together. "You didn't mean—"

Grey shushed her with a finger to her lips, which he slid down to her dimple.

Once inside, the apartment demanded a moment of stunned silence. Floor to ceiling windows filled with light, panoramic views of the city skyline—the Inner Harbor all the way out to the Key Bridge. Fully furnished in a style a bit warmer than the Halifax, and obviously livable. Pauline briefly tested the black leather sectional sofa, which faced the harbor. Then, stepping onto the balcony terrace off the main living area, a sharp wave of vertigo seized her, as if she couldn't rely on gravity to keep its promise. Grey wrapped his arms around her from behind, providing the ballast she needed. Returning inside, they explored the bedroom, which boasted a second, enclosed balcony to shield them from bad weather.

"Grey, what did you do?" Pauline asked at last.

"It's ours. We have a six-month lease. After that, we'll see."

"But I don't—"

"This is what money is for, Penny. Can you get used to it?"

She returned to the balcony terrace, gripping the railing this time, inhaling faint traces of the open water. Seagulls flew by nearly at eye level. She imagined they were a smidge closer to the sun.

"Yes. I think I can get used to living in the sky."

A month ago, she had nothing and no one. And now, an embarrassment of riches. It was almost too much to take in, each day more like a dream than a real life.

"We'll pick up whatever you need from your apartment, and then, that's it." He'd wrapped his arms around her once more as they watched sailboats and water taxis gliding across the harbor.

"What about you?"

"I'm living strictly in the future. The past doesn't count."

"That's funny coming from an archaeologist whose job is to root around in the past."

"As a means to an end, Penny. Anyway, we root around in *other* people's pasts, not our own. Who we *were* isn't nearly as interesting as who we're going to *become*."

"Right." She smiled inwardly. "That's so right."

They settled in quickly. Given how little they possessed, it wasn't difficult. The closets in the new condo were so large their new clothes barely took up any space. Pauline concluded there was nothing at her old apartment she needed or wanted. A clean slate seemed like a very good idea. Maybe she could wish her way out of her old life. Wouldn't that be nice.

Grey ordered groceries and wine to be delivered. Two hours later, a young man stood in the entryway alongside a cart filled with grocery bags and a carton of wine bottles. How effortless, living like the rich. Pauline opened a ruby red Barolo and hunted through the cabinets until she found two large, round wine glasses. *Their* glasses, now. How odd. The fully stocked kitchen contained a coffee machine with so many gold knobs, dials, and spouts, she figured a separate PhD might be needed to operate it.

"Here, babe, come take a look." While Pauline was learning where things lived in the kitchen, Grey had spread a new set of laminated maps across the spacious walnut dining table. She came toward him carrying the filled wine glasses, abruptly spilling a few drops on the table the instant she saw the maps. Her head exploded with images and urgent voices, banishing the tranquility of moments earlier.

"Hey," Grey said, quickly wiping away the red droplets. "The maps are laminated. The table is not."

"Sorry, I—"

"Never mind. We need a new site."

"Yeah." She looked away from the table, but already, she'd picked up a lot of intelligence. The maps spanned the Eastern Seaboard, making it possible for them to get just about anywhere within a day's drive. And there was plenty to get to; the pickings were rich.

"The money doesn't print itself," he said. His eyes

were cool and serious. This was the all-business Grey, in his smart new clothes.

"I know." She took her wine to the couch.

"After all our expenses, we've got enough left to feed ourselves for about two weeks."

"That's it?"

"That's it. So time to hustle. Time for Lucky Penny to work her magic." He massaged the back of her neck, which she needed more than she'd realized. How wonderful that he could read her so well, given how many secrets she kept from him.

"What if we don't find anything of real value?" she asked.

"We will. Of course we will."

"How can you be so sure, Grey? Doesn't this feel like a gamble?"

"Life's one big gamble, Pen." He flashed the crooked grin. "Stepping out onto that balcony is a gamble. If a strong blast of wind hits you at just the right moment—"

"I get it. I guess we have no choice."

"No choice at all. So what'll it be?" He turned back to the maps on the table.

Not a magical unicorn, buddy, like I told you before.

"I need privacy, Grey, so I can concentrate. Having you close by is...distracting."

"Will you let me distract you later?" A lusty smile.

"What do you think?" She clamped his balls and gave them a gentle squeeze. He kissed her, refilled his wine glass, and headed off to the bedroom. She heard him on the phone—the deep-voiced, all-business Grey. The only words she could make out were, *Yes, we're right on schedule.* What would eavesdropping get her? No. Don't go there. Trust is a two-way street.

She refilled her own wine glass, vamping for time before plunging into the chaos she needed to unleash. She'd struck a bargain and had to hold up her end— keep them on schedule, even. Otherwise, bye-bye luxury. Cinderella would flee the ball barefoot and in rags. And Scheherazade? Her tales would cease to enthrall the sultan, whose company she very much wanted to keep.

Taking a deep breath, she forced herself to focus on the maps, hoping to find the sure thing Grey was counting on her to find.

Ah, the wooden ribs of a spectacular seventeenth-century sailing vessel nestled in the mud of the Nansemond River in Virgina. Rebuilding the boat in her mind's eye, it sliced swiftly through the Virginia tidewaters, the breeze grazing her check. But excavating the skeleton of a sailing ship was not a two-person job, especially at night. She ruled it out. Grey would never know.

A flood of images followed: spear tips, ancient cutlery, ceramic fragments at least as beautiful as the face pot they'd already found.

Then a fresh image rose before her, clear and bright as a high-resolution photograph. This was the one. A curved saber with a carved brass hilt. Not old by archaeological standards. Made in France and exported to Virginia during the Revolutionary War. She guessed the piece had value. Weren't swords highly collectible? And didn't the so-called romance of war still hold many in its spell? Grey would be beside himself, but she'd parcel out the facts in dribs and drabs. If he were a fisherman, she'd be the one tossing tasty bait out into the water, making it easier for him to reel in a big whopper.

Before calling him in to learn what she'd found, she flipped open her laptop and used an erasable marker Grey had supplied to draw lines, arrows, and circles all over the various maps. All fake research. Hopefully convincing enough that he wouldn't wonder. He hadn't so far. She counted on that.

"I think I found it!' He was by her side in a flash, leaning over her shoulder as she showed him James City County, situated on the Virginia Peninsula jutting out from the Eastern Seaboard like the boot of Italy, surrounded by the James, York, and Chesapeake rivers. "This is where we need to dig." She pressed on a marked circle.

"What will we find?" He searched her face for answers.

"Well, I can't tell you exactly, can I? If I knew that, I wouldn't just be a genius, I'd be a friggin' fortuneteller, right?"

"Okay, but what's your best guess?"

"Based on all the sources I consulted, including some lidar images online, recent digs, and some other topo maps even more detailed than these, this area is a treasure trove of artifacts, ranging from the Woodland-era natives up through the Revolutionary War."

"How do we zero in? I mean, how do we find exactly where to go, like we did at the farm?"

"I tell you what." More vamping. "By the time we're packed and provisioned for the dig, I'll be able to say exactly where we should go."

"It's a deal, Lucky Penny."

"Lucky Grey."

"Someday, you must teach me…"

"Uh-uh. No way. Trade secret. You have yours, I have mine." She held her breath.

"That's fair. Secrets spice things up, huh?" Oh, that grin.

"Oh, yes. Absolutely."

They brought their wine out to the balcony terrace and watched the sun set.

Chapter 11

Pauline and Grey threw themselves into preparations for their second dig, which would be as illegal as the first and conducted under cover of darkness. Brazen nighthawking was an all-or-nothing proposition. No such thing as nighthawking just a little. They bought more gear, including a geology pick, brushes, a bucket, and a shaker screen to sort soil, sediment, rocks, and artifacts. The convertible, which Pauline had secretly dubbed "the dolphin" because it was so sleek and smart, was not the best vehicle for the new job, but they lacked capital to rent something plain and inconspicuous. Grey had spread their remaining cash on the bed. Three hundred bucks. That's all that remained of their one-hundred-twenty-thousand-dollar windfall.

The plan was to leave around nine at night and arrive at the dig site by midnight.

"We're poor again," Pauline said, loading gear into the dolphin's carpet-lined trunk. "I don't think I like it. What I do like is our new king bed and our killer view. I miss them already."

"We won't be poor for long," he said, putting in the shovels.

"Why are you so sure?"

"Because of you," he said, lightly.

"No pressure."

"I'm not worried." He slid behind the wheel and pulled the roof over them. Less conspicuous. She hated driving, and he loved it. No telling when the *pulse* might crash in, and the possibility of losing her bearings while driving had convinced her to drive as little as possible. "We'll have a new income stream soon."

"When you say 'income,' you make it sound like a sure thing."

"Isn't it?" he asked, pulling onto I-95 South for the three-hour trip to James City County. "Are you going to lose your magic touch any time soon?"

"I thought you didn't believe in magic."

"Well, your special genius, then. Isn't it bottomless?"

"Hmm." Was it?

"C'mon. You're Lucky Penny. The one and only. Patent pending." He squeezed her shoulder.

"The one and only. Don't forget it, mister."

The ride to New York had been a lark, pure adventure. This trip felt much more like a business trip, and she was the account exec expected to close the deal. The precise location of the old sword was securely stowed away in her head. But so much could go wrong. They could be struck by lightning in an open field. Or, more likely, they might get caught. The penalty for stealing antiquities was probably jail time. Enduring the *pulse* in a cell would be…difficult. Even if they found the sword without trouble, what if it turned out to be worthless? She pictured Grey packing up his stuff in the condo, shaking his head in disappointment, and then walking out on her without a backward glance. Scheherazade, beheaded after all.

Maybe this scheme was too risky. This wasn't like

digging at the far reaches of empty farmland. Grey's cocky confidence blinded him to the real dangers they could face.

"Look, do me a favor," she said. "Just don't ask any questions about my methods, okay? Let's just...do our own thing. For now, anyway."

"Listen, as long as you get results, no questions asked."

Pauline smiled ruefully to herself when he began fiddling with the fancy satellite radio settings. Fresh noise to quiet the doubts running on a loop. He flipped around from Pop2K to Caliente, the '80s and '90s channels, and more, before landing on Fantasy Sports, which sounded like gibberish.

"What's that about?" she asked.

"Investment strategies. Sports is just the excuse. Keeps me sharp."

Another side to Grey Henley, mogul-in-waiting.

As they continued south in the night, Pauline tried pushing worries aside. As a kid, she never went anywhere. The Hellers kept her at home, under foot, then complained when she moped around. "Stop sitting there like a damn plant," Nora would say. Countless hours spent in her room, waiting to grow up. Or, later, waiting for an episode of the *pulse* to devastate her.

Damn frosters.

Now here she was, running up and down the Eastern seaboard, having adventures with the best-looking man on the planet. If only she could go back and tell the young Pauline that everything would work out for the best. Because of course it would—it was.

She tore open a bag of chips and held them out to her driver.

At last, they entered James City County.

"Time to do your thing," Grey said.

"We're heading to the site of the former Kingsmill Plantation, which early white settlers built in the seventeenth century." She punched map coordinates into the car's onboard GPS. Grey glanced at the directions and nodded. "It's very fertile ground for objects spanning six centuries. The land is about to become a housing development, so our timing is perfect."

"You are a wonder."

Grey drove just under the speed limit on the nearly empty state highway. The dashboard clock said 12:26 a.m. Once they turned off onto narrower secondary roads, a light mist appeared in the headlights. The night was overcast and cool. A perfect night to dig. Pauline directed Grey to a field where they parked behind a stand of trees. Not fully hidden, but the best they could do, given the terrain. A row of construction backhoes stood like hulking shadows a few dozen yards from them.

"You were right again, Pen. Looks like they're getting ready to turn this place inside out."

"What a crime. Plowing up all this virgin ground, for what? Ticky-tacky houses and cul-de-sacs and ugly plastic swimming pools."

"Yeah, that's the *real* crime," Grey said as they shouldered their packs. "Yet somehow we're the ones breaking the law."

"When actually, our true mission is salvation."

"Nighthawkers to the rescue." Grey laughed softly. "Now where to, genius?"

Pointing to another stand of trees about an eighth

of a mile from where they stood, Pauline pulled out a laminated map, for his sake. Archaeology theater. She showed him the lay of the land.

"It's not an elevated site," she explained. "But the historical record is pretty clear that this is where the settlements were the most dense and active. And the penetrating ground radar images I examined back home confirm the basic coordinates."

At the tree line, she indicated the spot to begin digging, counting on her lover's single-minded pursuit of ancient treasure to prevent him from asking pointed questions. He'd reassured her he wouldn't, but he also wouldn't brook mistakes—especially not by her, not now.

They strapped on head lamps, the focused beams enabling them to work hands-free without lighting up the surrounding area, then started in on separate trenches. She positioned him directly above the sword, which stood hilt-side up in its soil coffin. She pictured it with perfect clarity, every facet as well as its precise position. Then, without warning, she left Grey behind.

She hovered just above a small brick factory outside Strasbourg, France, where weapons of war were hammered, smelted, and assembled for export to the American colonies battling to free themselves from Great Britain. A French worker in soiled breeches whistled a folk tune as he loaded horsemen's sabers into a wooden crate packed with excelsior for the journey across the Atlantic.

Now someone called her name. The Frenchman? No. Surely not.

"Penny! Penny! Hey!" Grey hissed loudly. "I hit something. Could be a rock."

She wrenched herself back to the present. "That was fast." As planned.

"I figure, eighteenth century, maybe." He tapped the back of his shovel against the hard object just beneath the surface dirt. "We wouldn't find Indigenous artifacts this far up."

"No, probably not."

"Maybe I should keep digging? See what else is down there? I hate to leave treasure behind."

"Grey, let's do one thing at a time, okay? Let's do this right. We shouldn't press our luck, out here in the open." She scanned the horizon.

Grey sighed, then switched from shovel to trowel and got on his knees to poke at the object. A small, knob-like shape the size of a grape protruded from the soil as he excavated its circumference. Over the next several minutes, while Pauline aimed her head lamp toward his trench to provide maximum illumination, he revealed more and more of the sword's hilt, which was gently curved with a decorative knob (the "grape") at the tip. She handed him a putty knife so he could begin to loosen the soil vertically beneath the hilt. They worked in silence, but Grey's rapid breathing gave away his mounting excitement. She continued scanning the horizon for…what?…Police? Competing nighthawkers? Or something else entirely?

He cleared the hilt, revealing the top end of the worn blade. At that moment, a gentle, unmistakable *whooshing* filled Pauline's ears, and she shivered. Looking up sharply, she threw off her head lamp and stepped away from Grey.

"Hey! I need that light. What are you doing?"

"Thought I heard something."

"I'm not stopping unless I absolutely have to. Check it out and let me know."

She began walking across the field under a starless, overcast sky, ready to confront whatever was heading her way, and dreading it too. The *whooshing* grew louder, as if the moths of the *pulse* beat inside her eardrums. Her heart hammered faster and faster, its insistent rhythm competing with the roaring in her ears. Not the *pulse.* Surely not.

The thrum of a harmonic chord, ringing her body like an instrument. The same chord she'd heard twice before. He was there, striding across the darkened field. A hulking shadow casting a faint silhouette against the night sky. Running away was pointless. She stood her ground, the hum growing denser, settling in her bones.

What do you want from me?

He was right before her now. Despite the darkness, she caught a gleam in his coal-black eyes. Not menacing, but warm and penetrating. He took her hands, and bolts of white lightning shot up her arms and out the top of her head. This figure and the *pulse* were connected somehow. But how? Why? Was he responsible for all the years of misery?

Together they rose off the ground, higher and higher, until they were floating above the Kingsmill land. There was Grey, far below, a small figure hunched over a trench. A tiny speck on the face of time. Almost insignificant, in the grand scheme.

The landscape slid away and changed...Small campfires, thatched houses and lean-tos built by the Chesepian people, members of the Carolina Algonquian and later the Powhatan Confederacy, who occupied and cultivated this land centuries before the white

Europeans arrived. The landscape shifted again. There, below, were the English colonists firing muskets on the Indigenous villagers. And then, red-coated British soldiers firing upon white farmers and settlers in the throes of the Revolutionary War.

The very sword that Grey was digging up, in the hands of its original owner, a civilian farmer who joined the Virginia Grenadier Militia to fight off British domination.

All this she saw from the sky, alongside her companion.

The sword's blade spoke: *Forged in the fires of France, I fight for my master's freedom from tyranny, my blade his instrument of victory.*

Suspended in mid-air, the edges of her body lost definition, her autonomy merged with his. Their breathing aligned. One body, one breath. She gasped, alarmed, fighting to hold onto her own flesh, bone, and blood. Yet she was slipping away somewhere...

No, no, no, no.

****

Another *whooshing*, and she was suddenly alone on the dark field, grateful and relieved to regain control of her own breathing. The stranger had shown her so much, and asked too much.

You are more.

Damn him for toying with her, dragging her from one world to another, and then back again. You live *here,* in this world, and *now,* in this time. And Grey is still yours, if you can keep him.

She trudged back across the field, head down, with no clue how much time had elapsed since leaving him behind. Once back by Grey's side, she observed he had apparently uncovered roughly half the blade, carefully pulling soil away with a tiny scoop to further expose the object.

"Well?" he asked, without shifting his gaze. "Anything to worry about?"

"Just...just a dog. A black Labrador. Very friendly. He had a collar, so he probably lives around here somewhere."

"I could really use some help. More light, especially."

Pauline focused her head lamp on his busy hands, willing the rest of the world to disappear. Just the two of them, in a small circle of light, retrieving a soldier's long-lost weapon.

Another hour passed before Grey finally freed the sword and laid it on a swatch of vinyl. Pauline used a small brush to wipe the crevices of the hilt and brush clumps of damp soil off the delicate blade itself. All the while, the sword continued speaking to her, boasting of exploits in battle, the feel of slicing through heart muscle, the way blood tickled as it dripped down the blade.

If only she could swat the voices away, like so many flies.

"It's magnificent," Grey said. He rubbed his fingers along the gold bands on the hilt and the pitted blade. "Pen, you've outdone yourself."

"You did all the work."

"You did all the finding. Look at the hilt, how it curves away from the blade. And look at how the handle is ribbed, for gripping, I imagine."

"I'm betting that the hilt is made from gold, silver, and copper, which corrode far more slowly than the blade, which is nickel, iron, and zinc. That's why the hilt is pristine but the blade is all nicked."

"You really know your shit. It's almost scary."

"Why do you think everybody at Carthage hates me?"

"They don't hate you, Pen. They're afraid of you. There's a big difference."

"What about you, Grey? Are you afraid of me?"

And what am I afraid of?

Grey laughed, began to speak, then stopped himself. He kissed her instead.

****

"Let's get out of here," he said, wrapping the sword in the vinyl. They shoveled dirt back into the trenches, packed their tools, and walked briskly back to the car. Pauline turned around once more to scan the field.

"Worried about the dog?" he asked. "Should we get a puppy?"

"Not while we're living in an apartment."

"So, when we buy a house?"

Right, like ordinary people.

The convertible pulled away from the dig site, the car's headlights switched off until they reached the state road. Pauline suddenly burst out laughing.

"What's so funny?"

She'd worried for nothing. Nobody was out to get them. The cops were miles away. Their nighthawking generated zero interest from anybody. There was only the little matter of the visitation, and the visions across time and space, and flying into the air, and the talking objects. Only that. She laughed until tears streamed down her face.

109

"What?" he asked again.

"Oh, it's just…it's just that I'm so happy."

"Me too. And you know what will make me even happier?" She had an inkling and clapped a hand on his inner thigh. He didn't seem to notice. "When we sell this thing."

After that, they drove in silence for a long while, each lost in private thoughts. As a gray dawn came up, they agreed to stop for coffee at a diner in Virginia.

Seated in an old-fashioned red-leather booth, Grey drenched his coffee with cream and sugar. Pauline, suddenly ravenous, devoured a plate of scrambled eggs and toast. Time travel would do that to a person.

"The sword will net us more than the face pot," he said. "I'm willing to bet. From now on, the sky's the limit. Start thinking big, Lucky Penny."

"Big about what?"

"The future. The digs. Our income. All of it."

She looked out the window. A light rain had begun to fall. The future that looked as bright to him as Christmas morning only sewed seeds of confusion. All she asked was to take the journey with him. *But is my future really my own?*

"Why is this so important to you, Grey?" He fidgeted, and she reached for his hand. "Tell me."

He sighed. "When I was twelve, my mom and I had nowhere to live. So for a whole summer, and fall too, I guess, we camped out. We pitched a crappy old tent in whatever campgrounds we could sneak into after the office closed. We didn't have sleeping bags. Just some old blankets. I lived on cold canned spaghetti. I hate that shit. The sight of it makes me gag."

"Wow. I had no idea."

"The past is the past, right?" He reached over and stole a piece of toast off her plate.

"Your mother loved you, though, didn't she? She did her best."

"Yeah, she did. Until she couldn't remember who I was."

"Oh, Grey." She thought he might tear up, but he didn't. "Which is worse? A home without love, or love without a home?"

"Let's not even go there." He fiddled with the salt and pepper shakers. "Like I said. I'm focused on the future."

"You're right. We should dedicate ourselves to being happy."

"And rich. You can't have one without the other."

"Both." No point in arguing the point just then.

Around seven that morning, they rode the elevator up to their condo, stripped out of filthy clothes, and showered. The wrapped sword sat on the dining room table, awaiting the next chapter in its long life.

They turned to one another in bed. She wrapped her legs around him, and they made love lying face-to-face on their sides, equal partners. She held his gaze, aware of being *here* and *now,* registering every wave of orgasm, longing to hold onto this reality and banishing any other.

Afterwards, Grey curled up next to her and fell instantly asleep. She listened to his soft, regular breathing, the breathing of the innocent. He had some baggage, but so did she. Exhausted, yet curled in a tense ball, she couldn't shake off the certainty that no matter how long they stayed together, or how much they loved each other, she'd always be alone with her secrets.

And whose fault was that?

Chapter 12

The all-business Grey was on full display, dressed in a navy-blue suit, rattling the car keys. He tucked the wrapped sword under his arm. Pauline would have undressed him then and there and dragged him back to bed, but sex was clearly the last thing on his mind.

"I still don't understand why you don't want me to come with you," Pauline said.

"Babe, look, like I said, it's best if we keep this simple. Negotiations are a one-on-one kind of thing. Don't take this the wrong way, but you'd just be a...distraction." It would be easy to take that the wrong way, but she let it slide.

"Are you meeting the same guy? The middleman? The one with all the rich buyers?"

"Yes. Same guy."

"What have you told him?" She filled a to-go mug with coffee, loaded with cream and sugar the way he liked it, and handed it to him.

"That we have an item of interest."

"And you know him how, Grey?"

Grey made a show of looking at his expensive watch. "Look, Pen, I'm sorry. I don't want to be late. He hates it when people are late. Wish me luck, huh?"

A quick kiss and he was gone.

He's coming back. I'm sure, now. Almost completely sure. That's progress, anyway.

Overcome by uneasy restlessness, Pauline walked in circles, staring out the windows filled with morning light.

Who am I without Grey? What am I?

She imagined him deep in conversation with the so-called middleman, haggling over the dollar value of the militiaman's sword, with its gold-ribbed hilt and pitted blade once flecked with the blood of living men. What would the sword's owner say, or its French maker, if they knew how their valued tool had become a valued commodity—the stuff of legend?

Don't let them in, the voices. Don't go there. You'll go mad.

Do something. Anything.

She pulled out her phone, looking for a distraction. A new text from Bette French. The two had kept up a long-distance correspondence primarily on social media, which conveniently lent itself to a carefully curated presentation of reality. Bette had seen pictures of Pauline's new clothes, the fancy apartment, the smiling couple. Bette claimed her prophecy was coming true: Marsh would turn out to be normal, just like the rest of them. Of course, Bette could only go by what she was told—and shown. Pauline didn't contradict her. Besides, Bette was busy making changes of her own. Last time they'd connected, Bette had joined a team of forensic archaeologists hot on the trail of a smuggling ring. So brave, so glamorous, Pauline reassured her, leaving out the bit about having a big, fat target on her own back.

Now it seemed Bette had moved on again, enrolling in law school "to catch more bad guys," she wrote. —*What about you?*—

Pauline typed an instant lie, telling Bette she'd landed an adjunct teaching gig at Carthage.

—*Makes sense*— Bette replied. —*Keep an eye on the crooked dean, okay?*—

Lying only ratcheted up Pauline's uneasiness. She stood on the balcony terrace and leaned out over the railing to take in the sailboats, kayaks, and ferries crisscrossing the placid waters between the harbor, Fells Point, and Locust Point. On the promenade below, runners, cyclists, and scooters darted among the pedestrians.

A new life in the sky, hardly hers, built on a series of coincidences. What if Dean Nojes hadn't called the pair of them into her mask-filled room? What would she be doing now?

Chance. Destiny. Magic.

You will have questions. Return to me when you are ready.

The dean's words—exactly what she'd said as Pauline left the little room with Grey—so loud and distinct that Pauline whipped around, ready to believe the dean herself had appeared on the balcony. But no. The voice, like so many voices, was only in her head.

She knew exactly what to do now: Find Dean Nojes and get her to explain—anything, or maybe everything. Pauline threw on a linen skirt, blouse, and sandals, then called Carthage University and asked to speak with Dean Nojes. A long shot, surely. School was on recess, and the dean could be lecturing anywhere in the world.

"Hello?" The dean's familiar alto, right there on the line.

"Dean Nojes? This is Pauline Marsh. You may

remember—"

"Pauline. You took your time. How soon can you get to my office?"

Pauline had forty bucks to her name. Too little for a roundtrip rideshare uptown. She caught a bus that would lumber its way up to Towson, about a dozen miles north. The slow ride gave her time to work up an indignant anger. Why should Dean Nojes know something about her life that she didn't know? What did she ever do to wind up a pawn in someone else's story—whether the dean's or the intrusive stranger who had nearly overpowered her? Why couldn't she just enjoy a normal love life—without choking on secrets?

By the time Pauline strode across the university quad, she was fuming, ready to confront the dean head-on. The diplomas had been mailed. The dean had no hold over her any longer. The dean's office occupied a corner of the administration building overlooking the university quad. Pauline had been in this office just once before, during the courtesy meeting the dean held with every incoming student enrolled in the graduate archaeology program. That was over two years ago. Nothing appeared to have changed. Even the crookedly stacked books on the floor appeared exactly the same.

Dean Nojes rose from behind a large wooden desk.

"Close the door," she said. "Take a seat." She pointed toward a green wingback chair, the ever-present bangles jangling as usual. She sat across from Pauline, a small coffee table between them stacked with back issues of *Archaeology Magazine* and *Antiquity Journal*. Pauline made sure not to look directly at the magazines' covers, which would unleash a flood of images and voices.

"I'm not going to hide behind my desk because you're no longer my student. This way, we're more like equals, you see?"

She did not see. What would the dean say if she knew about the nighthawking? And her decision, with her partner in crime, to profit from the fruits of their labor? None of the old woman's damn business.

"Of course, I knew you'd come. It was a matter of when, not if."

"Really?" Said with an edge.

"You think you're angry, but what you're really feeling is frustration." *How the hell would you know?* "Why don't you tell me what's going on?"

"I don't know what you're talking about."

"Then why are you here? I'll tell you why. I planted the seeds, and now you're germinating."

"Okay, Dean, so am I a geranium or a daisy? Or do you prefer something more exotic? A ghost orchid, perhaps."

Pauline half-expected the dean to boot her from the office for insubordination. But she smiled instead.

"I'm not the problem, Pauline."

"What problem? If you have something to tell me, Dean Nojes, then tell me."

"Call me India. I'm no longer your dean. Not *yours.*" Stony silence. "Okay, I'm going to share some observations and, if I say something that isn't true, say 'no.' Otherwise, I'll assume we're on the same page. Here goes. You possess secret knowledge about humanity's deep past."

Whoa. That can't be a lucky guess. She must know *something.*

"You routinely feel detached from your body.

Occasionally, you hear voices. You can locate any antiquity in the world, no matter where it's buried or for how long."

"Enough! You make me sound crazy."

"You're here, Pauline, so I can tell you to your face that you're not crazy."

"What, then?" She stood and tried pacing around the crammed office. "You're not allowed to know more about me than I know about myself!"

"What's it like?"

"What do you think it's like!" Did she really just yell at the dean?

"Sit down," the dean said sharply.

Pauline remained standing, gripping the back of the wing chair. "Tell me the truth."

The dean took a deep breath. "I'm a Facilitator for the Thread Continuum."

"The what?"

"Listen. The Thread Continuum is a world between worlds. Special in ways...well, in ways you'll understand some day. I barely understand it myself. As a Facilitator, my role is sadly limited as it revolves around finding you, one of the rare Elected, and making sure you don't do anything really stupid before...I've said enough for now."

Word salad. Nothing to hold onto. "I do not appreciate..." Pauline began, heart pounding. "You are not helpful, Dean."

"Time is like water—fluid, constantly in motion, with endless points of entry. You, in particular, may dip in anywhere the water flows. You will. You are. You have."

"I'm leaving."

"Not yet." The dean swiftly grabbed Pauline's wrist, the bangles cold against her skin. "You will remember this conversation later, and you will blame me, but that can't be helped, and I would do the exact same thing all over again. I was given a glimpse, at least."

"Please let me go."

"I would give anything to be you, even for a day."

"You have no idea what it's like to be me." She yanked her wrist free.

"Thirty years ago, I was teaching a freshman seminar when the Thread Continuum claimed me. One minute I was placing a view foil on the overhead projector, and then I wasn't. Suddenly, I was in a kind of blank space where the air shimmered, lemony yellow. I couldn't focus my eyes; everything looked fuzzy. I thought I was having a stroke and wondered who would take over my class. A large, dark figure appeared, though I could only see his contours, as if there were several layers of filmy plastic between us. I heard his voice in my head, explaining that I'd been chosen as a Facilitator to find and watch over an Elected. Nothing was the same after that. My life was no longer entirely my own. From that day to this, since the day you were born, in fact, you have been my responsibility."

The dean still wasn't making sense. Her words seemed like threads that could unravel until there was nothing left to hold onto, and then Pauline feared she might actually fly apart.

"Who are you?" One more try.

"I'm a talent scout," the dean said. "You're the talent."

"The graduation parties, the rituals behind closed doors…" A jumble of puzzle pieces.

"Merely a confirmatory test, which every Facilitator in the Thread Continuum is required to perform one way or another. I normalized the test by embedding it in an annual rite of passage for graduates. The university administrators just let me be me. Very clever on my part, I must say."

"My vision…"

"Not like anyone else's. The others made something up. The power of suggestion combined with peer pressure. And a bit of theatrical smoke. Works every time."

"I'm sorry, but that's not true. Grey Henley—"

"What about him?"

"He had a vision, a very clear vision."

"Is that what he told you?" She smiled skeptically.

"I believe him!"

"I watched you, blindfolded, and knew the instant you split off and left the room. And I knew when you had returned."

"I never actually left the room, though, did I?"

"You *did* leave—in astral terms—which is the same as leaving."

The dean walked to the window overlooking the quad, her back to Pauline.

"I've done the spade work," she said. "The rest is up to you."

There were no answers to be had here, were there? Pauline headed for the door.

"Wait." The dean turned around. "You'll do something for me before you go. You'll give me a consolation prize for pulling the short end of the cosmic stick."

Dean Nojes picked up a magazine from the table, opened to a page at random, and held it up to Pauline's face, so close she could practically smell the ink. "Tell me all about it." The dean tossed the magazine back onto the table. "Tell me about the artifact on the page I just showed you. Go on."

Pauline stood motionless. *Ask me to strip naked. Ask me to perform the dance of the seven veils. Ask me to confess my love for Grey Henley.*

"I have waited thirty years for this moment," the dean said. "You owe me. They *all* do. But especially you. You're different from the rest."

"What if I refuse?"

The dean's customary bravado vanished. She sank down in the chair, a little old lady running out of steam.

What the hell. I can always tell them she's batshit crazy, maybe senile. I can hold that over her, if need be.

"The object on the page you showed me is a *tajadero*, a chopping knife made throughout central Mexico by the Indigenous Aztec people. This particular piece—the one shown in the magazine—was made from copper in 1502 A.D. and used as a form of currency in addition to serving as an axe. It was worth 8,000 cacao seeds, and pieces like this were in widespread use before the Spanish conquistadores arrived. And, well, this *tajadero* was a source of bitter dispute between a profligate chieftain and his first wife, who resented him for making stupid trades when she knew she was the sharper negotiator."

Dean Nojes stared, eyes shining. Pauline looked away.

"Was that so hard?" the dean asked softly. "Now

get the fuck out of here."

In three strides, Pauline was out the door, down the hallway, and making a beeline for the exit. But she couldn't outrun the *tajadero*, sharing its plaintive tale. *They buried me with the human bones, alongside my axe-money brothers, all missing now. Where did they go? I'm alone in a strange land.*

****

On the bus ride home, Pauline fought a rising tide of nausea by intently studying the other passengers. All so damn normal. An old man in a straw-brimmed hat. A woman reading a paperback. A teen boy hunched over his phone. All real. No missing parts.

Back inside the apartment, she couldn't stand still. She pulled a white ceramic coffee mug out of the kitchen cupboard and smashed it in the sink, chips skittering across the counter. That felt good, for a moment. She smashed another one, and blood spurted from cuts to her knuckles. She poured hydrogen peroxide on the wound, relishing the stinging foam, then slapped on a bandage.

Grey caught her still cleaning up the mess in the kitchen. "What's going on?"

Breathe. Once, twice, three times.

"I'm a klutz. Broke a stupid mug."

"Poor baby." He kissed the bandaged fingers, then pulled her into his arms and danced her out to the balcony. "Wait here."

Pauline closed her eyes, trying to empty her mind, listening only to the horns of rush-hour traffic below. Grey returned in a pair of cotton draw-string pants and a polo shirt, looking younger than the businessman in the suit. He held a bottle of Barolo and two glasses.

Those glasses would do nicely, if the urge to break things returned.

"I need this," she said, lifting the filled wine glass.

"Isn't life amazing?" His smile couldn't get any wider.

"Amazing." A mere echo.

"On a scale of one to ten, how much do you like this apartment?"

Focus. You're with Grey now. He came back, after all. Everything's going to be all right.

"A nine. I'd give it a ten, but there's a lamp in the bedroom I don't like."

"The lamp with the rope wrapped around the glass base?"

"That's the one. We can replace it."

"I'll do you one better. After tomorrow, you never have to look at that lamp again."

"You know what, Grey? How about you just say what you want to say. No riddles. Not today."

"I'll give it to you any way you want it, babe."

He disappeared inside once more. Must they leave again so soon? Not another dig. Not yet. Couldn't she sit here, feel the coming June sun on her face, and never travel anywhere again?

He reappeared holding a new designer leather briefcase, which he lay on the small table, snapping open the shiny gold clasps. "Check it out."

The briefcase held neat rows of cash tied up in rubber-banded bundles.

"You didn't," she said.

"I did. The whiz kid did it again." He grabbed her face between his hands and planted a wet kiss. His breath was fruity and earthy, like the wine.

123

"Give it to me straight."

"It's not that complicated—not from our end. My source is connected to an international network of buyers, many of them billionaires. The competition for stuff your neighbor in the mansion next door doesn't own is really intense."

"And this source…"

"You'll meet him. Soon."

"The mysterious Mr. Middleman."

Grey laughed. "You can decide for yourself."

"How much we did make on this one?" An image of the short Virginia farmer, armed with the gold-hilted sword and primed for battle with the British, flashed by. She'd have to settle for Grey being perfectly happy to dwell in the world he knew. Her version remained off-limits.

"You ready?"

"Hit me."

"Four hundred thousand dollars."

"Whoa."

"It'll probably sell for more than twice that. But hey. Can't complain about our cut, can we?"

"What are we going to do with almost half a million dollars?"

"For starters, we're moving into the penthouse. Twelve floors above us. I already signed a year's lease, paid in full. The place is fully furnished—even better stuff than we have now. Can you cope?"

He flashed a red fob—the key to their new castle. Just then, the evening sun hit the multicolored glass panes on the aquarium directly across the harbor, setting off a sparkling light show that bounced between the wall of the building and the water's edge. So, the two of them were going to lord it over this breathtaking view.

"Everything's happening so fast, Grey."

"All according to plan, babe. And we're killing it."

"Rags to riches."

"Rags to *richest*," he said. "As long as we keep up the pace."

Throwing her arms around his neck, she nuzzled her cheek against his stubble. "Like Icarus flying up toward the sun. Except our wings won't melt, will they?"

"They wouldn't dare."

"Let's go tour our penthouse. I want to make sure they didn't sneak in any ugly lamps."

Chapter 13

The penthouse overlooking the Inner Harbor on the forty-second floor was as large as a house, with top-of-the-line appliances, a temperature-controlled wine cooler, and a spiral staircase with polished iron railings separating the main living space from the three bedrooms upstairs, one of which Grey said he planned to use as an office. The walls on the main level were practically all glass, affording panoramic views over the water and all the way out to the suburban hills.

Pauline figured it would take a while to settle in and stop wondering how this could possibly be home. She opened and closed drawers and cabinets, figuring out what went where. Her clothes barely took up any space in the walk-in closet that was twice the size of the first one. She was almost afraid to touch anything, as if she were a guest about to overstay her welcome.

Grey, on the other hand, left dirty plates and cups in the sink on the very first day. His dirty socks already lay on the bedroom floor.

"We'll entertain, of course," he said, spreading out across the enormous leather sectional sofa on that first evening.

"Well, la-di-da." Pauline stretched out on the other end of the sofa, so they could play footsy.

"Maybe a housewarming party."

"If only we had friends."

"Rich people don't need friends." He sounded dead-certain.

"Oh, really?"

"Anybody would kill for a chance to come up here."

"So we'll invite strangers, then. How about, we walk along Pratt Street and hand out tickets."

"I don't know why this is such a joke to you, Penny. We're building a life here, aren't we? What's so funny about that?" He pulled his feet away.

Stung that her flippancy had hurt his feelings, and wanting to make up for doubting him, Pauline rose and began a slow striptease. When she got down to her red lace bra and panties, she slid onto the dining room table—huge, glass-topped, big enough to seat a dozen. She lay on her side and drew up one knee, her leg flexing open to expose her crotch. Grey rose and stripped from the waist down, wearing only his tan piqué polo, biceps swelling beneath the short sleeves. He rolled her onto her back, the cool glass pressing against her flesh. He tossed away her underthings, then slid over top of her, pulling her arms over her head, their hands clasped. His cock was hard and insistent against her groin. She pushed against him and turned to get on all fours—an aroused centerpiece—and Grey took her from behind. Her breath caught in shallow gasps as the orgasm rode over her in waves.

The well-made table, streaked with sweat, did not even groan under their exertions.

Afterwards, they went upstairs to shower, the wall jets caressing them with its spray. Then, wrapped in thick towels, they sat on the semi-enclosed balcony just off the bedroom. Privacy *and* killer views.

Under the circumstances, she had a hard time feeling sorry for herself.

"Grey, I'm so lucky. You're so good to me. I can't imagine—"

"Ditto."

"And you were right. The past can't touch us now. This is who we are, right here, right now. This is what we deserve, isn't it?"

"This is a *fraction* of what I deserve," he said with surprising vehemence.

"I could stay up here forever and never leave. The demons can't find me—us—up here in the sky."

"Demons? There's no such thing. A demon is just a problem you haven't solved yet."

"Hmm."

Could Grey be right? Maybe everything Dean Nojes had told her, including about the so-called Thread Continuum, was a product of the old woman's jealous, over-active imagination. The *problem* was that the dean was nuts. End of story. There was, perhaps, another explanation for the *pulse* and everything that came with it. *Look on the bright side, for once.*

Curling up under the silky, high-thread-count sheets in their enormous bed, Pauline pleaded for innocent dreams involving parties, champagne, and caviar, not strangers who showed up unannounced and invaded her psyche. Not ancient burial mounds or hidden treasures. And definitely no episodes of flying apart.

****

In the morning, Pauline reached across the bed, only to find a cold pillow. A swift flicker of panic: Grey had left her, for good this time. Her innate weirdness,

128

and aversion to risk, had pushed him away. Then, the scent of fresh-brewed coffee wafted up from the kitchen below. *You idiot.* She padded downstairs, blinking in the bright morning light that flooded the condo. Grey fiddled with the complex mechanics of the espresso machine built into the kitchen backsplash.

"I've mastered it," he said with a boyish grin, holding a cup out to her.

They took their coffee and a plate of croissants out to the balcony terrace just off the main living area, nearly twice as big as the one on the lower floor. The early June breeze sent ripples scuttling across their filled cups and ruffled Grey's curls.

"You know what we need out here?" Pauline said, settling into a lounge chair. "A big, fat tomato plant. And some herbs, maybe. And geraniums. A whole garden. I've never had a garden."

"I think living here agrees with you."

"I'm beginning to think so, too."

"So, after we get back—"

"What?" Pauline set her coffee down too quickly, losing half the liquid. "No. I thought—we just got here, Grey. Why can't we just—"

"Go look and see if something's been slipped under the door."

She rose and gripped the terrace railing. "No more surprises. Enough is enough. Why can't we enjoy what we already have?"

"Penny, please. You won't be sorry. Go check."

"Why don't *you*?"

"Because that's not how I pictured it."

She gave him a look. What did that mean? Was everything Grey did premeditated? She pushed away the idea as repulsive. And not true. Their sex was spontaneous, after all. Nobody lived like that, planning out every minute of the day. Still, she didn't want to cross him over such a silly thing. She retrieved a large white envelope sitting on the floor near the door and handed it to him.

"This will be the last surprise for a while," he said, lifting the flap. "I promise. But *you*, Mademoiselle Boniface. Señorita Genius. You need to keep the surprises coming. Otherwise..."

"I know, Grey." Whatever the envelope contained would force her to plunge deeper into her secrets. An uncomfortable truth could no longer be swept aside. Grey wouldn't make a move that didn't involve her ability to *perform.*

I've made my bed. Time to lie in it.

"Yes!" Grey exclaimed. "He came through. I knew I could count on him."

He handed her a pair of large tickets and a handwritten note. The tickets, embellished with fancy gold script, represented a reserved first-class stateroom on the *Archimedes*, a luxury cruise ship sailing in a few days from Baltimore to Miami and then on to the Antilles. The note read: "As promised. See you both soon. Look forward to meeting P." Pauline couldn't make out the scrawled signature.

"What's going on?"

"That, my darling, is from Tyrone Lake. Our middleman. He's the guy with the golden touch."

"You should have—"

"I know, I know." He reached over to gently feather her bangs and tap the dimple in her chin. The warm tinglies did not follow, as they usually did when he touched her. "He sprang this on me a few days ago, and I didn't want to get my hopes up, or yours. But now, well, it's really happening."

Pauline attempted to piece together what any of this meant. A cruise?

"First class all the way," he continued, as excited as a little boy. "All the champagne we can drink. And all those treasures in Florida and the Caribbean, waiting to be liberated. We're going to get so fuckin' rich."

Grey had a fiery glint in his eyes. Energy and ambition radiated from every pore. His determination was strong enough to sweep anyone into his orbit and hold them there by sheer will. Pauline was living proof of that. Still, coming under Grey's spell was way better than coming under the *pulse*'s—or that of the stranger whose every encounter left her disturbed and confused.

Better the devil you know, than the one you don't.

The dean had told Pauline she'd been "elected" to something or other. Never mind all that. The only task she would commit to was this ride with Grey, wherever it led.

"It's going to be incredible," she said, kissing him to banish doubt. "I won't let you down."

"That's my Lucky Penny." He kissed her back. "The two of us are unstoppable."

Chapter 14

Once again, the pair were in a mad rush to be off. A day before the departure, they drove to the fancy mall at Tysons Corner to buy resort wear and more gear and clothing for the inevitable nighthawking excursions to come. Pauline refused to look ahead, taking each moment, each hour, as it came—tricking herself into believing she had some control over the future. Deep down, she wasn't fooled. But as they wandered through the over-lit mall, expensive luxuries shrieking from every store window, time seemed to stand still, and that helped, a bit.

Together, they bought matching sets of aluminum luggage before splitting up, as they'd done in New York. Surely, no self-respecting stranger from another dimension would visit her inside a suburban mall...would he? *Shake it off, Marsh.* Grey had handed her so much cash, she had trouble closing her new designer pebbled handbag. Unwilling to stand still in one place for long—an unfounded superstition—she wandered in and out of one name-brand boutique after another, until she arrived at the threshold of a gleaming jewelry store. Not just any jewelry store, but the one that was the stuff of legend, reeking of Fifth Avenue and romantic old movies. She'd never been inside a store like this. There, her eye was caught by an illuminated glass display case containing the jeweler's classic key collection. *That one.* A key-shaped pendant in rose gold studded with diamonds. She had to have it, and her longing telegraphed itself to the well-dressed man who helped her spend over two-thousand dollars for the key and a matching gold chain, which he slipped around her neck. The sparkling key between her clavicles, its heft and coolness operating like a calming talisman.

Leaving the store, fingering the key, she imagined an archaeologist thousands of years in the future unearthing the jewelry and marveling at its delicate curves, the clover-like loops of the key's head, and the skilled craftsmanship needed to manufacture something both intricate and simple. A different image followed, of Grey undoing the clasp, slipping the chain off her neck as his fingers wandered from clavicle to breast.

I will surprise him tonight, naked but for the key.

Reunited for the ride home, laden with packages, Pauline asked Grey to tell her about Tyrone Lake, going against her rule about not looking too far ahead.

"What about him?"

"You know. Who is he? How do you know him? Are we, like, formally in business with this guy?"

"Formally? No. But we have a gentleman's agreement."

"What does that mean?"

"It means, Pen, that he and I trust one another. We're onto a good thing here, and we both wanna take the full ride."

"But who *is* he, Grey?"

Grey shrugged and offered a Mona Lisa smile. "He's a very well-connected businessman."

"So you keep telling me."

"You'll meet him on the ship. I think you two will really get along." A brick wall. "You know I've got everything under control, right? We each have our jobs to do. Because you're so good at yours, genius, I'm able to do mine." He squeezed her hand.

"I suppose you want me to get started," she said, squeezing back.

"That would be awesome. Knowledge isn't just power, it's also profit."

"Tonight, then."

"Fantastic. You're the best. I don't know what I'd do without you."

"Starve?" She laughed.

"Well, it would never come to that." Frowning, he withdrew his hand.

The private elevator lifting them up to the penthouse was crowded with shopping bags and new luggage. They spent the evening packing, drinking wine, blasting oldies. The Camembert and Brie they grazed on cost nearly as much as Pauline would have spent on groceries in a week, in the old days. Around midnight, after procrastinating for hours, she shooed Grey away, telling him she needed privacy to do her research. For show, she opened her laptop at the dining room table they'd made love on days earlier and scattered a couple of important-looking archaeology textbooks as well as maps of Florida, the Keys, and the loose chains of islands floating all around Cuba and Dominican Republic.

A swift glance at the Florida map, and Pauline was awash in visions. She gripped the edge of the table, struggling to remain grounded. Mastodon bones grooved with human teeth marks, submerged in swampland. A knife carved from stone by pre-Clovis settlers who traveled to Florida from Alaska more than 13,000 years ago. Gold coins belonging to a Spanish admiral, Pedro Menéndez de Avilés, who settled in St. Augustine in 1565. Snippets of a dialect spoken by the Timucua—the Indigenous people dwelling in Florida before Europeans arrived. Their smoky fires scented the air. The vibrations of iron shot exploding from Spanish muskets rippled along her spine.

All the while, she sorted and catalogued, searching for the object she hoped would be of greatest value to Grey and...what was his name?...Tyrone Lake.

I have a job to do, and failure is not an option.

So much for being "elected."

And then it appeared. The One. She was certain. An ancient Peruvian funeral mask that dazzled with its intricate metal work. Retrieving it would be complicated. But one thing at a time.

Pauline removed her clothes and walked up the spiral staircase naked, but for the jeweled key around her neck. Grey, seated at the desk in his office, had his back to her.

"Hey, there," she said softly, standing in the doorway.

He turned around, eyes widening.

"Wow." He approached her and rubbed the key beneath his thumb and forefinger.

"Take it off," she commanded.

He undid the clasp, his breath hot on her neck, and the chain slid off with a slinky tickle. She led him into the bedroom, where he slid the necklace under a pillow. She undid his pants. He climbed onto her, teasing her nipples with his tongue, before moving down to her navel, then her cut. On fire, she gripped his hair and pulled him up toward her, pressing her hand on his buttocks as he thrust his way in.

Afterwards, he retrieved the key and held it up to the light.

"Imagine if this were an artifact," he said.

"My thought, exactly." She ran her fingers through his silver-flecked blond hair. "Speaking of artifacts…"

"Yes?" He rose on one elbow.

"I found it. In Florida, a bit south of Miami. But it won't be easy, especially at night."

"Tell me."

"Nope. I know how much you love secrets. Besides, I could be wrong. You know that, right? There's a chance, probably a good chance, that one day, my research, my map-reading, my hunches and triangulations, will fail."

"I don't believe that."

"I'm not infallible." *Only human.*

"You chose the perfect piece of jewelry, Penny," he said, fastening the chain around her neck. "You *are* the key."

Chapter 15

The *pulse*, again, and the timing could not be worse. Not that there was ever a good time to be turned inside out. Pauline squeezed Grey's arm so tightly, he asked if something was wrong. Nothing, really—except she couldn't see the steep ramp they were walking up to board the *Archimedes* docked at Baltimore's cruise ship terminal. Nothing, except she was scaling the side of a skyscraper without a safety net instead of taking a victory stroll up into the lap of luxury. Electric shocks made her nerves into live wires as moth wings beat against her gut, her feet lost touch with the ground, and her vision was jammed with fast-moving images.

Every stage of the *pulse* at once. Why? Why now?

Hey, Universe: How about a damn clue?

Pauline shut her eyes tight, willing the storm to blow over soon. She clung to Grey for balance.

"You know the ship is safe, right?" He held her close. "Safer than flying. You're not going to be like this the whole way, are you?"

"Uh-uh."

At the top of the ramp, she cautiously opened her eyes, relieved to see the real world returning in living color. She rubbed her shoes against the deck, reveling in its solidity.

Breathe in through the nose, out through the mouth.

A steward in a white uniform with gold buttons greeted them as part of a long line of boarding passengers. Pauline risked looking upward at the decks rising above them, like the layers on a wedding cake. With an effort, she leaned over the ship's teak railing and flung her arms wide. Rose in *Titanic*.

"See?" Grey said, throwing his arms around her middle. "Safe and sound."

"Let's go exploring." He'd never know the energy she expended to appear so carefree.

They grazed the ship's offerings, one after another: the sky-diving simulator, the rock-climbing wall, the water slide, and the planetarium. They poked their heads into the elegant champagne bar, with its gold-and-cream décor, sunlight streaming in from the deck. The ship's engine rumbled, and the massive vessel got underway. Pauline caught a reflection of the two of them in a window, startled by the transformation. She wore a flowing white-and-bone linen top, wide-legged pants, and designer flats, the light colors contrasting with her blunt-cut dark hair. Grey wore a light blue button-down shirt, neat khakis, and up-scale loafers. They'd come such a long way from their first week together. Fake it till you make it. That was one way of looking at it.

Grey swiped a keycard to unlock their stateroom on Deck 6. Evidently, someone had already unpacked the luggage and stowed the suitcases. A massive bouquet of flowers and an ice bucket holding a bottle of champagne sat in the center of a small, octagonal table.

"Oh, how beautiful!" Pauline inhaled the fragrant roses and other blossoms while Grey read from a small white card.

"Compliments of T.L."

"T.L. Who's that? The captain?"

"The captain, Pen? Really? The note also says, 'happy hunting.' Guess again." Grey peeled the foil off the champagne and expertly popped the cork.

"I don't...oh. Of course. Tyrone Lake. The benefactor."

"Business partner," Grey corrected, filling their flutes. "He's not giving us something for nothing."

"Oh, Grey, let's not talk about Tyrone Lake. Or business. Or even archaeology. Not now. Let's just pretend we're classy tourists." *And magically postpone the inevitable.*

"Okay, babe. We'll gawk at the ocean. How's that?"

The small balcony off their port-side stateroom offered an unobstructed view of the Atlantic Ocean. The sun bounced off the water as the *Archimedes* sliced through waves and a pair of seagulls dive-bombed the surface to catch fish.

"Is it just me, or do we spend an awful lot of time drinking on balconies?" Pauline smiled, restored, in part, by the bracing sea air.

"That's the awesome power of *us*." Grey flashed the crooked grin.

"To us." They entwined arms and drank from one another's glass, spilling, laughing, kissing. His kisses tasted of bubbles.

"Happy hunting," he whispered, licking her ear.

The black negligee she'd purchased for the trip would have to wait. They crashed onto the bed, skin on skin. Salty and delicious.

Falling in with Pauline's request, Grey did not

mention Tyrone Lake or business again during the two-day voyage to the Port of Miami.

"Let's go skydiving," he suggested over breakfast on their first full day.

"I was thinking, rock-climbing."

"Don't you want to fly? To float in the air like…like there's nothing holding you down?"

Been there. Done that.

"Uh, how about I watch you skydive. I'll record it, so you can see what you look like, my superhero."

"I don't get you sometimes, Penny. You don't think twice about risking everything, breaking every law, to dig up artifacts in the middle of the night. But you won't strap in for a ride that's safe for a ten-year-old? What are you afraid of?"

"I'm not afraid, Grey, I just…"

"You're afraid of heights, is that it? Is that why you hesitated on the gangway? Good thing all our digs so far have been at sea level. That could change, though. You'll have to face your fear head-on, eventually."

"And what about you?" She pushed away a plate of sliced mango. "What fears are *you* going to face?"

Grey paused, pouring coffee.

"I'll never be poor again. No matter what I have to do."

"That's not fear, that's ambition."

"You're wrong, Penny. When you were a kid, did you ever go an entire day without anything to eat? Did you ever spend a long night walking the streets, asleep on your feet, your mother dragging you by the hand until you thought your arm would fall off?"

"At least you *had* a mother."

"Okay, but you had a roof over your head and food

on the table, every single day. So don't tell me poverty isn't scary. You have no idea."

"Let's not play 'poor us.' It's stupid."

"You're right. It *is* stupid. I don't want to talk about it."

He rose from the little table on the stateroom balcony and turned his back to her, facing into the morning sun. She studied his perfect, muscular, blond beauty. He didn't cope with his damage very well, did he? *Then again, look who's talking.* But why let any of that stand in the way of romance?

She hugged him from behind, and he pressed his hand to hers.

"What a pair, huh?" She hoped his mood would lighten.

"I didn't mean—"

"I know," she said. "Forget it. But, uh, I'm still not going anywhere near that flying tube. You're on your own, buddy."

"Never mind. Let's climb the rock wall. I'll race you to the top."

The rest of the day unfolded like the storybook romance she'd hoped for. By lunchtime, they were splayed on teak deck chairs next to the infinity pool. The water's neat, horizontal edge was mesmerizing, almost hypnotic. Pauline stared at it in a white one-piece swimsuit with a plunging V-neck. Grey wore blue trunks with a white drawstring she couldn't wait to untie. She ordered ceviche for lunch, which arrived poolside in a wide martini glass, along with a crisp sauvignon blanc. Grey ordered a sirloin burger and a Belgian beer.

After lunch, eyes closed, a broad-brimmed hat

thrown over her face, she meditated on the ordinary sounds of kids and parents splashing in the pool. From deep in the ship's bowels, the faint purring of the engine vibrated against her back. Her thoughts drifted...

I wonder what's in store?...Charles Waters...A boy molding clay...Thatched roofs...Maps surging to life...You are more...

"Pen. Penny." Her shoulder shook. "Wakey, wakey, Sleeping Beauty."

Sitting up with a start, Pauline looked around. Two strangers sharing a chaise lounge had pulled alongside them.

"These are the Gillespies," Grey said. "Loretta and Ward. They both do something in finance that you and I will never understand."

The Gillespies looked about twenty years older than she and Grey, both tan, incredibly fit. Loretta's large diamond ring and diamond tennis bracelet caught the sunlight. Pauline smiled politely.

"Can you believe it?" Loretta's voice was low and modulated. Hollywood sunglasses hid her eyes. "We've never met an archaeologist until today. And now, a pair of them."

"Can you pull some strings and get us on a dig?" Ward asked. "Somewhere interesting, maybe Alexandria."

"He means Egypt, not Virginia," Loretta said. "Oh, Ward."

"Or Mesopotamia," Ward added, "if that's still a real place. Or Tasmania."

Ward raised his hand to catch a waiter's attention. He held out two fingers. "Two G and Ts." A guy clearly used to ordering people around. His narrow face was almost too pink with sun.

"The Gillespies have cruised all over the world, Pen," Grey said. "Isn't that amazing? We should do that, someday, after we, you know." He put his arm around her.

"Cruising is the way to go," Loretta said. "All the ship-board comforts you need and expect, with plenty of time to explore the best ports of call."

"We've been to Venice four times," Ward said matter-of-factly. "If you know what you're doing, you can avoid the tourists. Have you kids been?"

"Strictly private guides, private palace accommodations," Loretta said. "Can you imagine me on an overcrowded tour bus?" Pauline almost shook her head.

"I bet you've been on much fancier ships than this one," Grey said, clearly hanging on their every word.

"We prefer a private charter, but Loretta had a spur-of-the-moment hankering for Paradise Beach on St. Kitts and Nevis—"

"Have you ever tasted the honey from Nevis?" Loretta asked. "Something about those Nevis bees. Or maybe it's the flowers. Once you try it, you can't live without it."

"So, anyway," Ward continued, taking drinks from the waiter, "this ship was the quickest option from Philadelphia. Not top-of-the-line, but we can grin and bear it for a few days. More picturesque than flying."

Pauline didn't dare point out that this ship was the fanciest place she'd ever been. How much fancier could you get?

"Yeah, I think we'll step it up for our next cruise,"

Grey said. "Even the sheets and towels aren't quite what they should be."

Pauline almost burst out laughing, but pursed her lips instead, unwilling to risk mocking Grey in front of these people. She decided to take a dip and invited Grey to join her, but he declined, eyeing the Gillespies' gin and tonics. As she stepped into the pool, she heard Loretta asking Grey to tell her *simply everything* about archaeology.

****

At twilight, as the sun scattered bars of light across the water, they settled into a pair of curved white chairs in the open-air champagne bar. Couples filled the bar, the women showing off their tanned shoulders in flesh-baring pastel dresses, while the men, tie-less, relaxed in partially unbuttoned shirts and light sport coats. The evening breeze carried away their laughter and murmured conversations. The Gillespies were nowhere in sight. Probably ensconced on a huge balcony in a premium suite near the top of the ship. Or dining with the captain at his private table.

"You're stunning tonight," Grey said. She'd chosen the floaty, baby-blue chiffon sundress with spaghetti straps with an eye toward pleasing him. The jeweled key nestled around her neck.

"You too."

"What, this old thing?" In a white polo, summer-weight khakis, and thong sandals, his golden hair glowed against his newly bronzed skin. Sexiest man alive.

"Let's go dancing tonight," she said. "Dancing until dawn."

Grey stood and swiveled his hips, making her

laugh.

A bottle of Dom Perignon arrived, the flutes engraved with a silhouette of the *Archimedes,* like scrimshaw on glass.

"Can we keep these?" Pauline held up her glass.

"Penny, we can do whatever the fuck we want."

"You talk like a rich person. Like, uh, Ward Gillespie."

"Gettin' there. Everything's falling into place, can't you feel it?"

"Mr. Pollyanna."

"The glass," he said, filling her flute to the brim until bubbles foamed over the sides, "is more than half-full." She licked the rim to catch the bubbles. "Mmm." He swiped a finger across her lips to catch a bit of foam.

On the way to the disco, they scoped out a pair of grand curved staircases rising from the ship's central atrium. The stairs were flanked by a pair of tall columns, the surrounding floor inlaid with a tiled mosaic. The elaborately baroque space cried out for a dramatic gesture of some kind.

"Can't you see it?" Pauline mused. "The bride, her veil, the sweeping stairs. It's tailor-made."

"It's perfect."

An awkward silence followed. Pauline had spoken without thinking. She'd said more than she intended. Neither said another word on the subject, hurrying instead toward the propulsive *thump* of the disco lit by flashing white strobe lights and filled with a floor-pounding crowd. If ever Pauline longed to shed inhibitions, this was the time and place to do it. They threw themselves into the vintage rhythms of *Super*

Freak, Carwash, Heart of Glass, Billie Jean. Hips grinding, sweat dripping. The DJ changed it up, spinning Street People's *Wanna Slow Dance with You Baby.* She draped her arms around his neck, and they danced in slow circles.

Around midnight, they ordered cheesy nachos and margaritas at the after-hours bistro and stared out at a dark, moonless night, the sea visible only where the ship's side-running lights illuminated the black water. They spoke little, as if held by a spell, ending the night by making love on the stateroom balcony, Pauline gripping the railing, Grey folding himself from behind. Two hump-backed beasts saturated with pleasure. Neither said a word about the brief conversation in the ship's atrium.

Their second day aboard the *Archimedes* was given over to fresh pleasures. A swim. Another go at the rock wall, where she beat him to the top. A visit to the planetarium, where Pauline experienced a too-familiar sensation of being transported to another dimension. On the third morning, the spell broke when the *Archimedes* docked early at the port of Miami. The sounds of hurried footsteps and squeaky luggage wheels seeped into Pauline and Grey's quarters at first light, as passengers and staff rushed off in all directions. The two had barely finished dressing when there was a knock at the door. Housekeeping, probably. No. Grey opened the door to a slim man in a dark blue business suit and tie who, on first glance, looked a lot like an older, less muscular version of Grey, with some key differences. His hair was darker and threaded with silver, he had a thin mustache, and he bore a more cynical expression around his mouth and eyes. Pauline chalked up her initial impression to the fact that she'd only had eyes for Grey for so long.

"Ty!" The two men vigorously shook hands before clapping one another on the back.

Tyrone Lake sauntered toward her.

"Penny." He placed his hands on her shoulders and studied her face. His voice was high and reedy, nothing like Grey's. "So good to meet you. Grey has told me such wonderful things."

Chapter 16

Playtime was over. Tyrone Lake personally escorted them both down the gangway into a waiting black limousine with tinted windows. They cruised along Miami streets lined with palm trees that flitted like dim shadows across the car's darkened windows. Tyrone launched into a monologue aimed at Grey, seated beside him in the back seat. He barely glanced at Pauline.

"We need to jam as many deals through as possible, as quickly as possible. Capital is parking in the arts, billions every month. Anything you can find, as long as it's rare, one-of-kind, old as shit. I can sell it to the Russians, the Chinese, and the ruling families in Qatar. Americans too, of course. They've all got the best paintings, now they're hungry for antiquities—and not necessarily whatever's in their own backyards. But this only works if we lock up a unique supply chain. The better our sourcing, the quicker we beat everybody else to market with something nobody else has. Can you do that, Grey? Can *she*?"

What an asshole. Why did Grey worship this guy?

Grey squeezed her hand, and she hoped for damn sure he was silently apologizing on Tyrone Lake's behalf.

"You must keep your eyes open, Greyson," Tyrone Lake continued, his thin voice grating on Pauline.

"Never let an opportunity pass you by. Can you do that?"

"Greyson?" Pauline whispered.

"Tell you later," he whispered back.

The limo pulled up in front of the Intercontinental Hotel. Tyrone told them to head up to the rooftop restaurant, where he'd join them after making some calls.

"I bet he's got a direct line to the sultan of Abu Dhabi," Pauline said in a cutting tone, the moment they were out of Tyrone Lake's earshot.

"He might, actually," Grey said. "Don't underestimate him."

They rode an elevator up to a rooftop restaurant overlooking Biscayne Bay, affording a view through the hot, morning haze to where the *Archimedes* was docked. Grey ordered mimosas.

"So, *Greyson*."

"It's my legal name."

"Why didn't you tell me?"

Grey shrugged. "It's my father's name, and my grandfather's. I don't like to be reminded."

"How in the hell would Tyrone Lake know a thing like that?"

Grey looked out the window. "He asked. I didn't think lying to him was a good idea."

"You trust this guy?"

"Completely. We wouldn't be here if I didn't."

"He's a chauvinist pig, though, isn't he, Grey?"

"That's beside the point. Look, Penny, you'll do what you gotta do."

"What's *that* supposed to mean?" She gulped the champagne and orange juice.

"That came out wrong. I'm sorry. All I'm asking is, give Ty a chance. We need him."

"You both need *me.*"

"It's a team effort, Penny," he said, sharply. "You said yourself you have no idea how to sell an artifact. We wouldn't be sitting in this fancy place, wearing designer duds, if it weren't for—"

"I know, I know. I don't need a lecture."

"Even if you don't like Ty, you can still put your faith in *me.* Right?"

Pauline took a breath. "I want you to be happy, *Greyson.* That's what I want."

"I want the same for you."

They held hands across the table. Tyrone Lake arrived and pulled out a third chair.

"Don't get too carried away," he said, as if they'd been screwing on top of the table. He ordered food for the table without consulting either of them. Eggs benedict, bacon, toast, fruit, pastries. A waitress refilled his coffee several times, as though she were on his payroll. He didn't touch the food. Grey and Pauline ate in silence. She still remembered how it felt to worry about affording a decent meal. Tyrone ordered a second round of mimosas for the two of them, also without asking.

After dabbing his mustache with a white cloth napkin like a dandy, Tyrone Lake consulted his phone.

"It must happen tonight," he said decisively. "You can cope with that, right?" He stared at Grey, ignoring Pauline as if she were furniture. Surely Grey had educated him about her role? Her special talents? "The ship heads to the Antilles tomorrow, so we've only got one shot."

"Penny, I told Ty what you told me—that you'd found a site for us somewhere south of here."

"That's right." She wasn't about to give up more information until Tyrone Lake showed some respect.

"And?" the man asked, shifting his blue-gray eyes—like Grey's, only colder—to her.

"And what?" She stared back at him.

"Penny, all the resources you need to succeed are at your disposal," Tyrone said. "But I can't help you without the details. Now, come on, we're a team. I'm sure Grey has said as much."

"Grey knows I'm careful when it comes to, you know, illegally digging up priceless artifacts at night. The fewer people know the details, the better."

"Penny!" Grey said.

"It's all right, Grey. She's right—you can't be too careful. But Penny, first of all, I'm your partner, so I need to know what you know. Second, the stuff you find isn't priceless. On the contrary, it has a price, which I will set to attract the right buyers. So, you see, there's a lot more to this than you pointing to a map and saying, 'Dig here.' "

Is that how Grey explained to Tyrone what she did? Or did Tyrone boil it down to minimize her contribution?

"Mr. Lake, you can call me Pauline. That's my real name. Penny is a...private nickname." Grey bit his lip. Point made. "What resources can you provide?"

"Whatever you need, name it. But I need to know now."

She exchanged a quick glance with Grey. Toeing the line, buddy, just like you asked.

"The site is twenty-two miles south of here, just off

Melba Beach. The artifact—the prize possession, if my research is correct—lies on the sea floor as part of an unexcavated eighteenth-century shipwreck. There may be more than one item worth salvaging. I can't say for sure."

Tyrone tapped an expensive shoe on the tiled floor. "This all sounds too good to be true, Pauline. A shipwreck just offshore, filled with unrecovered treasure? Come on. This area has been crawling with shipwreck divers for years." He looked at Grey.

"Ty, we've given you no reason to doubt anything Penny says. We're already two for two, aren't we? You've turned a huge profit on the items we've brought you so far. Penny's archaeological judgment is extraordinary, but it's not a fantasy. We don't have to understand it, you and I, but we damn well should accept it. Besides, I'm not fucking around here any more than you are."

"Don't look a gift horse in the mouth, you mean," Tyrone said with a thin smile, his narrow mustache curving at the edges. "All right. We're all gamblers, aren't we? That's how we win. So, what do you need for this little outing?"

"A professional diver," Pauline said crisply. "Waterproof carry-alls. A cage that can be raised and lowered from the boat, to hold any objects too unwieldy for the diver to carry by hand. And of course, a skiff of some sort."

"Now, Pauline, was that so hard?" Tyrone's smile lasted a split second. "I'll make a few calls, and everything will be handled. You can provide Samuel—my driver—with directions when we meet tonight. Say, midnight?"

Tyrone Lake picked up the check for breakfast and then disappeared.

****

The pair were at loose ends, with hours to kill until the risky nighthawking began. Too much time to think about everything that could go wrong. Just because the Virginia gig went down without a hitch—not counting the unexpected nocturnal visitor—didn't mean their luck would hold. Grey, as usual, seemed unconcerned. They walked along the beach, letting their feet sink into the warm sand by the water's edge.

"Are we crazy?" she asked, breaking a long silence filled by the lapping waves.

"Relax. All contingencies are covered." How would he know that?

"We don't know the diver." She picked up a pink shell, then dropped it absently.

"He's part of Ty's operation. You let him worry about that."

"Ty won't be anywhere near this thing tonight, will he?"

"He doesn't need to be."

"So, if anything goes wrong…" Pauline said. She stopped and squinted out over the ocean, as if taking the full measure of the risks they were about to undertake. "If, say, a police boat or the Coast Guard spots us, you know who takes the fall. He's worked out all the angles, hasn't he?"

"You need to understand, Penny." Grey kicked up some sand. "Without him, none of this happens. He's in charge of…everything."

"Well," she said. "Not quite everything."

Once back on board the *Archimedes*, they ate a

light early supper before selecting and packing the tools they'd need for the expedition. Picks, brushes, trowels, headlamps, plus various maps and sea charts.

"What if the diver fucks up?" Pauline asked.

"Haven't we been through all this?" He tightened the straps on his pack.

"What if he breaks something? Ty will blame us. I mean, *me.*"

"You've never worried this much. What's wrong?"

"I like nighthawking when it's just us."

Grey's kiss was supposed to reassure her. She appreciated the effort.

"How about I give you some privacy to review your maps and stuff."

"Great idea," she said, well aware he wanted a break from her anxiety. "Take a stroll on deck."

With him gone from sight, she didn't have to pretend any longer. She sat on the stateroom balcony, gazing out at the bay in twilight.

Why am I doing this? Because I love Grey. Isn't that reason enough? And for financial security. But...is this all there is? Disturbing artifacts lost to time, cashing in, getting richer and richer...outlaws forever?

What do I want instead, if not this life with Greyson Henley?

Pauline's inner voice left her hanging. No response.

A knot of dread gathered in her stomach, as if something unexpected was about to happen. Maybe tonight, maybe not, but soon.

****

At exactly midnight, Tyrone Lake's limousine awaited them on shore, as it had that morning. Tyrone wore the same business suit he'd had on earlier, confirming Pauline's assumption that he had no intention of getting his feet wet. She and Grey were dressed casually in shorts, T-shirts, and deck shoes. The dig wouldn't be dirty, but it would be wet.

Tyrone dispensed with small talk. He held up his phone and leaned across the seat to look at Pauline.

"The diver's in a motorboat, ready to deploy to the coordinates you provide."

Maybe Grey had had a chat with him earlier that evening, about taking her into account. She had prepared for this moment of archaeology theater. She provided nautical GPS coordinates the diver would need to get close to the site. They planned to rendezvous with him on the closest stretch of Melba Beach. Pauline wondered if Ty had thought about police patrolling the beach late at night. Maybe he had the "muscle" to take care of such situations. This wasn't the time to ask. She wasn't sure she wanted to know, anyway.

Samuel drove them to the drop-off point at Melba Beach. Ty abruptly started firing questions at Pauline about what they were looking for, what it might look like, how big, how many. She calibrated her replies, sharing just enough to sound plausible, while holding back on countless details she could summon at will. Neither Ty nor Grey could possibly understand why she knew what she knew. She didn't understand it, either.

Grey beamed at her. Wasn't that all she really needed?

Chapter 17

The nighttime beach was warm, but the wind was picking up. An overcast sky would work in their favor, helping to render them nearly invisible. Tyrone Lake's parting words to Pauline and Grey when he dropped them off were nothing like "Be careful." He reminded them, instead, that there was a lot riding on this. "Don't screw it up, kids." He was looking at *her* when he said it.

They walked down Melba Beach toward the water until a light appeared and flashed three times. The diver signaling his location a few yards offshore. Grey took Pauline's hand as they waded into the surf. Warm waves slapped her legs, soaking her shorts. The water was rougher than she expected. The motorboat was tiny—barely bigger than their balcony terrace back home. A man in a wetsuit, almost invisible against the night sky, reached out to help them board. On the deck of the boat sat a square metal cage attached to a chain operated by a winch, just as Pauline had requested, along with a pair of scuba diving oxygen tanks and other gear she didn't recognize.

"Call me Max," the diver said.

"I'm Grey. This is Pen—Pauline. She's the mastermind."

"I've heard that, yeah," Max said. "But you're on my boat, and you'll do exactly what I tell you. Is that understood?"

"Aye-aye, captain," Pauline said. The boat rocked aggressively, making it difficult to keep upright. She and Grey spread their legs wide, seeking stability.

"Once we're out there, we'll have about two hours for retrieval," Max said in a gravelly voice. "We gotta make it back to shore before daylight. So, no room for mistakes. Is that understood also?"

Pauline guessed that Max was ex-military. He seemed just the sort Tyrone Lake would surround himself with.

"How can we help, Max?" Grey asked.

"Don't fall out of the fucking boat. Because fishing you out will waste time we don't have." He handed Grey an oar and said the two of them would row for about a mile before turning on the motor, to minimize attention. He led Pauline to a short bench near the transom and told her to stay put. She noticed there were no lifejackets in sight. She sure as hell wasn't about to insist on one and come off looking like a baby.

Max and Grey settled on the short bench running between the boat's gunwales in the center. The men grunted with effort as they fought against waves pushed onshore by the stiff breeze. The boat bobbed along in total darkness, as Max kept the running lights off until they were farther out in the bay.

"Pauline, I'm told you're the navigator," Max said, breathing hard. "You know what you're doing?"

"I've got a chart plotter, a compass, and GPS on my phone," she replied. "Plus, the NOAA chart for Biscayne Bay and beyond." She pulled a laminated map from her pack, along with a headlamp. She'd come well prepared—prepared to look normal, that is. She could easily envision exactly where they needed to go without any of these tools. But that wouldn't wash. So she relied on science most of the time, turning to pure instinct to make course corrections along the way. The men would not be able to tell the difference.

They rowed in silence for an hour. Pauline periodically called out instructions, telling them to turn a few degrees to port or starboard. Otherwise, the only sounds were the waves slapping against the boat and the men grunting against choppy waters. Pauline wondered how much Max knew about their objectives and the financial stakes. Would he get a cut of the profits? Or was he merely a minion on Tyrone Lake's payroll, willing to carry out any task? No matter what…no job too dirty, eh? Grey would not approve of her suspicions. He would vehemently deny them, surely.

Finally, when they were roughly a mile from shore, Max turned on the running lights before starting the motor and taking the tiller. He ordered Pauline to trade places with Grey. Seated together on the middle bench, they snuck a kiss in the dark.

"Excited?" Grey's lips grazed her ear.

She turned and bit his earlobe. "I hope Max knows he has to be careful, once we reach the shipwreck."

"Ty doesn't work with amateurs."

"How much farther, Pauline?" Max shouted.

She consulted the digital readings on her phone. "Ten minutes."

The wind grew stronger, causing the boat to rise a few feet in the air before slamming back down onto the water. The ride was rougher than before.

"Ohhh," Grey moaned. He leaned over the side and

vomited.

"Sweetie." Pauline rubbed his back.

"You okay?" he asked hoarsely.

"Right as rain. Be right back." She maneuvered over to Max and sat on the deck because she couldn't keep her balance standing any longer. She told him they were a quarter of a nautical mile from the site and instructed him to turn to port about fifteen degrees. He nodded and did exactly as she asked.

Minutes later, she told him to cut the engine and drop anchor. They were just beyond the outer reaches of Biscayne Bay, in the open Atlantic Ocean. The shore was long gone from view. The only visible lights came from a freighter, miles to the east. Pauline closed her eyes and traveled beneath the surface to the sunken ship, where its frame had cracked apart like broken ribs. The ocean wasn't too deep there, so Max shouldn't have trouble making the dive.

Grey groaned as the boat continued rocking.

"Amateurs," Max muttered.

"Don't let me slow you down," Grey called.

"You won't." Max prepared for diving. He sat on the gunwale in his flippers, his tank hanging out over the black water. "Tell me exactly what I'm looking for, Pauline."

"In the mid-eighteenth century, a Spanish sailing ship on its way from Cuba back to Spain was destroyed by a hurricane."

"Don't give me a fucking history lesson, Pauline. Tell me what objects I'm supposed to bring up."

"The main thing you're looking for is a Peruvian funeral mask."

"What the hell does *that* look like? Jesus."

"It's a piece of smelted metal, roughly oblong in shape, about the size of a dinner plate. It probably has artistic markings on it, like a face, maybe some other decorations."

"Metal dinner plate. Can't make out much more than that, down below. How do you know it's not buried under a ton of other junk?"

Oh, right. He would ask that, wouldn't he? She saw the object so clearly, she momentarily forgot he'd have no idea. Think fast.

"Well, I think, Max, the current down there keeps shifting the sand and debris like a broom—"

"Yeah, broom-like currents are a thing. Makes sense. What else?"

"You might find some coins, jewelry, pottery, almost anything, really."

"Is it the mask Mr. Lake wants most?"

"Yes," Grey called out. "Then coins and jewelry." He'd found a bottle of water and was seated on the deck near the bow. Despite everything going on, Pauline noticed that Max said *Mr. Lake*, while Grey uses the informal *Ty*. The two must know each other better than she assumed—or else had quickly reached a deep understanding.

"You better be right about all this," Max said, picking up one of the waterproof carry-alls. "Shipwreck my ass," he muttered. He inserted the breathing apparatus into his mouth, pulled the clear mask over his eyes, and tipped backward into the water, his splash drowned out by the waves.

"Penny," Grey called. She made her way unsteadily toward the center of the boat and plopped down on the bench, facing Grey on the deck, which seemed to be filling up with water sloshing over the sides. They were both soaked. "How come you're not puking your guts out?"

"Don't know. How are you feeling?"

"Shitty. But, no pain, no gain." Her headlamp revealed Grey's lopsided grin, which was replaced by another bout of vomiting. She slid down onto the deck, cradling his exhausted body.

"Close your eyes," she said. "Take deep breaths." She closed her eyes too and concentrated on the location of the Inca chief's funeral mask, which the Spaniards stole as part of an aggressive raid on a large tomb complex in Peru. They were crazy for gold and precious metals. Anything that might enrich the queen's coffers back home and line their own pockets in the process. The hurricane that sent their ship to the bottom of the ocean laden with contraband seemed like fitting payback.

Now, centuries later, the three of them were rescuing property that had already been stolen, so that at least it could be appreciated and enjoyed. What's wrong with that? She pushed away thoughts of repatriation—returning the object to the descendants of its Indigenous owners. After all, Dean Nojes had held onto the Cambodian dragon for decades. *I'm no better than the dean, and no worse.* And what would Bette say? Would she scoff and scowl at their illegal expedition, or admire their pluck? Maybe a bit of both. She'd never have a chance to judge.

She distracted Grey with his favorite subject.

"How much do you think the mask will be worth? It almost certainly contains copper, gold, and silver. I doubt there's anything quite like it. You always say the rarer, the better."

"Maybe a million, if it's everything you say," he mumbled. "Even if we see only half of that..." He pulled himself up out of her lap. "Imagine, Penny, if we can close four deals like this a year, pretty soon, we'll be free to do anything we want, go anywhere. We can charter our own jet, like the Gillespies, and fly to China, France, Australia. Machu Picchu! You name it."

"You really think so?"

"Wait and see. You work your magic, then Ty works his."

"Hey." Max resurfaced, his breather dangling free, his head bobbing at the surface. "Take this." He tossed the waterproof sack onto the deck, which Penny scrambled to intercept before a rogue wave swept it overboard. "Coins. They're everywhere. Hope they're what Mr. Lake is looking for."

"And the mask?" Grey asked.

"Not yet. But there's a lump of stuff I'm going back for. I'll give you this, Pauline. It's a helluva a shipwreck. Hard to believe we got to it first."

"That's why I call her Lucky Penny," Grey said.

"Yeah," Max said. "I wanna bring the cage down. Hand it to me, Pauline. Make sure the chain runs free while I pull it down." She placed a small trowel inside the metal cage, which Max might need, then lifted the cage, about two square feet, and lowered it over the side. The cage sank, and Max dove after it.

"He won't come back without the grand prize," Grey said. Maybe tough-guy Max was scared of Tyrone Lake. The waves grew taller, more water poured into the boat, and the two of them began bailing with their hands, until Pauline found a small bucket stowed in a box beneath the middle bench.

"At what point—" she began.

"Don't know. Don't think about it. We're still here, we're not sinking, that's all that counts."

Rain mixed with the waves, and bailing became pointless. Pauline could see from the uncoiled chain that the cage had been brought as far down as it would go. She focused again on the artifact, wishing she could guide Max telepathically to its precise location. But that was ridiculous, even for her.

Finally, the diver returned to the surface and swiftly executed a complicated, highly practiced maneuver to get himself back onboard. He shrugged off the tank and removed his flippers. Then, muttering a string of curses under his breath, he grabbed a bilge pump, which resembled a bicycle tire pump, and began pumping water out of the boat through an attached tube he draped over the gunwale. He told Grey to take over pumping so he could activate the winch to pull up the cage.

Without waiting for his irritated command, Pauline got in position to hoist the cage into the boat the moment it appeared, powered by the winch. She heaved and landed the cage, draped in seaweed, with a thud. Her headlamp illuminated a solid lump of material coated with green and brown layers of more seaweed, small shells, barnacles, and other marine material. A curved, jagged object protruded about three inches from the lump. This was the prize, though only she knew it.

"Well?" Max and Grey said together.

She ran her index finger along the eroded edge of the protrusion. A vivid array of images exploded: the Incan chieftain being laid to rest in his tomb, hundreds gathered for the ceremony. Another Incan official, in a long brown smock, carefully placed the gleaming funeral mask on the dead chief's face in the open coffin. The smelted mask was decorated with a raised facsimile of the chief's face framed by a fan-shaped headdress, his hands outstretched, and above his head, a series of radiating lines and other decorative symbols. Using a small pick, Pauline delicately chipped away the marine life encrusting a small portion of the exposed rim, all while trying to steady herself in the rocking boat, the rain nearly obscuring the light emanating from her headlamp. She was able to expose a few of the radiating lines on the oxidized green metal.

"You found it," she announced. "The mask. This is the one the Spaniards supposedly stole, then lost, when the ship went down."

"I knew it!" Grey said. "She's a genius, Max!"

Max didn't offer any further praise. He raised the anchor, restarted the motor, and turned the boat back toward shore.

Pauline looked past Grey. Her headlamp revealed a third person standing in the bow of the boat. Did the others see him too? Of course not. It's *him.* Larger than life, his bulk rock-steady in the rocking boat. His coal-black eyes bored into her yet again, and she could not look away, as her body began humming in tune with his energy.

"Your time here grows short," he said, his words filling her up, as if she'd been empty all her life, waiting for him to satisfy an unrecognized hunger.

He was by her side, wrapping her in his arms, suffusing her with the warmth of countless suns. In his embrace, Pauline expanded, the edges of her body dissolving. They became one breath. He spoke once more.

"I will be there to catch you."

And then he was gone, leaving her with a pang of loneliness, even as the man she loved with all her heart stood a mere three feet away.

She focused on regaining control over her own breathing, vaguely aware that Grey was examining the old coins in the pouch. She went over to join him, placing a hand over his heart to reassure her of its beating warmth as the boat raced toward shore, sending up plumes of white spray that mingled with the swelling waves.

Chapter 18

Pauline and Grey quietly entered their stateroom on the *Archimedes* around five in the morning, just as the rainy night was edging toward dawn. They'd pulled off another nighthawking expedition, guided by Pauline's secret store of knowledge. Once again, none of her fears had come true. Presumably, after this, Grey would never entertain another word of doubt.

He threw himself across the bed, wet and fully clothed.

"The bed's rocking," he mumbled. He was asleep instantly.

Pauline lay down next to him. His face was pale, his hair stiff with salt. She brushed a curl back from his forehead.

I'm not in love with a ghost. Only you.

She could not shut down as easily as he or dream as innocently. Wide awake, her mind's eye revealed men and women in woven shawls pulling carts loaded with fruits, vegetables, and bright textiles along the roads and trails running through Cuzco, the ancient capital of the Incan Empire. A man held up a quipu—a cord with knotted strings suspended from it, an Incan tool for recording information, akin to the abacus in the ancient Near East.

The Spanish vessel, *La Reina,* loaded with stolen Peruvian treasures, groaned and strained in rough seas as gale-force winds cracked the mast, sending the ship and its crew tumbling to their watery graves, screaming for God and Queen Isabella to save them. Max had not mentioned seeing bones, but perhaps those had been swept away by the currents long ago. Or perhaps human remains were beneath his notice because they were worthless to wealthy collectors.

At six o'clock, Pauline heard a sharp knock at the door. Grey was still out cold. She threw a blanket on him and hastily pulled on dry clothes. She cracked open the door. The thin mustache was unmistakable.

"Mr. Lake. You don't waste time."

Tyrone Lake brushed past her without waiting for an invitation. He was impeccably dressed even at this hour, in a light tan business suit, a brown-and-yellow striped tie, and the same expensive shoes she'd noticed the day before. Not a salt-and-pepper hair out of place.

"You must call me Ty," he said. She put a finger to her lips and pointed to the bedroom. "Ah, yes, a long night, I suppose. But you look chipper enough, Pauline. Can't the old boy keep up with you?"

He looked around the stateroom until his eyes alighted on the carry-all holding the funeral mask, still bound up in sea debris, and the smaller bag of coins.

"Show me," he commanded.

Pauline placed the objects on the octagonal table where Tyrone Lake's gift of champagne had welcomed them the first night.

"Should I wake Grey? He wouldn't want to miss this."

"Not necessary. What am I looking at, exactly?"

"The coins first." She spread them out. "Silver reales and gold escudos. Note the markings. The

167

queen…here. The royal coat of arms…here. All eighteenth century, I'd say. I assume you have people to confirm that sort of thing." He nodded, then swept up all the coins and returned them to the pouch. "There's probably a lot more where these came from. There's no way Max could have found all the coins that sank with the ship."

"You're saying a return visit could be profitable."

"Almost certainly, yes."

He nodded again. "And this…lump? What's this?" He touched the mound of material, still damp and smelling like musty salt.

"This contains the prize. The artifact I told you about." She fingered the rim of the metal funeral mask poking out from the mound. "An Incan funeral mask, probably smelted from gold, silver, and copper. Stolen by the Spaniards from the tomb of a chieftain or other VIP." She hesitated before adding another detail she could not possibly know by any rational means. A test of his astuteness. "I think you'll find that the mask contains iridium, a metal in the platinum family, probably taken from a meteorite."

"Did you say platinum?" Tyrone looked at her sharply, as if deciding how much to believe.

"A small quantity, but yes."

He smiled like a hungry wolf who'd found its prey. Ah, so the dollar signs in his eyes precluded any questions about how she could possibly know so much about an artifact still entombed in its oceanic prison.

"Excellent work, Pauline. Outstanding."

"Hey, Pen, why didn't you wake me?" Grey padded over, rubbing his eyes, still in wet clothes. "What did I miss?"

"Your genius girlfriend is going to make us all rich," Tyrone said, the wolfish grin on full view.

"I told you she would." Grey threw a damp arm across her shoulder. "She's the best thing that ever happened to me, Ty. Good thing I bumped into her when I did."

A surge of loathing for Tyrone Lake welled up in her gut. She hated the way he turned Grey into a striving, conniving, money-grubbing opportunist whenever they were together. Grey was not Tyrone. Grey was kind, thoughtful, compassionate, playful, loving…all the things Tyrone Lake was not and never would be.

"I need coffee," she said, irritably.

"I'll take care of it, babe." Grey picked up the room phone.

Tyrone took the plastic bag containing all the artifacts. "I'll be in touch," he said to Grey on the way out. The man was finished with her. She'd done her bit. She wondered if he had any idea how to recover and restore the mask, let alone properly clean and polish the coins. With a stab of guilt, she hoped for the best, bidding a silent farewell to the artifacts she knew so well. They began speaking to her, all at once, but with a huge act of willpower, she refused to listen.

"I know you trust him, Grey, but do you *like* him?"

"I respect him. It's got nothing to do with *liking*. It's business, Penny. He's incredibly connected and a really smart negotiator. I can't make you like him."

"Well, I don't."

"I think he likes you, though."

"He doesn't like me, Grey. He likes *using* me."

"I wouldn't put it that way."

They drank coffee on the balcony, just in time to watch the sun edge from dawn to daylight. The sky had cleared, promising a glorious day.

Grey pulled his chair around and clasped her hands.

"Penny, I'm not Ty. You're everything to me. Best friend, lover, partner. Let's get dressed up tonight and pretend we're the only people on the planet." He kissed her hands, then her shoulder, neck, and lips. He carried her to the bed, where he licked and caressed every inch, the pleasure of his touch bringing relief from the doubts and frustrations that had cast shadows across her love.

The *Archimedes* set course for the Antilles, and Pauline and Grey once again had time to waste. Poolside, the Gillespies had claimed the same lounge chairs as though they'd never left, both social-media-ready in perfect pastel resort wear. Grey got them talking about art and antiquities. Pauline looked on while he told a number of amusing lies to get the one-percenters talking about things like freeports—tax-free facilities where the uber-wealthy often stored their art.

"My grandfather is leaving me a substantial legacy," Grey said. "Quite soon, I imagine. I figure the best way to honor his legacy is by investing wisely."

"Good for you," Ward Gillespie said, sipping from an ever-present gin and tonic. "Most people your age don't think long-term. They want to spend, spend, spend."

Loretta left her husband's side to sit next to Pauline, bringing her drink with her.

"Grey told me all about these marvelous archaeological adventures you've been on together," Loretta began. Pauline raised an eyebrow. "Caves in

Spain," she continued. "Ancient ruins in Iraq. You must be fearless, Pauline." She shook her head, privately laughing at Grey's nonsense. "Don't be modest, my dear. I can only imagine the risks involved. And so much discomfort! Working in the heat, the cold, all that dirt and dust. In my line of work, eyestrain is the only real hazard. Well, that and a bear market."

Loretta cackled and sipped her drink, showing off flawless fingernails painted a nauseating shade of neon pink. The diamond tennis bracelet slid along her wrist.

"I couldn't imagine doing anything else," Pauline replied.

"Maybe in my next life, *I'll* become an archaeologist." Loretta cackled again.

"And that's why you need a balanced portfolio," Ward was telling Grey, who was rapt with attention. "Art, to be sure, but also real estate. If you want, Grey, I'll introduce you to my REIT guy, once your capital comes in. He'll set you up."

"That would be fantastic, Ward, thank you," Grey said.

"Honey," Pauline said. "I think we've had enough sun, don't you? Let's go in."

"You two are just the cutest," Loretta said. "Archaeologists on the *Archimedes*. What a trip." Pauline suspected she was drunk.

****

Grey wore a sharply tailored black tuxedo. He examined himself in the mirror.

"Is my bowtie straight?"

Pauline, still in bra and panties, reached up from behind to tweak the tie. He wore the cologne he'd purchased in New York.

"Wow." She inhaled him.

He turned around and placed his hands gently around the back of her neck, drawing her in for a kiss. A flame of need rose up as she pressed her groin to his, but he pulled away.

"Meet me in the atrium," he said softly. "As soon as you're ready."

Twenty minutes later, she made her way to the atrium with the grand staircases, which they'd admired on their way to the disco only a few nights earlier. Pauline's heels echoed on the hard tile flooring. Guests filled some of the upholstered chairs scattered about the brightly lit space, but on such a fine night, most were outside on various decks. Grey stood half-way up the far staircase. He smiled down at her. She still could not get over how handsome he was. How irreplaceable.

She walked up the marble steps to meet him: Cinderella in a white, one-shouldered Greek goddess dress and her formally attired prince. He kissed her hand and touched the jeweled key resting in the hollow of her neck.

"You're stunning," he whispered.

Grey Henley got down on one knee on the step of the grand staircase and removed a blue velvet box from his jacket pocket. He opened the box, revealing a large diamond ring that caught the light from the chandelier above.

"Pauline Marsh, will you marry me?"

Pauline was breathless. Literally breathless. The room spun upside down, and she was falling, falling, unable to get oriented, yet certain she was no longer in a room, on a ship. Nowhere and everywhere at once.

Moth wings beat in her gut, her body a sheath of

white lightning.

I am a rainbow, a grassy field, a cloudy sky.

Strong arms steadied her as she flew apart, the arms re-establishing boundaries where none had existed.

"I told you I would be here to catch you."

A familiar presence—beside her, inside her, a piece of her own soul.

You are more.

PART 2: DOCKING

Chapter 19

Have I died? she wondered. Has my soul departed my body? So noisy, this place between life and death...

Voices speaking over each other, making it hard to think straight.

The air, like silk against her skin.

Gravity, altered.

A single voice emerged, at last, but the words didn't register. Fingers clasped her temples—that felt real. Grey?... Not Grey.

Ahh, better. The voices, silenced.

"The souls of objects." She heard the words clearly, this time. Her eyelids—had they been closed?—fluttered open.

Where...?

A familiar place: the balcony terrace of the penthouse where she lived. She stood upright. Or, no, not quite. Shifting her head toward the speaker, the air shimmered lemon-yellow. The balcony shifted, as if loosened from its moorings.

He was with her, once again. More real, more solid, than before. Towering, with a bronze complexion, glossy black hair tied back, and eyes as black as his clothing. His gaze was penetrating, even mesmerizing. She looked down, the light shimmering, and noticed he was barefoot.

"I've quieted them for you, for now. The souls of

objects, speaking their truth." His voice rumbled like distant thunder.

She was dreaming, yes? She willed herself to wake up next to Grey, his crooked smile ready to reassure her that all was right with the world.

"Say my name," the deep voice said.

Your name? How would I...?

"Chaitanya," Pauline said, surprised at the sound of her own voice. Or was she speaking only in her head? *Chai-taan-yuh.* Other names and faces crowded in. Tucquan, born by the river. Charles Waters, from a Long Island farm. "Chaitanya," she repeated. "It means...universal soul or spirit. In Sanskrit. But how...?"

"Deep-time knowledge dwells inside you, and always has."

The man spoke in exhausting riddles, never making sense. She shook her head, as if to clear away the confusion, the lemon-yellow haze shimmering in response. Baltimore's Inner Harbor appeared below, indistinct through the haze. But the haze was pocked by moving objects. No, not objects, flying figures, hundreds of them, all clothed in black, like flocks of crows breaking formation. She blinked hard. The figures carried objects of every shape and size: pitchers, bowls, brooches, swords, masks, wooden chests. As they swooped close by, she caught tangents of chatter.

"...that summer day when my mistress filled me with cool water from the stream..."

"...my blade sinking up to the hilt in his breastbone...Ah! What a triumph!"

"...pinned to her ermine cape on the night he died..."

"What do you hear?" Chaitanya asked.

"So many voices, all talking at once."

"The souls of objects, telling their stories."

"Sorry, what?"

"Universal consciousness, endowed."

Make sense! She longed to shout at him, but held back, unable to shake the feeling there was something between them, drawing them together. She suddenly remembered that Dean Nojes had mentioned lemon-yellow air. Had she been here, after all—wherever "here" was? Pauline held up a hand, exploring the boundaries of her body. She looked down, touching her sides, surprised to learn she was wearing the white one-shouldered Greek goddess dress she had on when…when…

"Where is Grey!"

"He kneels on the grand staircase on the *Archimedes*," Chaitanya said, his voice warm and patient. "He is in his time space, and you are in yours."

The balcony swayed as if not properly anchored to the wall. No, Pauline was swaying, like a sapling bending with the wind. The weightlessness of the *pulse*: a familiar sensation in a foreign context. She gripped the railing, equally afraid of falling, which seemed likely, and of flying, which seemed impossible.

Chaitanya placed a warm palm on the top of her head, and a sense of calm well-being flooded her from head to toe, coupled with sympathetic vibrations—the hummed notes of the chord she'd experienced in his presence before. Her breathing slowed to align with his. One breath, together. This time, she did not panic. Under his touch—like a blessing—a lifetime of anxious secret-keeping fell away in an instant, offering a fleeting glimpse of a self she hardly recognized. Not a daughter, not a foster child, not a freak, not even a lover.

Someone…something…beyond each of those familiar identities.

He removed his hand, leaving her instantly diminished, less than she was, or might be.

"You will come to understand yourself, and your purpose, through the deeds you perform," he said. She waited for more, but instead of words, he spoke with his eyes, directing her gaze through the shimmering light toward the ground hundreds of feet below. A deep, neatly dug rectangular hole had been dug in the sidewalk at the corner of Pratt Street and Light Street. A black-clad female form rose up from the hole like a helium balloon, clasping pieces of fabric. Pauline *knew*. She just *knew*.

"Look!" she exclaimed. "She found Annabelle, the doll that Carolina Sewell loved so much, never let out of her sight, until the day she dropped it when she was seven and a carriage wheel immediately rode right over it, tearing it apart, pressing it into the mud. Oh, but down there, just now, all the pieces have been recovered, haven't they?"

"Listen, now," Chaitanya said.

A clear voice appealed directly to her:

Carolina's Auntie Mae sewed me from scraps of calico and gingham, burlap and twine, broken buttons, and filled me with straw. And when Auntie Mae gave me to Carolina for Christmas, we were together day and night.

"The soul of an object," she said, understanding for the first time what all the voices she'd been hearing truly represented.

"Many emissaries of the Thread Continuum hear the souls of objects—hear some of them. You, however, you hear them all, calling out from the well of deep time."

Too much. She tried to focus on one simple thing. "What will happen to her—to the doll fragments, to Annabelle—now that she's been rescued?"

"Such knowledge will unfold."

The air thickened and shimmered as Chaitanya looped his arm in hers—a surprisingly comfortable fit—and they left the balcony to enter the penthouse. Dizzy double-vision. Yes, this was the luxurious penthouse where she lived with Grey Henley. All the furniture was in place. But this was also someplace else entirely. The big picture windows did not look out on the Baltimore city skyline or the harbor. Instead, a series of images scrolled rapidly as if the windows were a movie screen. Villages, huts, fires, cave paintings, carved masks, woven baskets, objects of wood, beads, iron, jewels, animal pelts… Pauline experienced each fast-moving image in three dimensions, ready to reach out and touch, smell, or taste every item.

She turned to Chaitanya for an explanation. He smiled, his dark eyes warm, almost mischievous.

"All your doing," he said. "A fraction of your consciousness." She knew he saw it too, though she had no idea what the parade of images meant. "The others look out the window and see only sky and city."

The others. For the condo suddenly was not empty. Barefoot black-clad figures of all ages and genders—had he called them emissaries?—were everywhere: on the seat, back, and arms of the leather sofa, the hassocks, the floor, on the glass-topped table where she and Grey had made love...when? Some figures hovered in mid-air, bobbing gently. Pauline could not tell if their words and laughter rang out into the air, or if she only heard them in her head.

"This arrangement, these surroundings, will ease your way," Chaitanya said. All eyes—every pair dark like his—turned toward her. Chaitanya released her arm and arched his feet, his body rising effortlessly off the floor before gently touching down, like a feather falling to earth. He began to twist, slowly, elegantly, his arms and neck elongated, his trunk swaying. This large being, so filled with light and grace, combining masculine strength and feminine poise...he was dancing. Pauline stared at him, aware that all the figures in the room took up the dance, performing a slow ballet in the air, moving and swaying to silent rhythms. The air shimmered but was no longer mere air, only pure feeling, which Pauline inhaled. Beauty. Joy. And something more: a oneness, a unity, a sense of belonging *with* and *to* and *alongside.* Far deeper, even, than her connection with Grey. No! She tried to resist, to declare her loyalty, but found it impossible to do so.

The melody the others danced to vibrated in her now, also, a music belonging to no particular instrument or style or era. A timeless music composed of...souls.

The rhythm of her breathing changed again. They all—she, Chaitanya, and the emissaries—breathed together as one.

Pauline began to cry, tears floating off her cheeks and merging with the shimmering air. She rose into the air, arms swaying, as she joined the others in the dance.

I am me, and more than me.

The collective dance did not end so much as temporarily cease, as if on cue. Chaitanya took her hand and brought her to the center of the room. The emissaries encircled them, some on the ground, some hovering above, their arms stretched toward her like the spokes of a wheel—and she was the hub.

"Welcome to the Thread Continuum, Elected One," Chaitanya said. "Your true home, ever and always." He kissed the top of her head, a chaste kiss that nevertheless suffused her for an instant with the peaceful calm she'd experienced earlier. His touch was like a drug, easy to crave.

Bells began to ring out, like church bells pealing in a distant belfry. Emissaries darted in and out through the open door leading to the balcony—whether in response to the bells or for other reasons, she couldn't tell. Those who remained behind flicked their wrists, a motion that conjured bright golden balls, translucent and flickering like sparklers on the Fourth of July. A game? They clustered in small groups around the floating balls, gazing into them, discussing whatever was revealed there. Should she join one of these groups and see for herself?

Pauline was about to turn to Chaitanya for guidance when a sudden hollowing in her gut told her he had departed, his breath uncoupled from hers. A familiar twinge of panic, wounds of the old abandonment: Had he forsaken her? Or would he return?

Suddenly, she was wrapped in a stranger's arms, squeezed like a long-lost friend, or no, she was a child wrapped in a mother's love—a new and piercing sensation she never expected to experience. The stranger released her—too soon—and Pauline pulled back to look at the hugger, a woman with a wrinkled face and long gray hair streaming down her back. The woman's touch had briefly rekindled that sense of belonging, as if she were a member of a close-knit family, celebrating a reunion.

Is this what family *feels like? Isn't Grey my family?* Such a tangle of confused thoughts.

The woman took Pauline's hand. "In all my centuries, I've never met one like you," she said, her voice young, her movements lithe, despite her aged appearance. She wore a simple black unitard exactly like the others, her feet bare.

"Like what?"

The woman smiled, her warm eyes almost as dark as Chaitanya's. "Come."

Pauline followed up the spiral staircase, puzzled and even more confused, the warmth from that hug still nestled in her bones. Before they reached the last step, all traces of the condo vanished and Pauline occupied a white space, voices whispering all around her. No up, no down, no ceiling or floor. Then, an explosion of colors, sights, and sounds. Pauline and her companion soared over tree canopies, over fields, through mountain passes, skimming above rivers, whooshing in and out of clouds. Hadn't she done this before? But how? Ah, yes, the vision in Dean Nojes's room, when she'd left her body and soared through the world. Did that really happen? Was it really happening now?

I am the world.

No, no, of course not. A hallucination, surely. She was still on the ship with Grey.

The soaring ended. She was not aboard the ship, but on hard ground. A cottonwood forest in Winnipeg in the Canadian province of Manitoba. The trees' green leaves, arched above Pauline and her companion, grew like fat rounded triangles.

Pauline knew exactly where she was—but that's all she knew in the moment.

The woman smiled. "You know where we are, and you know who I am." She watched expectantly, her bare feet rustling the carpet of brush and fallen leaves.

Mother. No. Not mother, but someone like a mother. Maybe someone else's mother, daughter, granddaughter...

Pauline was barefoot too, though still wearing the white dress. Vibrations emanating from below ground tickled the soles of her feet.

"You're Helena."

"And?"

"You seem to think I know so much, but I don't know why I'm here, how we got here, or how to get back home. I'm lost, Helena."

"You are never lost, Pauline."

"I don't know who I am."

"You are you." Helena smiled encouragingly, giving Pauline the impression that this tidbit should unlock the mystery.

"I'm sorry to be such a disappointment."

"To see is to be," Helena replied.

"To see is to be," Pauline repeated. "But I *don't* see. What are we doing here, in the middle of a Canadian cottonwood forest, Helena?"

Without warning, Pauline once again was wrapped in Helena's arms, the embrace suffusing her with unconditional love. Helena was not a stranger, but a soulmate, someone she might have known in a past life—or another dimension.

Pauline made a mental leap. "Oh! We're here to retrieve the locket." Helena nodded. "The gold locket torn from your grandfather's neck at the start of the Beaver Wars, when the French and Ojibwe fur traders like him were fighting off British rivals. He ran through these woods, the British in hot pursuit."

"How does that feel, speaking your knowledge?"

"Wait, Helena, he wasn't really your grandfather, was he? But you cared about him, and he cared about you."

"He was like an adopted grandfather. He felt sorry for me."

"He also loved you."

"How does that feel, owning the truth?"

Pauline breathed deeply, freely, admiring the sunlight filtering down through the tall trees. "Lighter. I'm not afraid. I feel...like myself."

"What comes next, Pauline?"

Pauline had no clue—but then she did. The vibrations from the ground rose up through the soles of her feet to join the chorus of whispers—the souls of objects telling their stories, finding in her a willing and sympathetic listener. Eyes closed, she pictured the strata of soil below, compressed layers of organic matter: wood, leaves, bones, fragments of iron musket balls, shreds of tanned leather hides, crude stone spear tips. Her vision plunged deeper, toward Earth's ancient bedrock. She pulled back from venturing farther into the unknown, to focus on the task at hand.

With eyes open or closed—she wasn't sure—she

walked several paces southwest of where she and Helena stood. Helena followed Pauline's lead, and Pauline allowed emerging instincts to take over—to guide them in a quest they now shared. She held out her hands over a small clearing and the soil broke apart, the ground opened of its own accord, and a hole formed in the middle of the cottonwood forest. Soil flew out of the hole as if tossed by an unseen shovel. An object rose from the ground, a small gold locket, dented and tarnished, still attached to a thin gold chain. The locket landed in Helena's hands. She opened the rusted clasp.

"A strand of her hair is still inside," Helena said.

A sudden gladness filled Pauline, as if the locket held special meaning for her, though she'd never seen it before and wasn't aware of its existence until moments ago.

"Ah, you are experiencing the joy of recovery," Helena said. Pauline dared not reveal—tried not to think about—the recovery expeditions she had undertaken in her other life, her *real* life. Those digs did not flood her with happiness, like this one.

The locket spoke up.

I never meant for us to be apart, dearest. I long to hang close to your heart once again.

"Do you hear her, Helena, as I do?"

"Oh, yes." She caressed the locket. "Telling her story about the love between my adopted grandmère and grandpère."

"So I am not crazy, after all. Maybe not even a weirdo."

Helena hugged Pauline once more, an unspoken reassurance.

"I hope you'll return the locket to my grandfather,"

Helena said.

"What?"

"I am only a Recoverist."

"What am I, then?"

"So much more."

"More what?"

"To see is to be, and to be is to know."

"I don't understand when you speak in riddles."

"A riddle is a truth on the cusp of revelation."

How was it possible to understand so much, and so little, at the same time?

Helena handed Pauline the locket. An instant later, footsteps rustled in the leaves, and a man with long stringy hair and a weather-lined face, wearing a buckskin coat, stood two feet from the women, his heavy musket pointed directly at Pauline.

"What do you want?" He spoke in eighteenth century French, which Pauline readily understood. "You have no claim here."

"Helena! He's going to shoot me!" Pauline raised her hands and backed away.

"I can't see him, Pauline. Only you can. Speak to him. Explain you're here to help."

"Monsieur Roger," she began, his name tumbling from her lips as *Ro-zhay*, "I have something that belongs to you." She held the locket in her open palm, which the man quickly snatched.

"My dear Marie!" he cried.

Monsieur Roger put the musket on the ground and tried to open the locket, but his hands were too clumsy.

"Here, let me," Pauline said.

The man quickly retrieved the musket and aimed it at her. "One more step and I'll shoot."

Pauline understood now what was in his heart and knew there was no cause to fear him. She held out her hand. Slowly, cautiously, Monsieur Roger handed the locket back to her.

"Look, there," she said. The locket had sprung open to reveal a curled sprig of hair, half-black, half-gray. She held it out to him, careful not to let a breath of wind blow the keepsake away.

"What's he doing?" Helena asked.

"He's taking the locket, closing it up." Monsieur Roger kissed the locket before pocketing it deep inside his buckskin coat.

"Marie left me too soon," he said in a cracking voice. "This is all that's left of her. I despaired of ever finding it again. I must have lost it when that filthy, thieving English fur poacher jumped me, right over there." He pointed to a spot in the woods a few yards away.

"Pauline, is he still there?" Pauline nodded. "Do me a favor. Tell my grandpère that Helena is safe and well and misses him still."

Pauline relayed the message. Monsieur Roger blinked and wiped his eyes with his sleeve. "Tell her the same," he said. He walked a few paces into the woods and vanished.

"He's gone," Pauline reported. "He sends you his love."

"You did it!" Helena kissed her cheek.

"What just happened?"

"You are among the Elected."

"That's not an explanation."

"You are still docking. Clarity is rising."

"You're telling me to be patient, I think."

"Yes, while you become yourself."

This business of becoming herself—she didn't ask for it. She had no clue where it would lead or what she was supposed to do with all this knowledge—or her abilities. She felt out of place and yet more like herself than ever, as if she'd slipped on a dress made just for her, every tuck and fold tailored to her body.

"What happens now?" Pauline asked. "If there even is a 'now'?" The sun was still high in the sky above the verdant forest. Impossible to say how much time had elapsed since...since what? Since she materialized in the Thread Continuum? Since she and Helena turned up in Winnipeg? She felt neither hunger nor thirst. Was that a clue to time's passage? Or was she living in suspended animation?

"In the Thread Continuum, we do not dwell in time, rather, time dwells within us," Helena said softly.

"I don't—"

"Let us return," Helena said, taking her hand.

"Lead the way."

"I don't know how to do that."

"You do. Focus on any object in the space you have been calling home."

"Isn't it still my home?"

Helena simply smiled. "Go ahead."

Pauline pictured the glass-topped dining room table, special for reasons she wouldn't share with Helena. Maybe Recoverists couldn't read minds, either.

They soared once more, landscapes rushing by, leaving a trailing impression of countless objects, voices ebbing and flowing as they traveled. Pauline concluded that time was in fact not a relevant measure of the experience.

The condo dining room rematerialized. Pauline sensed they never really "went" anywhere. They were already wherever they wanted to be. Distance wasn't physical, but metaphysical. She couldn't have put any of this into words—to Grey or anyone in the real world. She touched the table's glass top, relishing the feel of something solidly familiar. Emissaries filled the room, as before, many peering into the bright, jagged-edged golden balls she'd seen earlier. The bells rang out.

Pauline missed Chaitanya.

No, Grey. She missed Grey. She longed for the excitement of his naked body pressed against hers.

Helena had remained by her side. "The souls of objects speak out as they are hidden, lost, buried, denied, destroyed, recovered," she explained. "Everywhere and always."

Helena flicked her wrist, and a golden ball materialized between them. Pauline peered into the light and gasped. The Susquehannock face pot. The Virginian's sword. The Incan chief's death mask. Each object talking nonstop and falling rapidly through time and space, as if heading for a crash. The bells rang out. No, they rang inside her, like internal alarms.

"This is my fault," she said. She covered her face with her hands, convinced something terrible was going to happen. She had failed them. She had failed *herself.* She couldn't bear to look Helena in the eye.

"Not your fault," Helena said gently, putting her arm around Pauline. "Your opportunity. The first of many."

"You're not angry? And Chaitanya...?"

"Anger has no purchase in the Thread Continuum."

"What am I to do?"

"Continue docking," she said. "And don't despair. The bells are ringing, and I am called. Be one with all, child. And thank you for helping him, the man I will always think of as my grandfather." Helena kissed her cheek and flew away over the balcony.

Pauline called after her—or wanted to.

Don't leave me.

Chapter 20

Pauline stood on the balcony in the shimmering air, barely contained by the hazy space. A figure waving from Light Street down below caught her attention, yards from the site where Annabelle, the doll from 1854, had been recovered—or fragments of her, anyway. No question, she was the one the figure was waving to. Why? Emissaries filled the air, traveling in all directions as the bells rang out. On the harbor, figures stood on the water's surface, peering down, waiting for what? Signs of buried treasure like those she helped excavate in Florida? Could she have managed that expedition entirely on her own, without help from Grey or Max? Could she have said to them—and to Tyrone Lake—"Relax, I've got this, guys."

The waving figure spoke inside Pauline's head. Did she need to censor her thoughts? Was everyone a mind-reader?

Pauline, come down, I'm excited to show you.

She thought of the condo elevator—assuming it even existed. The voice told her to forget that. Was she expected to fly down? Or teleport, as she'd done with Helena? She wasn't prepared to test her flying powers, not yet. So instead, she closed her eyes and pictured herself standing next to the figure on Light Street.

And just like that, she was there.

"I'm Bex," said a young man. "But you already

know that." Bex looked about sixteen with a medium-brown complexion and short dreadlocks. His eyes were dark and warm, like everyone else's. He was slight, about Pauline's height, wearing the typical black unitard with bare feet. He held fragments of Annabelle. She nearly laughed at the sight of this teenaged boy clutching a tattered doll. "Dance with me."

Bex released the doll fragments, which hung suspended in the air, gently nudging one another. He reached for her hands, and together they rose off the pavement, slowly spinning. The air dance gave birth to friendship, creating bonds of trust that would have taken years to develop in the world she came from.

And oh, her world began to crack wide open.

"You grew up in an orphanage in Philadelphia," she said, as if she'd known him forever. "You never knew your parents."

"Nope. Same as you."

"But Bex, it's not just that. My God. You're the first person...Nobody adopted you because of the *pulse*. They all thought you were weird or sick, and they worried they would catch whatever you had. Even your friends in the home shut you out when they were old enough to realize you were different."

"The *pulse*? Oh, you mean the *shadows*. Yeah." He shrugged as they continued spinning around one another. "Mr. Cotter, the warden—I secretly called him the warlock—he wrote stuff in my record, about my dizzy spells, and blah, blah, blah. So, the parents shopping for kids wouldn't look at me."

"Do you have any idea what this means?" She spun away from him, making her own circles in the air, inventing her own dance. She'd never felt so light, so free, and aching with a joy that was almost too much to bear.

Bex laughed. "It's the way."

"I'm not the only one!"

"In the Thread Continuum, many are one."

"Is everyone here like me? Like you?"

"We are all born to it."

"So…there's nothing actually wrong with me."

"Nothing could ever be wrong with you," he replied.

Bursts of deep knowledge alternated with surreal disbelief, leaving her giddy with possibility. They returned to the ground, standing in the middle of Light Street, which ought to have been teeming with cars, but there were none. Every office building and apartment complex stood where it belonged. The aquarium too. Yet everything was altered—and so was she. The Thread Continuum seemed to be an in-between place, asking her to straddle two realities. Could she believe in both, or would she have to choose?

Could she love two very different kinds of men, or would she have to choose?

But really, there was no choice. She sobered up.

"Let's motor," Bex said. He jumped on a scooter and began zipping across the Inner Harbor, heading east. Annabelle was tucked under his arm. Pauline hopped on a scooter, pursuing him.

"I thought we didn't need things like this to get around here," she shouted.

"We don't," he said. "But it's fun." Oh, right. He was sixteen.

They sailed over the footbridges, no pedestrians in sight, only emissaries overhead, or raising objects from holes in the ground, or hovering above the harbor. Images scuttled across Pauline's vision: plate ware, basket fragments, opium pipes, rusted iron shackles.

In Fells Point, they dropped the scooters and sat on a small, grassy parklet near the waterfront. The air shimmered, its lemon-yellow glow obscuring the Domino Sugars plant on the far side of the harbor. Reality, illusion, or both? Did the distinction even exist?

Pauline turned to Bex. "I wish you didn't have to go through all that crap at the orphanage. My frosters—my foster parents—were mean as dirt."

Bex put a hand on her shoulder. "P, really, everything's okay. The Thread is my family. The family I never had before. It's all good."

"But Bex, you must have been so lonely."

"The only way through a tunnel is through it. First the dark, then the light."

"More riddles. What are you hiding? What are you *all* hiding?"

"You're still docking."

"Yeah, so I keep hearing. What does that even mean?"

"Once Chaitanya came and got me, everything got better, everything made sense."

"But before...before you got here, can you tell me one real thing?"

Bex looked out at the hazy harbor. "Sometimes...I thought I was...flying apart."

"There!" Pauline said, standing so abruptly she rose a few inches off the ground before settling down. "That's right. Flying apart. That's exactly it. Was that so hard?"

"That wasn't real, Pauline. *This* is real." He gestured broadly to the harbor which hardly seemed real.

"Well, *this* isn't real to me, Bex. I mean, yes, flashes here and there, but... Let me ask you this: Are you really, truly happy here?" He flashed a broad grin. "And you don't miss anything at all about your real...I mean, your other life?"

"The mission *is* my life."

"You're only sixteen, and you talk like you're a hundred."

"You'll see."

"But I'm only passing through, Bex. No offense, but I have a life, someone who's waiting for me."

"Passing through?" He laughed. "I don't think so, P." He stood and held out the doll fragments.

She held off. "What does she tell *you*, Bex?"

"She misses Carolina like crazy. It doesn't get any easier for her. It's sad and terrible, to ache like that all the time. She doesn't understand why it had to happen—why she fell off the carriage, why no one stopped to rescue her."

"So Annabelle is railing against her fate?"

"See, yeah, you get it." He laughed again. "Good way to put it." He held out the pieces once more. "At least you can put her back together, good as new."

"I can? What about you? Can't you do that, Bex?"

"I'm a Restorationist, so yeah, I can, but I thought, uh, you'd want to, you know, check it out." She took the fragments. "Imagine how she looks whole, how she looked brand new. Hold her tight."

Pauline pulled the pieces of Annabelle to her chest. The doll lurched as if an animating spirit had suddenly entered its doll body. Her fragments reunited seamlessly. Pauline held her at arm's length. The doll wasn't alive, but she was whole, and she most definitely possessed a soul. Even her gingham dress looked freshly starched, her button mouth smiling.

"Whoa." Who was this person, full of magic tricks? Opening holes in the ground, reading peoples' minds, traveling at the speed of light, and now, putting broken things back together. "What happens to her now? I mean, what's the future of an old doll that's been repaired? Even a doll with a soul?"

"What do you want to happen?" Bex wore a cheerful expression. Not a trace of teen angst. Everything he'd gone through in that orphanage, he seemed entirely over it. Putting the past in the past, where it belonged. Isn't that what she and Grey set out to do, together?

"What's this place done to you?" she asked.

"Gave me to myself."

"But was it your choice?"

"My path *is* the path," Bex responded. "It's not a choice."

Not a choice?

Wasn't she a grown woman, empowered to make her own choices in life?

Bex took Anabelle from her. "She wants you to figure out her next step." Silence. "Reparations."

Pauline couldn't see where any of this led. All the earlier euphoria suddenly seeped away.

"Pauline, you know she won't be happy until she's reunited." Another emissary appeared. Bex didn't flinch, as if this were planned. "This is Cheyenne, a Reparationer." He greeted the emissary with a friendly,

"How you knowin'?"

"Knowing great," Cheyenne replied.

Cheyenne's long red hair, piled high on her head, looked Victorian. Almost against her will, Pauline allowed the woman to pull her in for an all-knowing embrace. Cheyenne was 125 years old, raised by a great-aunt who was friends with Edith Wharton. They rose into the air together and danced a loose waltz.

Bex hopped on the scooter. "Try not to think so hard. Feel your truth. Own it." He was gone.

"Bex will restore what the Recoverists retrieve. Is that right?" Pauline asked.

"You're still docking," Cheyenne replied, giving a non-answer.

"And you reunite objects with owners."

"Yes, but when you see the larger picture—and you will—you'll know we are realigning the universe. Your contribution is incredible."

Pauline began walking back toward the Inner Harbor, Annabelle dangling in one hand, Cheyenne holding the other.

"You didn't know your real parents, did you?" Pauline asked.

"You know I didn't." They passed a group of Recoverists on Thames Street bringing up wooden planks from a sailing ship that Frederick Douglass worked on as a caulker.

"Oh, wow." Pauline stopped to watch.

"You know what they found, don't you?"

"Of course. Don't you?"

"I'm only a Reparationer, so, no, I don't. If it comes to me for homegoing, then I'll know."

Pauline wondered what the rebuilt sailing vessel

would be worth to a wealthy collector. What an absurd idea.

She continued her line of questioning. "And you didn't get along too well with your great-aunt Polly, did you?"

"Oh, well." Cheyenne waved away the ancient history. "I was a disappointment to her. Not especially interested in the whole debutante coming-out-to-society thing. Kept to myself, mainly, reading in my room. My great-uncle left an extraordinary library. All the classics in English, Greek, Latin, Arabic. The books were a great comfort, especially on the days when I was, well, indisposed."

"What did you call it, Cheyenne, and don't pretend you don't know what I'm talking about. We're friends now, right? Friends don't lie to each other."

"The *vapors*."

"Very Victorian of you."

"Edwardian, actually."

"The *vapors*. What did that feel like?"

"Well, you know," she said. "Disorientation. Fainting spells. The terrifying feeling that I was..."

"Flying apart?"

"Of course," she said. "The doctor wanted me to take all sorts of medicines, but Aunt Polly insisted I was malingering, shirking my duties."

"So you were miserable. Like me." And like Bex, she thought. Maybe like everybody in the Thread Continuum, once upon a time.

As they reached the Inner Harbor, Pauline looked up at the penthouse, shimmering in the opaque air. "And what happened to your parents?"

"I never knew them. But once Chaitanya

appeared…well, after that, everything made sense."

Same story, over and over, but Pauline didn't quite feel the fit. She had every reason to leave here and return to…what was it?… Oh, yes, a marriage proposal. That.

"That's far too much about my irrelevant time tracks," Cheyenne said. "Let's talk about Annabelle. She's perfect, Pauline. Great job. Now let's bring her home."

"Aren't we a bit late for that?"

"It's never too late for reparations. Not ever. As an Elected, Pauline, this is of the utmost importance."

"To see is to be, and to be is to know."

"Yes! Hold onto that."

Hold onto what, exactly?

"I don't know what you expect me to do with Annabelle, Cheyenne." She may as well have been back in the forest with Helena, expected to possess knowledge she did not have. Like trying to find the light switch in a dark room where you've never been before.

"Hold her close," Cheyenne said. "Ask yourself who she belongs to. Then go deeper. Ask, who has been longing for her without realizing it? If Annabelle is the answer to a question, who is asking?"

Pauline took a deep breath, closed her eyes, and held the doll tight. A kaleidoscope swirled—voices and faces by the hundreds, all looking for answers. They streamed by so fast, like the images on the maps that rose off the paper and assaulted her senses.

But then one voice grew louder than all the rest.

"Luisa," Pauline declared. "Brownsville, Texas. She's eight. Annabelle will help her sleep and chase away the nightmares. And Luisa will pour out her hopes and dreams and fears into Annabelle's ears. They will grow up, together."

Cheyenne beamed, and Pauline felt like a prized pupil, a bit of good humor returning. They danced again together, rising languidly into the air, celebrating the union of Luisa and Annabelle.

"Let's go," Pauline said, again letting instinct take over. She and Cheyenne stepped across the thresholds of time and space. In the small room Luisa shared with her mother, Pauline placed Annabelle on the girl's pillow, where she would be discovered after school and proclaimed a miracle.

Thank you for bringing me home, whispered Annabelle.

A breath and they were back in the penthouse, bells ringing, orange balls flashing to life between emissaries floating around the room. Cheyenne flicked open a golden-orange ball, revealing Luisa hugging Annabelle and confiding in her. Pauline could not help smiling, though she would not call herself a miracle worker, not by a long stretch. The glowing ball quickly changed to reveal a succession of objects crying out from dark and lonely places, begging to be rescued, remembered, restored to their rightful inheritors, and made whole.

Her conscience spoke up, more real than an object. *I've betrayed you all.*

"You are a force for good, Pauline," Cheyenne said with such certainty. Pauline wanted to believe her.

"I don't know." She shook her head. "I just don't know, anymore."

Emissaries encircled her, hands outstretched.

"Dance with us!" they cried, pulling her away from

her center of gravity, pulling her out over the harbor, like a clutch of helium balloons rising into a formless yellow sky. Arcs and twists, bodies entangling and disentangling. A new sort of humming, the wordless conversation of a unified consciousness.

Helena was there. "You are woven from the Thread," she said. "The one in the all, belonging to the fabric of forever. Soon, you will fully embrace who you are."

Pauline felt a sudden rift, body and soul splitting apart, like a cell undergoing mitosis. She was drawn to the collective ecstasy coursing through her, while still longing for the clear rules of her earthly life. Two competing forces, no clear winner.

"Who am I?" she screamed into the void.

Chapter 21

Pauline broke away from the cloud of dancing emissaries, spinning end over end, wondering if she were tumbling back to earth, to her first world, or even to her death. Perhaps the hallucination of the Thread Continuum would end if she survived the coming crash.

She'd return to Grey's arms, where she belonged.

In free fall, still, moving from one time and space to another, until all motion stopped. Pauline took in her surroundings, trying to get her bearings. A nondescript living room. She'd been here before.

"You're back. I knew it."

Pauline whipped around.

"Dean Nojes!" The dean's house. The dean sat by a lamp, reading a book. "Did I frighten you?"

"Not in the least. Couldn't if you tried. I always knew it was a matter of when, not if. So you have always been expected. Seems all I'm good for is waiting around."

The dean wore narrow reading glasses that made her appear older than Pauline remembered.

"I don't know how I got here, or why I'm here, Dean."

"What are you wearing?" she asked. "Is that some sort of special costume for the Thread Continuum?"

Pauline, though barefoot, still wore the white one-shouldered gown.

"Uh, no." Laughter bubbled up unexpectedly, a chuckle, then huge, sobbing gulps. Tears rolled down her cheeks.

"Would I understand the joke?" the dean asked. "Or is this only for insiders, the really special people, like you?" She pulled off her glasses and glared.

"No, no," Pauline said, catching her breath. "Everybody up there…over there…wherever 'there' is…they all wear black. And nobody wears shoes. Can you explain that, Dean?"

"You're the expert."

"This what I was wearing when he, uh…"

"When he took you away."

"Yeah." She snorted again but suppressed it.

"I know why you're here. So do you. Don't play dumb, Pauline. Not for my sake, anyway."

Dean Nojes disappeared into the room where the visioning experience took place, a lifetime ago. Pauline would give anything to relive those moments with Grey, when their attraction was new and infinitely exciting. Oh, could she fly to him now—and forget everything else that had just happened? She pictured him, his blond curls threaded with silver, the mole, and the crooked smile.

Nothing. She was blocked, as if a wall had been erected that she couldn't smash through.

The dean returned holding the small bronze Cambodian dragon, her treasured possession. Pauline instantly understood: she was tasked with returning it to its rightful inheritor.

"You've always known this day would come, haven't you, Dean?" she asked.

"Since the moment you were born."

Pauline absently took the familiar dragon, puzzled by the dean's remark. "Since I was born? You knew my birth parents?"

"No, of course not. I only knew you. And I knew you would be my responsibility from afar. Your parents...well, they quickly went out of the picture. Because of who you are."

"I don't understand. Did I do something...to them?"

"You need to take that up with *him*. Far above my pay grade."

The dean had retaken her seat, and Pauline stood over her.

"What do you know about my parents? What aren't you telling me?"

What was the point of traveling through space and time, if you couldn't learn the basic facts of your own existence?

"I don't know anything, Pauline. I've told you everything. I'm a tiny cog in a machine that surpasses my understanding."

Pauline unconsciously closed a fist around the dragon and felt the object shift. Its rough-edged green coating disappeared to reveal a dark bronze patina, smooth to the touch. The worn spikes of the dragon's mane regained their points, and the decorative scrollwork on the dragon's face—whiskers and eyes—regained definition. She re-opened her hand.

"Holy shit," the dean said, peering at the figure. "What did you do?"

"I restored it. Not on purpose."

"No one's seen a specimen in this condition in over a thousand years. Let me see."

"I can't let you hold it. I'm sorry, Dean. It's just that—"

"Oh, never mind. Go on. Get out of here. You got what you came for."

The dean picked up her book.

"You didn't do a very good job, you know," Pauline said.

"What?" She peered over her glasses.

"Looking after me, or whatever you were supposed to do as a…what do you call it?…a Facilitator. You could have found me nicer foster parents, at least. They made my life miserable. Did you even care?"

"It's better that you weren't too attached. Emotionally, I mean."

"Better for whom?"

Pauline thought of Bex in his Dickensian orphanage. Cheyenne and her mean great-aunt. Even Helena, who didn't seem to have any close kin. Why? Why were we all deprived of family and a loving home?

What did I ever do to bring the Thread Continuum into my life—to ruin my life before it had even begun?

This wasn't the dragon's fault. He deserved a good home. She thought about what Cheyenne had taught her. To whom does the dragon belong? Who is asking for it, without realizing the question had been posed? Possession is only sometimes about bloodline. More often, it's about a seeker and their quest.

She'd barely formulated the question before she found herself standing outside a small brick house in Ninh Binh, near Hanoi. A woman named Long was getting ready to leave for work. Her name, in rough translation, was "dragon," but that's not the only reason the artifact belonged with her. Long had recently lost both her parents and her brother (her only sibling), and she was wondering whether to leave home and start over someplace new, alone, or whether to go on at all.

Pauline approached her, speaking Vietnamese.

"Please," she said, holding out the dragon. "This belongs to you. You cannot ask me how or why, but it is yours, and yours alone. Of that, I am certain."

Long took the dragon and slowly turned it over. Then she held it up to the light and let the sun illuminate the bronze surface. She began to cry.

"I prayed for a sign this morning," she said. "You have brought it to me. My journey is not over, as long as small miracles are still possible." Long threw her arms around Pauline's neck, melting Pauline's troubled heart.

Okay. The Thread Continuum was not ruining her life. It was a gift. And a burden. And an unsolved mystery. Or was she, herself, the mystery?

Why could she transport herself half-way across the world in the blink of an eye, yet was unable to reach Grey? Did the universe have it in for her, or what?

She had barely formed these questions before Chaitanya was with her, in her, part of her, their bodies vibrating to the same frequency, their breaths aligning. The familiar balcony in Baltimore was shrouded in a thick fog, or perhaps the fog was a void in space itself. No bells, no emissaries, just the two of them, nearly as one. Yet the atmosphere was not shrouded in silence; a thrum of communal voices, like the sustained chord of a far-off organ, provided a reassuring backdrop to their sudden togetherness.

"You are a maker, a creator, a unifying force, and

my soul's completion." Chaitanya spoke without words.

Pauline's central nervous system nearly convinced her this might be so, yet she fought to hold onto her own construct of reality. He must have sensed her resistance.

"I was as you are, in another time and place," he told her.

"What were you?"

"A carpenter. A builder of houses and markets."

"Like Jesus."

Chaitanya's laughter rumbled through her. "Hardly. My time began before all that. But time is only a construct of convenience. It's irrelevant to the Thread Continuum."

"What happened to you?"

"I was born," he replied. "As were you."

"We are *all* born. Stop hiding."

"I was born to become, as you were born to become."

Pauline wanted to scream, helpless and frustrated, and still powerfully drawn to this being. "I do not understand. Anything." She could barely frame the words.

"You are the essence of understanding."

Giving in to Chaitanya, merging to the point of relinquishing her individuality, would require almost no effort at all. But she wanted to fight—for herself and for Grey.

"I've been manipulated," she said, trying to re-establish her own breath. "Have I been your pawn my entire life? Ripped from my parents' arms? For what? You tell me I'm more. I never asked to be more—only to be loved. And now you would deny me even that.

It's you, isn't it, who prevents me from returning to the man I *actually* love."

The balcony faded altogether, and Pauline felt herself suspended, neither in air, nor on land, but somewhere between both. The quiet undertone of voices receded but did not disappear.

"Knowledge transforms us, and soon, we cease to be who we once were."

"Tell the truth! Did you steal me away from my mother and father? Did you do the same thing to Bex and Cheyenne?"

"You were all born with gifts that marked you—especially you. The Thread Continuum is a genetic condition. You are the first Elected of your kind in thousands of years. Before you, there was me. You are a rare gift."

She forced herself to look into his eyes, so dark they seemed to absorb the light. How easy it would be to sever old ties and slip into him.

She could love him because he felt inevitable. As if she really had no choice—or, rather, as if he were the only choice. She could join with him, forever. Her body craved connection with his, as her breath fell back in sync.

But no, no. This wasn't right.

"Tell me," she demanded.

"Your parents were empowered to forget. They suffered no sense of loss, no pain."

"I was unloved as a child, and now you tell me I was also forgotten by the only people who might have loved me unconditionally. You are a monster!"

She wanted to strike him, but that would feel, despite the revelation, like striking herself.

"Gifts impose their own laws, just as the sun warms the soil." He spoke calmly, but she summoned every ounce of will to press on.

"You brought me here without my consent."

"I brought you home."

"I already have a home—and someone there who loves me, needs me. I'm not giving that up for this nowhere land. You're not taking that away from me— when you've taken so much already. The souls of objects can survive without me."

"My parents, also, were denied me, and I grew to manhood in the lanes and alleys of our village. I understand your difficulties, Pauline, but they are passing, even now."

"Your ancient backstory has nothing to do with me. I'm not staying. You blocked me before. But you will not block me now."

"You may go back, Pauline. The Thread Continuum is not a prison. But believe me when I tell you, your path is unchanged, for you cannot alter who you are or escape your true calling."

Destiny be damned. She would forge her own path.

PART 3: LOYALTY

Chapter 22

Her head spinning, the voices banished, Pauline stood on the staircase in the grand atrium of the *Archimedes*, looking up at Grey Henley on one knee holding a blue velvet box containing a sparkling engagement ring.

"Pauline Marsh, will you marry me?"

Chaitanya's words still echoed, but she was determined to defy them. She searched her heart and concluded that after everything she'd been through, everything she'd learned or been told about her fate, she wanted only to marry this man and spend the rest of her life with him—on Earth.

"Yes! Yes, Greyson Henley, I will marry you!"

He took the ring from the box and slipped the perfect teardrop diamond onto her fourth finger, then took her in his arms and they kissed long and deeply.

"I love you, Lucky Penny," he murmured.

"I love you too. My first, my last love. Promise you'll never leave." Wrapping her arms around him, appreciating the solid bulk of flesh and bone, she vowed to banish the Thread Continuum from her thoughts. A strange dream, from which she had now awakened.

Walking arm-in-arm down the staircase, she held out her hand to admire the elegant ring.

"Uh, Pen, why are you barefoot?"

Oh. She still wore the white goddess dress, but her shoes had not made the return trip.

"I, uh, kicked them off in the corridor. I'm only willing to suffer so much for beauty, and they were killing me."

Grey laughed. She swore never to tell him another lie. He'd been honest with her—clear about his needs and wants, his hopes and dreams. She owed him the same. She couldn't help wondering, however, if her sandals were floating somewhere in the cosmic void, or perhaps a Recoverist had found them and was handing them off to a Restorationist, who would polish them up and give them to a Reparationer, who would find them a new home.

No. Stop. You're not thinking about this anymore.

They strolled onto the deck just as the moon was rising over the water, casting ribbons of white on the dark ocean. Other couples wandered by, but they barely noticed.

"I'm so glad you said yes," he said. "Because if you had said no, I don't know what I would have done. Yes, I do. I would have hurled myself overboard, right here, right over this railing. I can't imagine life without you, Penny. Not after all we've been through already, and the incredible future we're going to build together."

"Who can say no to you, Grey?" She looked up at him, smiling. "You're awfully persuasive."

"Listen, I hope you don't want a long engagement?"

"I know you, Grey. You're already plotting something, aren't you? Every time you ask a question like this, you're already two steps beyond the answer. So, I'll tell you what you want to hear, because, lucky for you, buddy, it's what I want too. Let's get married as soon as possible. I don't want to wait."

She could not risk Chaitanya swooping down and whisking her away, forever. He wouldn't do that, would he? She couldn't be sure. All she could do was double down on anchoring herself to *this* life, so that leaving somehow became impossible.

"Fantastic!" He let out a whoop, heads turning to regard the happy couple. "I've already asked the captain, and he says he can officiate, and it's legit."

"Of course you did." She took his hand.

"And Ty has agreed to be our witness."

"Oh."

"Oh, c'mon, Pen. Ty is thrilled for us. He really is."

"What do you mean he's thrilled for us? You only proposed five minutes ago. Did you speak to him before—"

"I did, uh, I did tell him I was going to ask you."

"Why? What's he got to do with *us*? Why would you involve him in our personal life, Grey?" She turned away, looking out on the moonlit sea.

"I'm sorry." He pulled her close, caressing her hair. "I look up to him. He's my mentor, Pen. I want his approval, is all. But if you don't want him to be our witness, we can find somebody else."

"No, no. I get it." She leaned into him, inhaling his cologne. He was *hers*. "I've been alone all my life, Grey, so I'm not used to letting people in. It's the same for you, isn't it?" She looked up into his eyes.

"Yes, Penny. I need a man like Tyrone Lake in my life. I feel lucky to have him, after everyone else…after being on my own for so long."

217

"We *are* peas in a pod, Grey." She smiled. "It's all about trust, isn't it? Trusting each other, most of all, but also building our own circle of people, together. Right?"

"Exactly."

"Shouldn't we be drinking champagne now?"

"A whole magnum."

Arms linked, they made their way to the champagne bar, aglow with intimate golden lights. Pauline wiggled the fingers on her left hand, enjoying the feel of the ring's band. After a private toast, Grey rose to announce their engagement to the entire room.

"I am the luckiest man in the world!" He lifted his glass, signaling everyone else in the bar to join him. "To my almost-wife, Pauline Marsh. The smartest, cleverest, sexiest woman I have ever met. She is positively…magical."

Embarrassed yet flattered, Pauline kept her seat and raised a glass. She basked in the superficial admiration, relishing its lack of complication.

"To Pauline!" A group toast from a roomful of strangers, all happy to celebrate the couple's good fortunate.

"The world's a pretty nice place, after all, isn't it?" She posed the question to her fiancé, whose own warm glow matched her own.

"Yeah. Turns out it's not half-bad."

"I'd hate to leave it."

A slightly worried frown marred Grey's perfect face. "Silly girl. Nobody's leaving anybody."

As if on cue, they both began laughing hysterically, unable to hold back.

"When're we getting married, almost-husband?"

"Tomorrow, wifey dear."

"Th' sooner the better!"

"Sooner's always better!"

"To the captain!" She raised her glass again.

"The captain!" Grey threw back his glass of champagne.

By the time they left the bar, they were both so drunk they took a wrong turn on the way to their stateroom and found themselves in a deserted service corridor. Grey kissed her, then pushed her up against a metal locker, its cold surface searing her back, but she didn't care. He hiked up her dress and seized her thighs until she was off the ground—it made perfect sense this time—so her legs could squeeze his middle. He thrust into her. Harder, she begged. Harder. Pauline let her screams of pleasure ring out. She didn't care who heard. She was home, with Grey, living for the moment. Nothing else mattered.

Once they reached the room, Grey threw her onto the bed and slid off her dress. She watched him get naked in front of her, his cock swelling once more. They made love again, slowly and quietly this time. Sex as love, not merely lust. They fell asleep, limbs entangled.

In the middle of the night, Pauline woke to drink some water. On the short walk in the dark from the bed to the bathroom, she tripped on something, nearly tumbling to the ground. The strappy sandals she had lost on her journey to the Thread Continuum lay askew on the floor, as good as new. Suddenly, she was stone-cold sober.

Chapter 23

On the second day of their three-day voyage aboard the *Archimedes* to Nevis in the Antilles island chain, Pauline Marsh and Greyson Henley were to be married at noon by Captain Jon Argent in a small office called the ready room, adjacent to the ship's control room. Pauline wore a sparkling silver sheath dress purchased from an on-board boutique. Grey wore his tuxedo.

Tyrone Lake knocked at the ready room door a few moments before the simple ceremony. He wore a light gray business suit and pale pink tie, his thin mustache impeccably groomed and his silver-threaded hair looking well brushed. The sight of this man practically made the hairs on the back of Pauline's neck stand up. She couldn't say why. The man was not especially likable, but that didn't account for the strong feelings he provoked in her. But she had to accept him, for Grey's sake. *Maybe he'll grow on me. Maybe I'll simply get used to him.* This man was making them wealthy, and she supposed she should be grateful to him for that, if nothing else.

Unfortunately, Grey stepped out for a moment to have a private word with the captain, leaving her alone with their business partner.

"Aren't you a vision," he said, stepping into the ready room. "I'm very happy for you, dear."

Don't "dear" me.

"Thank you, Mr. Lake."

"Please call me Ty. We're practically family now, aren't we?"

"Are we? I'd prefer to keep our business and private life separate."

"Yes, Grey has told me that you—"

"Do you and Grey discuss me on a regular basis?" The ready room was small, too small to put more than a few feet between them. She hated feeling trapped.

"He's madly in love with you, Pauline," Ty said. He smiled, but his eyes were like ice. "And he admires you a great deal. As do I. You're remarkably good with maps and so forth."

"You sound surprised." He lounged in the doorway, while she backed up against a built-in desk, with no more room to maneuver. "If I were a man, would you question my ability to read a map?"

"Pauline, I always seem to be on the wrong foot with you. I'm sorry. I wish you'd take my compliments at face value. No need to be so touchy. Hopefully, as we spend more time together—"

"I'm happy to let Grey handle our business affairs with you directly. I trust him."

"But…" he said.

"But what?" *What does he want from me?*

"But you don't trust me, Pauline, do you?" He offered an apologetic smile, which felt like a performance.

"It's important that I do," she said. "For Grey's sake and mine."

"Well, then, let's work on that together." He stepped forward and took her hands in his. His were cold, and she gratefully pulled away as Grey and Captain Argent entered the ready room.

"And here's the bride!" Captain Argent strode over and clapped her shoulders in a fatherly way. "The most beautiful bride of the season, I must say."

"Surely, Captain Argent, that's what you tell all the girls," Pauline said.

"I mean it every time," said the captain. They all laughed, even Tyrone. Captain Argent was in his mid-fifties with a fringe of light brown hair and a ruddy complexion. He wore the standard white shirt with insignia patches on each shoulder and black pants.

"I'm so glad you two had a few minutes to chat," Grey said, his arm around Pauline's bare shoulders.

"I think Pauline and I are beginning to understand each other," Ty said. "Aren't we?"

"Oh, yes." She refused to return his pointed gaze.

"Well, shall we get started?" Captain Argent asked. He donned a pair of reading glasses and took a small black book from his desk. "Bride and groom, please stand over there. Mr. Lake, you're next to me."

"Are you okay with this?" Grey whispered. "It's not elegant, I know."

"It's perfect," she whispered back. "And so are you."

Ty took out his phone. "I guess I'm the photographer. I'll do my best." He aimed the phone and started snapping, while Captain Argent recited a standard text, the kind you hear in the movies and never think is real. "Greyson Henley, do you take…" and "Pauline Marsh, do you take…"

Ty took a velvet pouch from his pocket and passed it to Grey. Prompted by the captain, Grey removed a thin gold wedding band from the pouch and slid the ring onto her finger. Then she did the same for him. Had he brought the rings with him on the voyage—so sure of his plan, and sure of her response? Or did he procure them during one of their rare episodes apart during the voyage? Or—and she hoped this wasn't the case—did Grey ask Tyrone Lake to pick up the wedding bands for him? If so, that would spoil an otherwise perfect wedding. She'd rather wonder than know for sure. Living with a lot of unanswered questions was hardly new.

In ten minutes, the ceremony was over, and the newlyweds kissed.

"Congratulations, Mr. and Mrs. Henley!" Ty said, taking another photo.

"I'm not Mrs. Henley," Pauline said sharply, breaking away from the marital embrace. "I mean, I'm not changing my name." She looked at all three men, half-expecting them to challenge her decision. "My last name, Marsh, is the only thing I own that belonged to my birth parents, and I'm never giving it up."

"That's fine, sweetheart," Grey said. "The Henley name isn't great shakes, anyway, is it?" He glanced at Ty, who nodded imperceptibly. What had Grey told him that he hadn't told her? *No more secrets!*

Captain Argent kissed her on both cheeks and then excused himself to tend to other duties. Pauline had no idea what came next. All of this had been Grey's doing. All she'd done was say yes. A champagne toast? Wedding cake? Grey and Ty led her to another part of the ship.

"You know I love surprises," Grey said, winking and grinning. Ty led the way, as if this was *his* show now, not theirs. They entered a room used for shipboard lectures, with rows of folding chairs, a projection screen, and a long table. The captain's ready room was positively romantic compared to this.

"We have just enough time to set up," Ty said. He leaned over a large black storage box, and a sharp jolt tore through Pauline. In the box lay the Incan chieftain's funeral mask they'd brought up from the shipwreck, partially cleaned and mounted on a polished nickel rod attached to a black lacquered base—the better to display the piece on someone's sideboard, or coffee table, or trapped inside a fancy glass-walled cabinet of curiosities. The artifact lay encased in a custom-shaped foam cushion. It was still green with oxidation, but the decorative center showing the face with its fan-shaped headdress and large circular earrings had had layers of dirt and grime lifted. All this she knew—saw—before the box was even open.

Ty placed the artifact on the table, while Grey set out a stack of glossy flyers, containing information on the object's provenance and historical importance. Somebody—or an army of somebodies—must have worked incredibly quickly to pull all this together. Next to the flyers, Grey set out business cards printed on heavy cream stock:

Tyrone Lake LLC
Private Investment Advisory Services

What had any of his to do with her wedding? She looked at Grey, intently organizing stacks of paper on the table. *Is this really my husband?* It all felt so right, so inevitable, a moment ago.

Guests streamed into the room, welcomed by Tyrone. She recognized many by sight, as they'd all lived on the same ship for days. The only people she'd spoken to, however, were the Gillespies. Loretta made a beeline for her. There was no turning away.

"Pauline!" Shrieking as if they were long-lost friends. Loretta wore clouds of pale linen and silk, her aggressive tan giving off a strong floral scent. "When we reach Nevis, you must let me introduce you to the local honey I've been raving about. You can put it on everything you know. It's magical in cocktails. You look incredible, by the way." Pauline held out her left hand. "Oh, my God. You didn't. Did Captain Argent do it? He's such a gentleman. Ward! Ward, look!" She grabbed Pauline's hand and held it up as if it were an artifact. "The kids got married. Isn't that sweet?"

Ward was studying one of the flyers. He looked over and waved when his wife called out. *Will this be us in twenty years? No. Impossible.*

Ty called the room to order, and Grey gestured to Pauline to sit up front with him.

"Just wait," Grey whispered. "This is gonna be amazing."

Ty was clearly in his element, relaxed and confident, the striking artifact stationed behind him.

"As you know," he began, "this event is by invitation only to shipboard guests interested in new and unique opportunities for investment portfolio diversification. To call this object you see before you unique is an understatement. This pre-Columbian Peruvian funeral mask, fabricated roughly two thousand years ago, is not only the largest fragment of its kind ever recovered, but its provenance is also extraordinary. Whoever purchases this piece will happily dine off the tale for decades. While storytelling is not in and of itself an investable asset"—the room erupted in knowing laughter—"it is a highly desirable benefit of owning the piece."

Ty went on to paint a glamorous picture of the Spaniards stealing the mask from a "special tomb" in the eighteenth century, along with other treasures, only to lose the plunder in a shipwreck off the Florida coast. He got some of the details wrong, but no one else would know that, let alone care. The two dozen guests hung on Ty's every word, with dollar signs in their eyes. Watching them, Pauline began to understand the dynamic at work. People like this loved a dramatic story, didn't they? But they thought with their wallets, not their hearts. If they believed an asset was likely to appreciate over time, they'd fall in love with its worth as an investment vehicle. Not as a work of art or a reflection of the human spirit.

In the midst of all the acquisitive wealth, Pauline could not have felt farther removed from the Thread Continuum, which she vowed again not to think about.

She watched Grey, who was watching Ty with undisguised admiration.

The presentation ended, and people swarmed the table, eager for an up-close look at the mounted artifact. An irresistible urge came over Pauline—more instinct than urge. As a Reparationer, she scanned the world for the rightful inheritor of the funeral mask. Who was asking questions? For whom did this object provide an answer?

Ah, yes. In this case, bloodline won out. He was an Indigenous Peruvian toymaker, forty-six years old, planing wood in his small workshop in Puno, near the shores of Lake Titicaca. The mask should be his.

I can make this happen, set the world right, in this small way. What was the feeling welling up in her? Power, and the right to exercise it? Or was it responsibility? The notion that she was supposed to be giving back. And what about the wrongs that had been done to her—all the years with the Hellers? All the years enduring the *pulse,* alone with her affliction?

She could seize the artifact and bring it to its deserving owner in a heartbeat.

But she wouldn't. Pauline remained in her seat, watching strangers run their fingers along the fragment's ragged edges and across the carved lines and curls on its face.

I did not choose to be the guardian and savior of this object, just as I did not choose to be ripped from my parents' arms and dropped into a household devoid of love and affection.

I chose Grey. He chose me. And now we are married, and my loyalty lies with him.

Her husband nudged her and smiled. "So cool. They're really into it. Ty is a genius at this stuff. I'm gonna learn from the master."

"Is this our honeymoon?"

"Oh, babe."

"It's fine, Grey. Really. What happens next?"

"Hopefully, a bidding war."

"Really? Right here?"

"It starts here. Look." Grey pointed to several people filling out paperwork. "Bid sheets. They submit them to Ty, he and his team do some fast due diligence, then they choose the winning bid."

"How do you know all this?"

"I've made it my business to know, Penny. I don't

just stuff cash in a briefcase, you know."

"Clever boy." She kissed him. A wife supporting her husband. Wasn't this how it was done? "So, these rich people take everything Ty says at face value? They believe him?"

"There are always buyer's remorse clauses built into these deals. But yeah, they wouldn't be here if they didn't know his track record in the antiquities market. You *can* trust him, Penny."

"If you say so."

"Hey, who wears the pants in this family? No, don't answer that."

Later that afternoon, the newlyweds climbed the ship's rock wall for the third time, in keeping with their unorthodox wedding day. Grey rappelled down to take a call from Ty. He called her down.

"He sold it, Pen."

"How much?"

"A million dollars." Grey was beaming.

"You're kidding."

"The Gillespies bought it for their house on Martha's Vineyard."

She pictured the mounted mask on a sleek table in a light-filled contemporary house near the bay. It was all wrong. It didn't belong there. But why should she get the last word?

"Pen," Grey said, helping her unclip her climbing harness. "You won't believe it. He's giving us half. Our commission is—"

"Half a million dollars."

"Because he knows how hard we worked—how hard *you* worked—to pull this one off. And he knows there were risks involved. So it's an even split. How's that for a wedding present, darling?"

She refrained from mentioning how little Ty did for the money. He delivered a slick talk to a bunch of rich people—a captive audience in the middle of an ocean. Oh, and he prettied up the artifact a little. That was it, really. As for the coins that were also recovered, she guessed he kept the profits from those transactions for himself. She shook her head a little, to banish these uncharitable and disloyal notions. *Love him for who he is—how he is.*

"We can't stuff all this cash under the mattress, Grey." She couldn't decide how she should feel as a half-millionaire.

"I know." He chuckled. "I'm opening an off-shore account. Maybe a couple. Ward is going to advise me."

"In both our names?"

"Of course. What's mine is yours, and vice versa."

A new surprise was in store when they returned to the stateroom. The room was strung with twinkling lights and white and gold helium balloons touching the ceiling. The octagonal table held a three-tiered wedding cake and a bottle of champagne. The bed was covered with red rose petals and, on each bedside table, a dish of chocolate-covered strawberries.

"Did Ty arrange all this?" She forced herself to accept the generosity.

"No. Your beloved husband arranged this with the captain this morning. I knew you'd be a good sport about the auction."

"Oh, Grey. You really *are* a romantic at heart, aren't you? Business isn't your only turn-on." She pushed him down on top of the rose petal-covered bed.

"Well, they run neck-and-neck," he teased, letting

her climb on top of him and pin his arms, rubbing her crotch against his. She concentrated on his strong thighs, flexing to her rhythm. She unzipped his fly and rode him, her hands pressed against his chest. He smelled like earth and sweat and metal. Before coming, he surprised her by flipping her over and taking her from behind.

"Do I satisfy my wife?" He licked her ear.

They sat naked on the bed feeding each other cake, licking white frosting off one another's fingers, washing it all down with champagne and strawberries.

****

In the morning, Pauline wondered how long she could put off retrieving the note that had been slipped under the door. How long could she put off that sinking feeling? She knew she couldn't. She handed the note to Grey without reading it, forcing herself to listen.

"He says congratulations, again, and if we're not too tied up with newlywed duties, would we please meet him in the central café for coffee this morning to discuss business opportunities. He's funny, don't you think? Very dry sense of humor."

"He's a laugh riot."

"We will, of course, resume our newlywed duties later."

"Of course."

"But let's get going. I don't want to keep him waiting."

Surrounded at the outdoor café by the ship's tourists in casual summer wear, Tyrone Lake stood out in formal business attire. He sipped espresso, staring down at his phone, looking up only once they were seated across from him.

"You look surprisingly well rested," he said, flashing a lascivious grin. He waved, and coffee appeared along with a basket of croissants. "What do you think of your most recent paycheck, Pauline?"

"It's an awful lot of money."

"We really appreciate the split commission, Ty. That's really generous of you."

"You'll find I can be extremely generous, when everyone does their part." He dabbed his mustache with a napkin. "Can you do it again, Pauline? Can you find something as valuable as the mask?"

The men's eyes cut into her like lasers.

"Under the right circumstances."

"And what are those?" Ty asked.

"First, fertile ground, meaning, a site with a long history of human occupation." She paused to pour cream in her coffee. Let them wait. "Second, secure access at night—no disruptions or disturbances. And third…"

"Go on," Ty said. "Third?"

Grey squeezed her hand under the table. *Third is my good will.* Did she want to keep playing this little game of theirs? Could she hold onto her husband's love and affection if she didn't? What a pointless question.

"Third is, time to do my research. And fourth, of course, is luck. Don't forget luck."

"So Nevis is perfect then," Ty said. "Which is exactly where we're heading. A tiny speck of an island, but I think it satisfies your first requirement. I'll take care of the second, give you time for the third—but not too much time. Don't want you overthinking things. And as for luck, well, I'm not too worried about that."

"Fantastic," Grey said, nodding as though they had

231

a real plan in place, as opposed to a general intention. *And as though I weren't lying through my teeth.*

"Now, I need you both to sign this." Ty pushed a piece of paper and a pen across the table. It was a multi-page contract granting Tyrone Lake LLC ("hereinafter, the Corporation") "exclusive access to all material finds of any externally verified value greater than $100 on any venture financed in whole or in part by the Corporation. Furthermore, the Corporation retains the exclusive right of possession, valuation, representation, and sales of any aforesaid material finds, without exception."

There were a few more clauses and conditions after that, including one that guaranteed a commission to the "lead excavator's team." Meaning, the two nighthawkers. Pauline pointed to that line, which did not specify a commission percentage. Grey picked up on the cue.

"Ty, we should spell out a base commission—a minimum. I suggest thirty percent."

"Twenty-five," Ty countered.

"Forty," Pauline said. They both looked at her like she had two heads. "Up to fifty, depending on the difficulty and complexity."

"It's twenty-five on the next one," Ty said in a steely voice. "We'll see how that goes. Then I'm open to renegotiating the base."

"Done," Grey said quickly. How easily he overrode her. She had to let it go.

They signed the contract. Ty immediately turned to Pauline. "So, how quickly can you find us an artifact worth a bloody fortune?"

Chapter 24

Hours before the *Archimedes* was scheduled to dock at Nevis, Pauline asked Grey to leave her alone so she could research plausible sites for their next dig.

"Are you sure you have everything you need, babe? It's a tiny island, and obviously, this isn't like finding something in Virginia. If you need resources, you know Ty would be happy—"

"You'd be amazed what you can find online if you know where to look. There're all kinds of declassified military satellite imagery available, for example, and a mess of other stuff. Not to mention all the detailed terrain maps I can get online for free. I'm building quite the database. So, no worries."

"Okay." He ruffled her hair. "You're the genius."

I'm the liar, you mean.

"Now go, get out of here," she told him. "Let me work my magic."

Alone, she stared out the stateroom window for a long time. She knew, now, what she was capable of achieving. And what she had to do. No—not *had* to do, *chose* to do. Putting her gifts to work for the two of them, to build the life they chose, together. Wasn't that her motivation?

She sighed. Time to begin. To let go. Pauline allowed herself to fly apart. The sensation she'd once feared had become part of who and what she was. She accepted it as integral to the bargain that enabled her to remain with Grey on Earth as she knew it.

She projected her consciousness outside of her body, traveling all through Nevis, peering into its deep past, above ground and below. Nevis—Nuestra Señora de Las Nieves, Our Lady of the Snows, to the Spanish conquistadors. Dulcina, Sweet Island, to the Arawaks. And Oualie, Land of Beautiful Waters, to the Caribs. She soared over the Caribs' blacksmith's shop, rum shop, and the shoemaker's shop. And there, below, was also the stone ruin of the Montravers estate and Cottle Church.

Her partners would not be satisfied with an ordinary object. They expected her to find something spectacular, by any means necessary, she supposed. If they truly cared about her methods, they would question her more closely. But her methods were of little interest to either Grey or Ty. All they wanted were results that would eventually yield cold, hard cash. Her husband believed the ends justified the means. Within reason, she assumed. It wasn't something they'd discussed.

Ancient words from lost languages, roasting fish, the dry rustle of a roof being thatched—all that and so much more filled her senses, which expanded to meet the multiple experiences thrust upon her. A reprise of the fast-moving images against the windowpanes in the ersatz penthouse in the Thread Continuum.

Her attention was caught by a lost coin lodged several inches beneath the floor of an eighteenth-century cottage on the island's high ground. Not just any coin, but an exceedingly rare Brasher doubloon, a gold coin minted in the United States before the U.S.

Mint itself began releasing coins for public circulation in 1793. Her archaeological training told her this was an extremely valuable find, while her gift of second sight revealed the two faces of the coin. On one face, an eagle clutched an olive branch in one claw and arrows in the other; on the other face, the sun rose over a mountain in front of a sea. The doubloon circulated on the island at a time when the British, Americans, Spanish, Dutch, and other colonial powers were commingling in the Caribbean, and their currencies moved around with them.

To preserve a veneer of plausibility, she would not tell Grey or Ty for another day. Let them think she was hard at work. Also, she needed a cover story. How could she possibly know precisely where this coin hid? Did anyone ever actually find a needle in a haystack? She had to concoct a story that was entirely believable (if no one checked), with a healthy dash of speculation thrown in.

By the time they'd docked at Nevis, Pauline had a game plan, from which she was temporarily distracted by the island's breathtaking beauty. Sweeping beaches, aquamarine water, and looming above everything, Nevis Peak, a volcanic mountain covered in lush dark greenery, white clouds piled above its rim like whipped cream atop a chocolate cake. They made their way to a luxury resort sprawled along the beach. Pauline asked Grey to tell Ty to meet them for drinks at sunset, to discuss what she'd found and what they'd need for the dig.

Grey, obviously delighted, wasted no time. He whipped out his phone and relayed the message. He was in high spirits, as giddy as a little boy.

"Let's go swimming!" he suggested. "Better yet, let's go surfing!"

"Surfing? Do you know how?"

"No. So we'll learn."

Pauline had her doubts, but Grey was undeterred. They changed into bathing suits, tossing their clothes onto the king bed in their room, which opened wide onto a breezy terrace overlooking the beach. They borrowed boogie boards from a shack on the beach. The sun was high and hot. It felt good to be off the boat, back on land, with room to maneuver.

"This seems doable." Pauline held the short boogie board to her chest, perfect for body surfing.

"Someday, I'm gonna learn to surf for real," Grey said. "This is kiddie stuff."

"Well, it's enough for me." She relished feeling incompetent, even a bit scared. She didn't want to have mastery over *everything*. That was no way to live. Let Grey be braver than she, and better at something.

"This feels like a honeymoon, doesn't it?"

"Are you asking me or telling me?" She laughed. "It's beautiful. Wonderful. I'll race you to the water, husband."

They dashed into the lively surf, waded out until the water was chest-high, then rode the crest of white-tipped waves back to shore atop the short boards.

"Whooo!" Grey yelled.

They made several runs together, until Grey decided to paddle his board farther out so he could ride bigger, longer waves back in. Pauline decided a lounge chair on the beach was calling her. For the next half hour or so, she watched her husband riding the waves, getting better and better at judging how to catch the peak of the wave for the longest ride. He was the most determined, single-minded person she'd ever known. She loved that about him. And she didn't want to think what might happen if she should ever come between him and the object of his desire.

And she didn't mean herself.

****

Tyrone Lake had once again beaten them to the table at their appointed time for cocktails. Perhaps he thought arriving early, or first, gave him more power. She couldn't wait for the day he'd show up late, for one reason or another, forced to prove he was human and fallible, like the rest of them. She and Grey approached the terrace bar where their partner awaited their arrival, the surrounding palms swaying in the breeze, the crash of the surf providing a rhythmic backdrop. Pauline wore a seafoam green sundress that billowed as she walked and a wide-brimmed straw hat. Loose and relaxed from the day's exercise, she felt she had the upper hand in the coming conversation. Grey was more handsome than ever in linen trousers and a light blue button-down shirt, his dirty-blond hair still wet from the shower, his skin golden brown from the sun.

"I'd say you kids have been having fun," Ty said, crisp in an off-white linen suit. "Working on your tan, Greyson, I see." Ty was as pale as a vampire. "Ah, the carefree days of youth. I never really got to experience that, myself. But good for you."

This was the first time Ty had dropped a bit of personal information in Pauline's presence. Maybe he'd be more tolerable if he'd open up. Did he like anything besides money? Did he grow up poor, like Grey? Was that why they were so devoted?

Once drinks arrived, Ty got right down to business.

"So, Pauline, what's the plan, and what do you need to make it happen?"

She hadn't said a word to Grey and was grateful he hadn't pressed her. Both he and Ty gave her their undivided attention.

"You may find this hard to believe," she began, "but I'm reasonably confident that a rare Brasher doubloon is buried on this island."

Ty's eyebrows shot up. "How confident?"

"Holy shit, Penny."

"As you know, many colonial powers had business interests throughout the Caribbean at the time Ephraim Brasher's doubloons were circulating in the late eighteenth century, including here on Nevis." She licked her lips, coated with salt from her icy margarita.

"Go on," Ty said.

"Various historical and numismatic records suggest that particular currency was passed around here, and one of the likeliest places is in an old inland tavern, where the landowners and royal representatives frequently met, and where moneylenders and others conducted a lot of financial transactions. The experts think a couple of these rare coins are still out there, somewhere, and evidence suggests this is a likely spot."

"And you know where this tavern is, or was?" Grey asked.

"Yes. The building still stands on a somewhat remote part of the island, but the problem is, the house is in private hands, now. I checked."

"You let me take care of that part," Ty said.

"But Ty, this isn't like diving in open ocean." She knew her push-back would irritate the hell out of him.

She didn't care. "We'd need to dig up the floor of this place, or get in through the foundation, somehow. What homeowner would let us do that?"

As a Recoverist, she could bring the coin up herself, but she'd ruled that out even before the ship had docked.

"Maybe we could offer the owners a royalty," she said. "You know, a nice chunk of change in exchange for granting us access to their property."

"Penny, you don't—" Grey began.

"That's not your concern," Ty cut in sharply. "Tell me what you need to do the job. To confirm the site."

"For starters, an XP Deus metal detector and headphones." A key item on her pre-planned list. "Also, we'll want to have the proper solvent on hand, so we can spot-clean the coin—if indeed we find it—right away. Do you know how to recognize the markings on a real Brasher doubloon?"

"I don't," Grey said. "But I'm guessing you do."

"*I* do," Ty said. "To be authentic, the coin must have the EB punch mark on the eagle's breast. I've seen one of the surviving doubloons up close. I know what we're looking for."

"Exactly." She already knew the minter's initials were on the coin. She was reluctant to admit that Tyrone Lake knew his shit.

"I'll have the equipment for you in two days," Ty said. "As for accessing the property, give me the details and I'll make the necessary arrangements."

"You'll strike a deal with the owners?" she asked.

"What did I just say?" Ty snarled.

"If Penny's right," Grey said, clearly eager to shift the conversation, "and she usually is, what's the market value of a newly discovered Brasher doubloon?"

Ty put down his martini and leaned forward across the table.

"Ten million," he said softly.

"Holy crap," Grey said. "Penny?"

"We'll have to see, won't we?" The value was indeed startling. "Don't start counting chickens."

Chapter 25

Waiting wasn't difficult—during waking hours. Sun, surf, sex, island hikes, and cocktails at sunset all helped to pass the time before the next illegal dig would begin. Grey checked in with Ty by phone several times a day. Pauline made a point of not eavesdropping. She simply had to trust them. She also made a point of avoiding Ty's company during the two-day interlude.

The nights were a different story. Once again, Pauline felt herself split in two, her very soul spreading between different worlds. Chaitanya monopolized her sleeping hours—if indeed she really slept. Grey may have lain next to her, been the one to commandeer her flesh, but Chaitanya possessed her soul. They roamed the world together, sailing through time on one breath, their senses united. They hovered above the ancient village where he had lived the Earth-bound portion of his life. Bleached white stones, watering holes, open-air markets displaying dried meats, hides, fruits. The scenes of his childhood, he told her.

"What do you miss?" she asked wordlessly on one of their dream-time voyages.

"There is nothing to miss. The threads bind us and cannot be unraveled."

"To see is to be." She was still stretching to grasp who or what she was whenever they were together.

They raised ancient treasures buried under a long-

241

forgotten estate in Andalusia, bringing into daylight for the first time in centuries a variety of pendants, hairpins, chains, necklaces, rings, dress ornaments, and a golden Star of David. Side by side, they found new homes for every artifact, uniting objects with caretakers who valued their ingenious beauty, not their worth.

Tapping into the rare power of the Elected, Pauline and Chaitanya visited the Shigir idols—carved wooden totems over twelve-thousand years old, older than the Pyramids. The faces on the tall idols, carved from the trunk of a larch tree, bore mouths in the shape of an "O," as if expressing perpetual astonishment. Pauline gently straightened one of the totems standing at the edge of an ancient Russian lakebed. The gesture was akin to touching time itself.

Chaitanya was a portal to the realm of human expression, its endless capacity for creation. And so was she. Denying her genetic destiny seemed increasingly futile.

But those feelings, the tug of her Elected companion, arose only at night. Pauline used the daylight to rationalize away her vivid dreams, byproducts of her inexplicable journey to the Thread Continuum. Her brain was simply processing information. She worked hard to believe her own explanation. And she marshalled every ounce of willpower to resist probing the inner recesses of her own mind, for she knew the questions lying in wait: How long could she keep up this dual life? One creature by day, another by night? Who would win, in the end—and would she have the strength, let alone the opportunity, to make that call?

Thus, the days belonged to Grey and to the

reassuring feel of normal living—the smell of frying fish, the sound of crashing surf, the groans of Grey's orgasms. Pauline had let Bette know in a private direct-mail message that she and Grey were married. Bette's reply was a mix of snark and affection. *Leave it to you to win the class's other big prize, Grey Henley. Nice going, Marsh.* She went on to report that she'd landed a fellowship through law school with the U.S. Department of the Interior, working in a unit that specialized in art-related crimes, focused, of course, on archaeological artifacts. Pauline could read between the lines of Bette's sarcasm. She was clearly elated. None of Bette's news would get back to Grey or, God forbid, Tyrone Lake.

On the second and final day of waiting, Pauline dodged Loretta Gillespie cutting across a veranda. She couldn't bear to hear yet again about Nevis honey. Nor would she risk answering endless questions about the Incan funeral mask that now belonged to the Wards. As if they could ever properly "own" such a thing.

The island began to feel claustrophobic. Pauline was almost grateful when Ty summoned them for drinks on the terrace at sunset.

"Tonight at midnight," he said. "We will be able to enter the premises."

"And actually dig a hole in the floor?" Pauline asked.

"Whatever you need to do, you will be able to do it. I've got the equipment you asked for, and I've hired a Jeep to take us out there."

"What did the owners say?" She pressed him. "Are they getting paid if we find the doubloon? Will they be there?"

243

"Pauline, I'm tired of repeating myself. That's not your concern. Your only job is to find us an artifact I can sell. That's it. Period. There's absolutely no reason for you to know every detail. You've seen that I get results, and that should be enough for you."

"Seriously, Pen," Grey said. "Don't worry about any of that. Ty and I would never walk into a situation like this without knowing in advance what we're up against. And we'd never expose *you*, either."

"It's all about minimizing risk and maximizing opportunity, Pauline," Ty said. "Maybe someday, you'll understand that."

She stood and looked at the two of them. "There's something you're not telling me. Either of you." Grey wore an innocent expression. She couldn't "vision" her way through this.

"That house—" Grey began.

"We're going in alone, Pauline." Ty practically spit the words. "End of discussion."

Later that evening, as Pauline and Grey were putting on dark clothing to minimize the risk of detection, Pauline shared a fraction of her doubts.

"I could've sworn I was right about this house we're about to destroy. That it's owned by a couple, who've lived there for years. I saw the courthouse records online. What if I'm right and you and Ty are wrong? What if we get there and scare the shit out of the owners? What if they call the police? Law-breaking tourists usually end up in jail."

Grey shook his head. "You're wrong about this one. You're awfully good at what you're good at. But like you always say, someday, you'll make a mistake. And now you have."

"I hope you're right. I hope *he's* right."

"Don't lose your nerve." He pressed her dimple. "You're so good at being brave. Remember that. I promise not to vomit this time."

"There's that," she said.

At the appointed time, the pair climbed into a black Jeep parked on the road just outside the resort. Ty was driving. Grey slid in next to him.

"You're coming?" she said.

"You're surprised." Ty looked at her in the rear-view mirror. "I'm hands-off when I want to be, hands-on when I need to be. This project is too important to leave to anyone else."

Ty seemed to know exactly where to go. Had he scouted the property without them? That was not a question to be asked.

"The equipment is in back," he said, "along with shovels and other things I assume we'll need."

They rode in silence for about forty-five minutes over rough local roads, far from the island's main arteries. Nevis Peak was a faint silhouette in the clear night sky.

Ty pulled up to the house, which sat on a gentle rise. Their flashlights revealed the former tavern to be small and white, with turquoise shutters and a matching front door. Wordlessly, they broke out gear from the back of the Jeep, each of them arcing their lights across a neat walkway lined with broken seashells. Palm trees and other well-cultivated vegetation Pauline didn't recognize surrounded the property. No question, the house had been well-maintained, as if someone lived there, or at least, cared for it regularly. Even the front door's brass handle looked polished. Was this really an unoccupied dwelling?

Ty inserted a key into the door and led the way inside. He was dressed casually all in black, rather than his customary suit. A lean thief ready to slip away unseen in the dark. Which made her and Grey...also thieves, of course. They dumped the gear and shone their lights into a large, rectangular room with wooden floors, a stationary ceiling fan, and no furniture. So, the place was in fact vacant. Pauline opened the refrigerator in the small kitchen off the main room. It was empty and unplugged but didn't smell as if it had been sealed up for long. Grey tried various wall switches, proving the electricity had been cut.

"I guess you were right." She was still only half-convinced.

"That didn't hurt too much, did it, Pauline?" Ty asked. What a bully. Grey laughed—more at her than at him, she supposed. "Where do we begin?"

Pauline easily visualized the Brasher doubloon about six inches under the floorboards in the room where they stood. A man with one eye, a heavy drinker who frequented this place back in its heyday, had lost the coin—ordinary at the time—through a hole in his pocket as he was booted out for perturbing the government dandies in their frilly shirts. It had fallen unnoticed between the looser floorboards that had long since been replaced. And there it lay on the thin edge, as if standing and waiting to be noticed.

Pauline gave orders. "Grey, take the metal detector and begin sweeping from the center of the room. Try to move in a spiral, widening out as you go." He took the rod and put on the headphones. "You're listening for high-pitched tones. Ignore the low- or dull-pitched sounds. That's just nails and other junk. We can adjust the instrument's sensitivity if we need to."

She pretended to consult her phone for information. Let Ty think she was studying maps and other data. She explained that most of the tavern's tables and chairs had been arranged in the center of the room, with the bar along the room's southern wall. A simple scullery stood where the kitchen was now, semi-detached from the house.

"I hear something!" Grey said.

"Low or high?" Ty asked, concentrating on Grey.

Grey continued sweeping in a slow spiral. "Low...low...low." He paused right over the spot where the coin was lodged. "Different now. A high beep, much higher than the others."

"That's where we should begin to dig," Pauline said.

Ty made a few quick trips back to the Jeep, returning with a small jackhammer, followed by a portable generator, both of which had been covered by a tarpaulin. Oh, so having this equipment at the ready suggested that Ty already knew the electricity was off, confirming Pauline's suspicion he'd already been out here—at least once.

"Good thinking, Ty," Grey said, holding the disc of the metal detector over the spot on the floor.

"That's going to make an awful lot of noise," Pauline said.

"So what?" Ty snipped. "We're alone here."

Ty fired up the jackhammer. He handled the equipment with ease, as if he'd done this sort of thing before. The motor's loud, growling grind pierced the night. So crude. So messy. She couldn't forestall the memory of the quiet elegance of the Recoverists in the Thread Continuum, bringing up buried artifacts without making a big commotion. The memory unleashed a pang of unexpected nostalgia.

Ty hammered into the floor, carving out a rough rectangle a little over a foot wide. Using a sharp-edged shovel, Grey began prying up the cut floor and the underlayment beneath it. Remnants of the old, original floorboards remained, the wood rotting and splintered.

Ty stopped drilling. "Check again." Grey positioned the metal detector over the exposed area, now a mix of splintered flooring from different centuries, tar paper, and a top layer of soil.

"High-pitched and strong," Grey reported.

Pauline knelt beside the hole with a small trowel and gently scooped up loose material and deposited it on a thick sheet of plastic.

"Ty, we should clear a bigger field," she said. "A little deeper, too."

Ty restarted the jackhammer and enlarged the rectangle until it became a square, roughly two feet wide. He paused while Grey again checked to see if the gold coin was pinging the detector. He hovered over a particular spot.

"It's really strong right here."

Pauline scooped more dirt and debris onto the plastic sheet, well aware that the coin was a few inches below. She brought it up on the trowel and laid it on the dirt pile, a tarnished Brasher doubloon roughly the size of a U.S. half-dollar. Ty was literally breathing down her neck. He soaked a rag in cleaning solution and gently rubbed the coin. The sharp odor of mineral spirits permeated the room.

The coin spoke. *The men passed me around in their grubby hands, shifting me from pocket to purse, until I escaped to the dark place, unmolested.*

Pauline chuckled.

"What?" Grey asked sharply. "Something we should know, Penny?"

"Nothing."

Ty unwrapped the cleaned-up coin and held it flat in his palm, eagle side up, while Grey kept it under the spotlight of his flashlight.

"Is that it?" Grey asked in a loud whisper. He leaned in for a closer look, then shot Pauline a look of excitement.

"The EB stamp is there," Ty said, touching it lightly. "This is the real thing." His eyes narrowed. "How'd you do this, Pauline? What's your angle?"

"Angle?"

"She's a certified genius, Ty," Grey said. "I told you, and now you see I wasn't kidding."

"You're too good to be true," Ty said, his face dark.

"It's just smart detective work, Ty. Nothing more, nothing less."

"My Lucky Penny," Grey said, with a kiss.

"These finds," Ty continued. "They seem…improbable. Like it's all rigged." He turned to Grey. "Are you sure she's not working for someone else? Being fed intelligence from another source? Because if that's the case…"

"If that's the case," she said, "then what?"

"What do you really know about this girl, Grey?" Ty spoke as if she were invisible, which she damn near could be. "If this is a sting operation…if she's working undercover..." Ty shot her another hostile look, the coin clamped in his right hand. "Don't underestimate me, Pauline. You don't want me for an enemy."

"Whoa," Grey said. "Ty, you gotta know I'd never have brought her into all this if I wasn't sure—"

"Brought me in?" Her voice rose. "What's that supposed to mean?"

"Nothing," Ty said quickly. "Forget it. You're working miracles, Pauline, and I'm a cynical guy. I don't like surprises, and you keep surprising me."

"As long as we're making money, and nobody bothers us, what's the problem?" Grey asked the boss.

"No problem," Ty said, tossing the coin in the air and catching it. "Right, Pauline?"

She turned away from both of them and left the house feeling dirty. The men followed, tossing the jackhammer, the generator, and the other gear into the truck.

"What about the mess?" she asked.

"Don't worry about it, Pen," Grey said quickly. "Not your problem."

"Not that it's any of your business, Pauline, but I've got people coming in to clean up and remove any fingerprints," Ty said. "It's all been handled."

"Oh, great. Covering up our criminal tracks."

"What's your point?" Ty asked sharply.

"Nighthawkers, Pen," Grey said in a much lighter tone. "Let's stick with that. What happens next, boss?" The coin, wrapped in a rag, sat in Ty's back pocket.

"I'll show it to my people." He pulled onto the bumpy road, which lacked streetlights. The stars glistened densely, witnesses to their illegal adventure. "Then we'll see."

Back at the resort, Ty dropped the pair at the front gate. The moment he was out of sight, Pauline found herself twirling in Grey's arms as he let out a triumphant *whoop.*

"Do you know what this means, Penny?"

"Which part?"

"Ty says this coin could sell for ten million dollars. We get twenty-five percent. That's two-and-a-half million dollars, Penny. Think about it! We're gonna be multimillionaires! I told you I'd be rich before I'm thirty. I did it. *We* did it."

I should be happy for him—for us.

"Aren't you going to say something?" he asked, bouncing around.

"It's almost...too good to be true."

"But it *is* true, baby. Dreams come true!"

"Do they?" His words were more loaded than he could imagine. She had to focus on the upside, for his sake. They'd never need to worry about money again. And Ty would cover their tracks so thoroughly the nighthawking could never be traced back to any of them.

Pauline was free and clear, and set for life. What would her younger, lonely self say about that? She'd have been astonished and relieved, no doubt. Pauline felt neither. They walked across the grounds of the resort toward their room, Grey chatting about the future, holding a one-sided conversation, which he didn't seem to mind. Pauline stood on the terrace adjacent to their room, listening to the waves and the breeze rustling the palm trees. Grey came up behind her and wrapped her in his arms.

"What's wrong?"

"Let's go home." She nearly choked on the words, tears springing suddenly.

"Let's charter a boat, explore the islands, and find more treasure."

"No," she replied quickly. He turned her around and tipped her chin upward, forcing her to look into his handsome face.

"We're nighthawkers, Penny. It's our job. Hell, I'll even say it's our destiny. We were born to do this, you and I. I've had my eye on you since our first semester at Carthage. I could tell you had something special, and I wanted a piece of it."

"A piece of what? You make me sound like a…a slab of meat or maybe a lucky slot machine at a casino."

"No, no," he protested, fingering her dimple. "You're twisting my words."

"Where is all this leading, Grey?"

"What do you mean?"

"Do you want to spend your whole life digging, stealing, and selling to the highest bidder? Is that what our marriage is about?"

"You know my number one goal is getting rich. I've always been clear about that."

"And now we are—or we will be, once Ty sells the coin. Isn't that enough?"

"It's never enough." He frowned.

"Well, it's enough for *me*. I'm going home tomorrow." The words were spoken before she had time to reckon with the consequences. She pictured their luxury penthouse in Baltimore, not in its fuzzy Thread Continuum incarnation, but the real place, a sanctuary with a gorgeous view, where her new life with Grey had barely begun. "I hope you're coming with me."

A silence passed between them.

Grey sighed. "I'll tell Ty you need a break."

She pulled away. "Do I need Ty's permission now to live my life?"

"We signed a contract."

"I'm not his property! Besides, that's business. This is our life."

"That's not the point," he said.

Another brief silence passed before he spoke in a calmer tone.

"Look, let's not fight. Why should we? Tonight was incredible. I can't wait to see what we find next. You still feel that way, don't you?" He pulled her close again and whispered in her ear. "Soon, we'll be rich beyond our wildest imaginations. Untouchable. We'll build our own castle. Sail around the world. We'll discover where all the world's most precious artworks are hiding—and no one will know how we do it."

"How do we do it, Grey?"

"I don't know, Penny, and I don't care, as long as we keep it up."

"For how long?"

He stepped away and looked at her hard. "Is there something you'd rather be doing instead, Penny? Because this is it, for me."

Pauline was suddenly exhausted. "Do you love me, Grey?"

"Of course I love you. I love *us*. I love who and what we are together. What we're capable of. Do you doubt me?"

"No." A black pit was opening deep inside her gut.

"You've made your feelings perfectly clear."

Looking at him, she recalled how his face took on a haunted look when he spoke about roaming the streets, homeless, with his mother, as a little boy. *He needs this, just as I need him.* She hugged him tightly.

"That's better," he said gently. "You're not, uh, flying apart, are you?"

"No. This is…just because."

An hour later, they were making love, but Pauline's attention wandered far from the thrusts of her husband's body. The souls of objects issued calls of longing and remembrance, loneliness and hope. Bowls, knives, boots, buttons, bones, talismans. All these "things" wanting something from her. And what had any of that to do with real love, sweating flesh, the give-and-take of marriage?

Deep in the night, Chaitanya beckoned again, his large presence an amalgam of the elements of earth itself—fire, water, air, soil. They strolled along a beach together. No, they did not stroll, they floated, skimming the water where the foam-inflected sea met the sand, a moonless night enveloping them in a forever darkness. Pauline exceeded the confines of her body as the boundaries defining day and night, space and time, fell away.

Come home, he said.

My home is with Grey.

Your forever home is with me.

Chaitanya hummed, low and deep, the warm notes filling her in places she didn't realize were empty.

In the morning light, as her eyes flickered open, Pauline was briefly disoriented, her dreams bleeding into her waking life. Who is she—was she—with?

I am torn asunder.

Grey climbed on top of her and even as he grew hard, she could not stop thinking of Chaitanya.

Chapter 26

Pauline and Grey stood on the tarmac at the Nevis airport, where she was about to board a private charter to Miami, and from there, fly home to Baltimore.

"Are you sure you won't come home with me?" She had to ask, one last time. He responded with a kiss and a smile.

"I have so much to learn from the master."

Tyrone Lake, master of nothing but his own limited self-interests. She worried that Grey was in the man's thrall, blind to all his faults. Maybe leaving Grey alone with him wasn't such a good idea.

"He's promised to teach me how to pitch to potential buyers," Grey continued. "I want to understand how his network operates—where he finds all these billionaires tripping over themselves to buy off-market antiquities."

"You're beginning to talk like him."

"I hope so. I gotta learn how to talk the talk."

"Promise you'll come home soon."

He kissed her again. "I promise. You know what you can do in the meantime."

"Pine for you? Send naked selfies?"

"That too." He laughed. "When you're not busy planning the next dig."

"Oh. Right."

"Hey, we're on the same page, aren't we, Lucky

Penny?"

"Yes."

"Then what's wrong now?" A hint of impatience.

"Nothing's wrong. I'll surprise you. How about that?"

"You know I love surprises." The crooked smile returned. "And Ty will—no, never mind about him. I'm going to miss you."

"Me too."

The engine on the small prop plane roared to life, and they embraced one last time.

"Our first real separation since the day we met at the dean's house," she said.

"But not for long. And we'll be a lot richer the next time I see you. Think about that."

She would try *not* to think about that, in fact. She watched through the plane's small window as Grey walked back toward the terminal, his back to her. She willed him to turn around and wave one last time, which would somehow mean that everything would turn out fine. But he didn't. He kept on walking, his head down.

****

Pauline walked into the penthouse condo in Baltimore and stood motionless in the dark. Coming home alone was maybe not such a good idea. With Grey by her side, she wouldn't be assailed by the eerie feeling that she stood in two places at once: this place and the shimmery approximation she visited in the Thread Continuum.

Had they entered together, he'd be flicking on the lights, sprawling on the leather sofa, maybe pouring a Scotch. They'd have a nightcap together on the balcony terrace and admire the city lights rippling on the harbor.

Pauline was afraid that if she turned on the lights, she'd somehow trigger a return to that other dimension. She'd find herself floating amid emissaries consulting golden balls, while the bells rang out. Chaitanya would somehow convince her to stay.

She looked at the large picture windows, relieved to see hard-edged steel, glass, and concrete, not a movie reel of ancient objects. *This* was home. Her real home. The home where her future would unfold.

Here, Bex would never call to her to race scooters across the harbor. Helena would not invite her to heal broken hearts—or embrace her as only a mother can. And Cheyenne would not accompany her on time-bending trips to unite lonely objects with deserving caretakers.

So what? None of that was real. Just the stuff of dreams and nocturnal wanderings.

Finally, Pauline screwed up the courage to walk up the spiral staircase to the bedroom, the suitcase trailing behind her. She turned on the lights, breaking any lingering spell, and ran a hot bath. Later, in bed, she wanted to postpone sleep as long as possible to hold her other world, the world that took over during the night, at bay. She turned on the television, growing drowsy against her will.

When a newscaster mentioned Nevis, Pauline came wide awake and turned up the volume to hear the report.

"Questions and concerns tonight on the island paradise of Nevis, which has some of the wealthy tourists here on edge. A local couple, Lawrence and Gertrude Hemphill, have gone missing, and foul play has not been ruled out."

The TV showed a photo of a middle-aged Black couple, smiling and standing in front of the very house where she and her partners had dug up the Brasher doubloon. The small white house with turquoise shutters. She shivered under the covers.

The Hemphills were lifelong residents of Nevis, the reporter explained, well known among the small residential community. Both worked at a local hospital. A man in his twenties came on—their son—pleading for information about his parents, who had no plans to travel and wouldn't leave without telling him if they did.

"Please," the young man said. "I just want my parents back safe and sound. They're good people. This makes no sense. You can keep the furnishings you stole. I only want my mother and father."

Pauline jumped out of bed. *Think. Think.* This was a misunderstanding. Perhaps the Hemphills had agreed to let Ty put them up in a hotel for a few nights, while…while what? They ripped up their floor in search of a priceless artifact?

No, that explanation made no sense.

What if Ty, or someone he managed, had told the Hemphills that their home had a gas leak, and they had to move out until the necessary repairs were made?

The couple wouldn't buy that, would they?

And wouldn't they have told their son if they had to leave the house unexpectedly? Their loving son, worried to distraction about his parents. Pauline imagined how that must feel.

She pulled out her laptop to learn all she could about the Hemphills' disappearance. There wasn't much more than the news had already reported. She was able to confirm one chilling fact: the couple disappeared the night before the dig. Thinking back to that night, Ty obviously had a key to the front door. They didn't need to break in. She wondered then how he'd obtained it. The question loomed ominously now.

There had to be a reasonable explanation for the turn of events.

She called Grey. He barely had time to ask if she'd arrived home safely before she blurted out, "What happened to the Hemphills?"

"The what?" The noise in the background suggested he was at the resort's terrace bar. "Guess what, Pen? I took my first surfing lesson today. On a *real* board. So cool. And even better news: Ty might have started a bidding war over the doubloon. So incredible. Wish you were here to see it all go down."

She almost told him she didn't care. "Grey, the Hemphills live in the house where we dug up the coin. I was right."

"Sorry, what? Can't hear you."

"The house." She shouted into the phone. "The owners are missing."

"Who's missing?"

"Grey! Ask Ty what happened to the Hemphills, okay? Can you do that for me?"

A pause on the other end. "I'll call you back in the morning, okay? Love you."

The line went dead. What did he know, if anything? She briefly considered calling Tyrone Lake directly, but he'd never share the truth with her. Plus, calling him would put Grey in an uncomfortable position. Tyrone Lake might think his partner and protégé couldn't *control* his temperamental wife.

Sleep was out of the question now. She went downstairs and paced from window to window, wondering what to do and refusing to believe the worst—that Tyrone Lake did something terrible to the Hemphills. Worse still was the notion that Grey knew anything about it, or even had an inkling.

Pauline moved out to the balcony and suddenly realized she wasn't helpless. Not by a long shot. If ever there was a time to test her wildest abilities, this was it. Nervous, she closed her eyes, drew in a deep breath, and pictured herself standing in the Hemphills' house on Nevis.

A *whoosh*, followed by the sensation of flying apart, as if her molecules were coming unglued. Perhaps the *pulse* had been a warm-up for exercising this power, a set of muscles she flexed for years before the real trials began.

Cautiously, she opened her eyes and she was there, in the very room where they'd dug up the coin. She wished she could tell Chaitanya. Or maybe he knew. Maybe he was always watching her, waiting for her.

Never mind that. The hole had been filled and the floor refinished. The new floorboards were nearly identical to the older ones but, upon closer inspection, she saw the contours of the repairs. The house was hot, stuffy, and quiet, filled only by a sad emptiness that brushed her skin.

Car tires crunched on the shell-strewn driveway. She crouched beneath a front window as a man got out of the car and strode to the front door. *Should I leave? Can he see me? Am I even real in this space?*

There was no time to do anything before the key

turned in the lock and a brown-skinned young man entered. The Hemphills' son, of course.

"What the hell?" he said, clutching car keys. "Who are you? How did you get in here? Are you with the news? I'm done feeding you scandal. Get out."

"I'm not...not a reporter. I'm...a friend."

"I don't know you," he said, angrily. "Do you know my parents?"

"I may be able to find out what happened to them."

"What do you know?" he shouted. "Tell me!"

"Nothing yet. But I can find out."

"I'd call the police now, but they're useless."

"Please don't involve the police. I wouldn't have come if I didn't think I could help. I want to find your parents almost as much as you do."

She was digging a deep hole, but she didn't see another option.

"I doubt that. You're an American. A tourist, I suppose, sticking your nose where it doesn't belong. This is island business."

"Things are not what they seem, Mr. Hemphill."

"Meaning what? My parents are blameless. They've done nothing wrong. Someone must pay for whatever's happened to them." Sweat poured down the man's face. Or perhaps he was crying. "Now get out of my house. And don't come back."

The front door slammed shut behind Pauline the instant she walked out. She blinked in the bright sunlight, contemplating her next move.

The souls of objects will speak their truth.

Of course. The souls of objects: they fill the universe with clues, and she could find those clues, hear them, touch them.

Where to start?

Something related to the Hemphills…

I miss the soft warmth of her finger. Here inside the box, I'm lonely and cold.

An opal ring belonging to Mrs. Hemphill, a gift on her tenth wedding anniversary. The ring lies…where? Concentrate. Inside a wooden box alongside other miscellaneous jewelry. And the box sits…in a drawer…in a room…belonging to Tyrone Lake.

Before forming another thought, she was standing in the man's room at the resort. Startled, she whirled around, relieved to find herself alone. She couldn't waste time worrying what might happen if Tyrone Lake found her there. Mrs. Hemphill's opal ring sat inside a larger box made of sandalwood, which held scores of rings, loose gems, cufflinks, diamond studs, and several of the Spanish coins rescued from the shipwreck. The contents must have been worth a small fortune. Where did Tyrone Lake obtain all this treasure, and why was he hoarding it?

And Mrs. Hemphill's ring: Why was it in his possession—and how did it get there?

She pocketed the ring and considered rifling through other drawers, looking for papers, anything to incriminate him. Grey deserved to know the truth about his—their—partner. But Ty might return at any moment, and she was done taking chances.

Wrapped in the cloak of time and space, Pauline willed herself back to Baltimore, where night had turned to morning. A troubled night, without Chaitanya's company. More immediate problems pressed in, along with deepening confusion. Pauline stood before the full-length mirror in the bedroom and confronted herself, searching her face and body for clues about her existence.

Who are you?

What are you doing?

The phone rang, and for an instant she mistook the ring for the calling of the bells in the Thread Continuum.

"Penny!" Grey shouted over the line. "Are you sitting down? Never mind. Guess what? We did it, babe! We sold the coin to a Swiss banker for...are you ready?...ten-and-a-half million dollars. He says he's been looking for a Brasher doubloon for years, and he had to have it for his collection. I'm super-pumped!" Grey paused, presumably awaiting her response.

"Wow."

"You're speechless, right? I don't blame you. Like, it's almost too good to be true. But this is real life, babe. This is how it's all going down from now on. So I'm thinking...you there?"

"I'm here."

"I'm thinking we should top ourselves. You know, come up with something so rare, so priceless, the whole world will fight over it. You think you can find something like that?"

"Are you coming home soon?"

"Ty and Ward are gonna help me set up some off-shore accounts tomorrow. Then, yeah, I'm gonna charter a private plane all the way home. Then we'll celebrate together. Can't wait! I love you."

"Love you too."

After the call, Pauline picked up Mrs. Hemphill's opal ring, listening to stories the ring was eager to share about her adventures on the hand of a nurse, a mother, and loving wife.

Chapter 27

The sight of Grey in rumpled linen, his chin overgrown with stubble, melted her heart once more. He was eager and ambitious. That didn't make him a criminal. Still…

"Miss me?" He threw himself down on the leather sofa and kicked off his shoes.

"Not too much."

"Come here, you." He motioned for her to sit beside him. Reaching into his pants pocket, he removed a small, velvet drawstring bag. "To let you know I was thinking of you every minute."

Pauline withdrew a bracelet sparkling with diamonds and sapphires.

"Oh, Grey. It's…it's too much."

He fastened the bracelet around her wrist. "You can stop thinking like that, Penny. Stop worrying about what things cost. Those days are behind us, forever."

"I don't need to live extravagantly to be happy."

"Then what *do* you need?" He undid the top button on her blouse.

She paused, taking the question seriously. "What I really need…"

"Yes?" He continued undoing her blouse.

"What I really need from you, Grey, is…honesty."

He stopped undressing her. "What are you talking about?"

"There are a few things I'd like to know. To clear up any confusion."

Grey rose and fixed himself a drink. "You used to be a lot more fun. What's gotten into you?" He didn't wait for a response. "Listen, Ty and Ward gave me a crash course in high finance, so we can put our money to work for us. I learned all about off-shore tax havens. And Penny, I know you don't think much of Ty, but I'll bet he knows more about the antiquities market than all those so-called experts at Sotheby's, Christie's, or Bonham's put together. The man's a walking encyclopedia."

"I bet." She watched him pace around. Maybe he was walking off nervous energy. After all, he'd had a long trip and a lot of excitement crammed into a couple of days.

"He comes from nothing, you know. Ty is totally self-made. You can respect that, can't you?"

"He's an awful lot like you, Grey, isn't he?"

Grey stopped pacing and looked at her. "Yeah. Yeah, you could say that."

"But you're not nearly as greedy, are you?"

"That's not fair, Penny." He plunked down in a wing chair opposite her on the couch. "To him or to me."

"Sorry." Catching his restless mood, she moved out to the balcony terrace, watching the sun on the water. The soul of an object broke into her thoughts, unbidden.

I am a button meant to be sewn onto René's best leather jerkin, but I was orphaned, instead...When the clasp came loose and I bounced to the floor, he caught me up and dusted me off...The little boy's mother insisted he trade me for a handful of seeds...

Grey joined her on the balcony.

"I must ask you, Grey."

She framed her questions carefully: about the missing Hemphills, their easy access to the unfurnished house, and whether he knew who owned it. She did not mention Tyrone Lake by name. Nor could she mention the opal ring, as there was no way to explain why she had it or how she obtained it.

When she'd finished, Grey gave her a totally open, guileless smile that suggested he had nothing to hide.

"You and I," he said. "We didn't do anything wrong. You found the artifact, which nobody else knew anything about, and we took it. We don't owe anyone anything, let alone any sort of explanation. And I don't know anything about these people. Who are they, again?"

"Lawrence and Gertrude Hemphill. I saw them on the news. It's their house." She almost told him about meeting their son but stopped herself in time. "You must have heard or seen something down there. It's big news."

Grey shrugged. "The house was empty when we got there. Ty had a key. It's over and done with. And we scored a huge payday. Why are you obsessed with these irrelevant details? Why don't you focus on our success? I mean, we pulled this off without a hitch. That's pretty damn impressive. And I didn't have time to watch the news, in case you were wondering."

"Don't you care?" She felt queasy.

"About what?"

"They disappeared, Grey, the night before we went into their house. Doesn't that concern you? Aren't you worried that Ty might have...might have...?" She couldn't keep him out of it any longer.

"Tyrone Lake is a businessman."

"I'm not talking about business."

Grey shrugged again. "Sometimes, business is cutthroat. You do what you have to, to get what you want."

"Including...murder?" Instead of waiting for an answer, she could teleport to a far-off time and place, so she wouldn't have to face whatever was coming next. A stupid fantasy. And cowardly.

"Really, Penny? Don't be ridiculous. I don't understand where all these crazy theories come from. You're almost scaring me." He placed the back of his hand against her forehead, as if a fever could explain away her concerns.

"I don't think you know Tyrone Lake as well as you think you do."

"I don't think you know him at all," he replied sharply. A moment later he softened and put his arms around her. "I don't want Ty coming between us. I don't want *anyone* coming between us. Can we agree on that?"

Pauline nodded.

"Now," he said. "I have an idea. Let's throw a housewarming party. A big one. We'll invite everyone we know from Carthage who's still around, and our neighbors in the other penthouse, and anybody you can think of."

"Are you going to invite Ty to fly in from wherever?" He looked pained. "It's okay. I know he means a lot to you. I don't want to come between you two, either. That isn't fair."

"You're the best," he said.

A plan was coming together, sparked by Grey's desire to host a party. Pauline couldn't tell him a thing about it, which nearly broke her heart.

Chapter 28

Grey surveyed the champagne chilling in the wine fridge.

"Babe," he called up from the kitchen, "I don't think we have enough. I'm going to order another case."

"Whatever makes you happy." Pauline was in the bedroom putting on her two pieces of statement jewelry, the jeweled key and the diamond-and-sapphire bracelet. She went down to the kitchen holding up two different earring options. "Which goes best, babe?"

"The dangly gold rings, for sure," he said. "You look fantastic."

"Thanks. So do you."

Grey wore a light-colored, button-down shirt and slacks that made him appear like a carefree lord of the manor. Informal, but elegant; relaxed, but in charge. Pauline wore a classic little black dress and red pumps.

The penthouse was bathed in the orange glow of early sunset. The wide open balcony doors let in a welcome summer breeze. Pauline had lit candles floating in shallow bowls and placed them around the room. They cast a warm, mellow glow. The mellow lighting did not soften her mood, however.

"Stop pacing," Grey told her. "Relax. This is gonna be a great party."

"Just breaking in new shoes."

There was a knock at the door. *Not a guest, please. Not yet. I'm not ready.* She opened the door reluctantly, relieved when it turned out to be the wine delivery.

Pauline would not confess to Grey how much she hated parties, spoiling Grey's fun. *This* party, most of all. But all parties, in general. She hadn't had a lot of practice, as her foster parents, the Hellers, hated people and never hosted a party. The only good to come from *any* party was Dean Nojes's forced gathering for graduate students, where she'd met Grey. But that hardly counted, as she had no choice.

Then again, tonight's affair was not really a choice, either, in more ways than one.

Grey massaged her shoulders.

"Why are you so tense? This is supposed to be fun. Our coming-out party. Our we-rule-the-fucking-universe party."

"We don't have any friends. Not real friends."

"Isn't your friend from grad school, Bette—isn't she coming?"

"Yeah." Bette was doing her a favor by coming, but Grey didn't know that.

"This will help." Grey popped the cork on a bottle of chilled champagne and ushered her out to the balcony. "This is our happy place, right here."

"It is, isn't it?" The balcony was a complicated space, which there was no way to explain.

"We make a great team, but we need more now. We need allies even more than friends. Connections. That's how we get ahead. Someday, we'll be able to make our own deals. It will all depend on who we know."

She looked at him in surprise. "You mean, you

want to break away from your boss and mentor? Go out on your own?"

"Eventually." He smiled. "But not yet. I still need Ty. We both do."

"Here's to getting ahead." Pauline raised her glass, telling him what he wanted to hear.

"Here's to winning."

The doorbell began to ring, and kept on ringing, as the penthouse filled up with people Pauline didn't know. Among them were their neighbors, a couple in matching seersucker jackets.

"I'm Dick, this is Dave." Dick handed her a large bouquet. "We thought maybe you didn't exist!"

"You're never here," Dave added. "Are you spies, or what?"

"They can't tell us *that,*" Dick said, swatting Dave's arm.

She thanked them for the flowers and encouraged them to get a drink, which would preclude a long conversation.

"Oh, so tasteful," Dick said, running his hand along the glass-topped dining room table. "We could use a piece like this, Dave, couldn't we?"

Dave had already wandered off to get a drink.

Grey had been in charge of the guest list, with the exception of Bette French, so Pauline had no cause to feel uneasy about all the strangers in her space. What if Helena, Bex, and Cheyenne were to show up all of a sudden? Would they blend in, dressed all in black? The bare feet might raise questions. Would they creep everybody out or entrance them? *Would I want to hang out with them, and only them?* They could perform for the crowd—a jaw-dropping, gravity-defying dance, perhaps.

But not Chaitanya. Not here.

"And this is my wife, Pauline." Grey introduced a middle-aged man in an open-necked shirt that revealed a hairy chest. "This is Chip Hendrix. He's a financial advisor. Lives a few floors down from us. I told Chip we'd be happy to sit down and let him pitch us some investments. Good idea, right, Penny?"

Chip shook her hand and flashed white teeth before handing her a business card.

"You've done a lovely job with the penthouse," Chip said. She didn't bother mentioning that the place came furnished.

"Thank you." She took the card, which she'd stick in a drawer at the first opportunity. "It's nice to meet a neighbor. I wonder how you two found time to meet. You see, Chip, my husband works all the time."

"Because I love what we do so much," Grey said, putting a proprietary arm around her shoulder. "Pauline and I run the business together. It really doesn't feel like work."

"Money doesn't make itself," Chip said with a chuckle. "Not at first, anyway. It's nice to meet a young couple like you, with such a sense of purpose. Gives me hope for the younger generation."

Moments later, she pulled Grey aside and asked him what he told people they did for a living.

"What do *you* tell people?" he asked, turning the tables.

"I haven't said a word to anyone, yet."

"Well, tell them we're archaeologists who invest in art and antiquities. Tell them anything you like. All that matters is you make a good impression."

She dutifully mingled, imagining the room filled instead with floating Recoverists, Restorationists, and Reparationers, all of them engaged in benevolent work with no expectation of personal gain.

Looking across the room, she caught a glimpse of Chaitanya. There, in the briefest flash, then gone. *Come home.*

Bits of conversation swirled around her. People talking about money, stocks and bonds, cars and houses, and the best places to vacation. Who were these people, and where did Grey find them?

Sue Rios turned up. Pauline had no idea Grey had invited her. "Pauline!" Sue exclaimed, as if surprised to find the hostess at her own party. They air kissed. "You have really come *up* in the world." She looked enviously around the penthouse. "I never pegged you as the monied type. I mean, you didn't dress the part at school, that's for sure." Ah, yes, same old Sue. She explained she was on her way to a conference in Washington, and so glad she could stop in.

"How is Princeton treating you?" Pauline had to say *something.*

"Oh, you know." Sue shrugged. "Academia, and all that jazz."

"Sure."

"Oh, there's Grey," Sue said, looking over Pauline's shoulder. "I must say hello. Keep in touch, yeah? *So* great to see you." She flounced off.

Pauline was impatient for Bette French to arrive, while dreading it at the same time.

The doorbell rang again. Maybe Bette, finally. But no. It was Tyrone Lake in a sharply tailored pinstripe suit, flanked by two big men with coiled earpieces.

Bodyguards? Was that really necessary? The room was dominated by men, she realized, with only a sprinkling of women mostly hanging on their arms.

Grey made a beeline for Ty. They embraced warmly, like old pals. Again, Pauline caught a resemblance, something in the shape of their heads, even the way they each stood with one foot slightly in front of the other. Then again, Grey practically wanted to *be* Tyrone Lake, didn't he? The mimicry could be entirely unconscious. Ty nodded in her direction, a thin smile barely playing on his lips. As Grey handed him a drink, she caught the flash at Ty's wrist—one of the diamond cufflinks she'd seen in the box that held Gertrude Hemphill's opal ring in his room on Nevis. It was unmistakable.

Pauline felt as if a dam was about to burst. She could no longer pretend that nothing was wrong.

If only Grey had never met Tyrone Lake. If only she and Grey had continued digging for private thrills, finding buyers on their own, even at a fraction of the prices they'd achieved. They'd be scrappy and hungry together, a pair of nighthawkers defying convention, breaking the law, and doing it all on their own terms. They'd never be able to live in a swanky place like this, but so what? She didn't need the trappings, only Grey.

The doorbell again, and this time it was Bette. Pauline rushed her up the spiral staircase and into Grey's office. They stood awkwardly, assessing each other as the sun began to sink and the room dimmed. This was their first meeting in person since grad school. Their social media friendship had barely held them together. But Pauline had prevailed on Bette to come up from Washington—as a friend, sort of, but also on official business.

"You've changed," Pauline said. Bette's hair was brown now and pulled into a simple ponytail. She was conservatively dressed in a boring blouse and skirt. The only nod to her former flamboyance were her rainbow sneakers.

"Not really," she said. "But you. You're very different, somehow. I can't figure it out. You're still too goddamn beautiful. But...maybe it's marriage. I'm not sure it agrees with you."

"You still don't pull punches, do you?"

Bette turned to the window, watching the setting sun light up the clouds with an orange glow. "Wow. How can you afford all this? Sorry. That's rude."

"It's a long story, and I don't want to talk about it. But you wouldn't be you if you didn't ask. You still have a suspicious mind, which I'm counting on."

"You and your squishy ethics," Bette said. "That much hasn't changed, has it?"

"Are you working on any interesting cases?" *Cut to the chase.*

"Did you know there's a huge underground market for shark fins?" Bette shook her head in disgust. "And don't get me started on the thieves robbing Native burial grounds. I mean, who does that?"

"Plenty of people, I'm guessing."

"Sad but true. So, Pauline, how's teaching going?"

"Teaching?"

"Aren't you an adjunct at Carthage? Working under Dean Nojes's thumb, I imagine?"

"Oh, right." She waved dismissively, recalling her lie. "My last course ended in the spring. Not sure I'm going back, to be honest. Hey, would you like a drink?

277

I'm a terrible hostess."

"Do I need one? I mean, I know you didn't invite me just to pretend we're best friends. Or to show off this place."

"No, you're right. Wait here."

Pauline retrieved the drawstring silk pouch from the back of her night-table drawer—the very one that had held the bracelet from Grey. "If I speak to you in your official capacity, can I remain an anonymous source?"

"That depends," Bette said.

"On what?"

"I'm only a criminal justice fellow, Pauline, and a mere student of the law."

"You were never a 'mere' anything, Bette. Did you ever report the dean for making us all hang around to play her game?"

"I did." She smiled at the memory. "The administration told me to fuck off. Though not in those exact words." They laughed. "I never told you, the dean matched me with Sierra Dobbs. For that stupid ritual she made us all go through in the room filled with masks."

"Sierra Dobbs? A piece of work, huh."

"Yeah. She started crying the instant we entered the room. Such a drama queen."

"What did you see, Bette?"

"When?" She looked puzzled.

"In the room with the masks. When she told you to close your eyes. You remember."

Bette shrugged. "I didn't see anything but the back of my eyelids. But I sure felt something."

"Tell me."

"I was angry. Like white-hot angry."

"About what?"

"It was weird. All of a sudden, I was enraged. People don't think twice about stealing from ancestors, stealing other people's birthrights, desecrating graves, and yanking sacred objects out of the ground. Turning this mysterious gift, human culture, our ability to make objects we invest with meaning—turning that into cash. It's sordid. Ugly. A nasty business."

Pauline could not look her old friend in the eye just then. Her own hypocrisy stung like a snake bite. Better get on with the business at hand. She was about to open the drawstring pouch when Grey popped in.

"Here you are," he said. "Hiding out. Gossiping. Hey, Bette."

"Hey, Grey."

"Pauline, some of our guests are leaving, and they want to say goodbye."

"In a minute." He nodded and disappeared. Pauline closed the door, then removed Mrs. Hemphill's opal ring from the pouch and held it out to Bette. "This is stolen property. Something might have happened to the owner."

Bette took the ring and examined it.

"It's contemporary," she said. "Not an artifact. I don't understand."

"It's connected with a nighthawking event. On private property."

"Look, Pauline, I'm not a cop, or anything. You know that, right? But if you're serious, if that type of crime has been committed, I know who to take this to. Where did this happen?"

"In the Caribbean."

"That makes it way more complicated. I'm not sure—"

"Bette, I know this is weird, between us. And I know asking you to help is a long shot. But I think...I think it's quite possible...the owner of this ring was murdered for the sake of an artifact that's worth a lot of money." She couldn't take it back, now. "I trust you. I need you to believe me—to believe this is serious. And find a way—"

"You don't want me to ask how you know all this," Bette said, angrily. "You want me to keep you out of it. No. You want justice, as long as you keep your own hands clean. Isn't that right?"

"It's complicated."

"Of course it's complicated," Bette said, her voice rising. "Archaeology and murder don't play well together. Tell me yes or no: You know the suspect or have a pretty good idea who it is."

Pauline looked away and nodded.

"Not Grey?"

She shook her head. But was she sure? She couldn't bear to name Tyrone Lake, or even point him out to Bette downstairs, because that was really the same as accusing Grey. Besides, if the authorities did their job, then the evidence would almost surely lead them to Ty, anyway, without any further interference from her.

"I think I'll get that drink, now," Bette said, pocketing the pouch containing the ring.

"Sue Rios is here."

"Oh, great," Bette said, rolling her eyes. At least they enjoyed one more laugh together.

Chapter 29

Alone in the huge lecture hall at Carthage University, Pauline sat down front where she could not escape the wrath of Dean India Nojes, who was no longer short. She was over ten feet tall, looking down from a raised podium, screaming at Pauline for what felt like hours on end.

"You know what you must do!" the dean yelled, slamming her hand on the podium. "What are you waiting for? Do the right thing, Pauline! DO IT!"

I will! I will! The words stuck in her throat.

"What did you say?" The dean continued to yell. "Quit stalling! Every moment you delay makes you an accomplice. You're guilty, Pauline. Guilty, guilty, guilty."

A man and a woman appeared on either side of Pauline in the lecture hall.

"We're so disappointed in you," the man said.

"We had such high hopes," the woman added, shaking her head. "We sacrificed everything, so you could become your best self."

"You see?" the dean said from on high. "Your parents agree with me. You better turn this thing around, Pauline, before it's too late."

"Don't turn your back on your destiny," said the man—her father.

"Quit hiding from yourself," said her mother.

"You're not doing yourself any favors."

Pauline strained to speak to her parents, so much she wanted to ask them. But her jaw was locked shut and her throat muscles refused to cooperate.

"NNNNNo!" she cried out. The strangled words, uttered out loud for real, woke her up, and Grey, too.

"Bad dream?" he asked, running a hand along her arm.

She swallowed hard and peered into the dark bedroom, looking for…what?

"I saw my parents. My real parents." Her voice cracked.

"Maybe you drank too much at the party," he said. "I'll get you a glass of water."

Pauline hardly drank at all at the party, but his tender gesture moved her.

"Try to go back to sleep," he said. In an instant, he was snoring lightly. She fingered his curly hair. *My husband isn't guilty of anything except wanting his dreams to come true. I can't hold that against him.*

She lay on her back, staring up at the ceiling. The dream felt too real. A shot across the bow, somehow. Was she afforded a glimpse of her real parents? Were they out there, somewhere, wondering about her? The dean had said her parents were "out of the picture." What did that mean?

What was Chaitanya hiding from her? So many secrets, and so many secret-keepers. She among them.

She lay awake most of the night, searching for answers that never arrived.

At daybreak, she sat on the balcony, staring into space, her eyes gritty with exhaustion. Right *there*, about a dozen feet away, was where an emissary had flown by carrying the metal fragments of a mechanical bird built in Leonardo da Vinci's workshop. She tingled, existing in two places at once, between two realities competing for her loyalty and love. And maybe her soul.

"My poor darling." Grey brought coffee an hour later. "Are you hungover?" She shook her head. "I thought the party went spectacularly well. Don't you?" She nodded.

"Who were those burly men with Ty?"

"Dunno. Associates, I suppose. I didn't talk to them."

"You really don't know much about him, do you, but you trust him all the same."

"I *do* know him, and I *do* trust him. We've been over this. Actually, you seem kind of obsessed with Tyrone Lake. I don't know why. Is it because he's drastically changed our lives?"

"He despises me because he needs me. And that frightens him."

"Don't play armchair psychologist. It doesn't suit you."

"He didn't create this in a vacuum." She waved vaguely toward the condo. "Don't give him all the credit."

Grey sighed and put down his coffee. They had barely touched one another in three days.

"I'm going to check in on our money, and watch it grow," he said.

"Maybe I should buy you a plant, a nice little orchid that you can fawn over and tend to. You can make *that* grow."

"Mmm, you tend the plant, I'll tend the money. I

may have a green thumb—but not where Mother Nature is concerned. And you? What are you up to today?"

He didn't need to come out and say what he meant. She read between the lines easily enough. He wanted her to find the next dig. A big one—a multi-million-dollar score.

"I haven't decided yet."

"Well, I'll leave you to it." He kissed the top of her head. "You know where to find me." Translation: Come tell me when the next artifact is within our grasp.

"Grey." She called out as he stepped back inside. "Let's go nighthawking together, just the two of us, like we used to. I'll find something, somewhere fun. We can make it a thing. We dig at night, then check into a romantic inn somewhere close by. And whatever we find, we'll keep for ourselves. Display it in the living room. Like the Gillespies. No reason we can't also become collectors."

"Penny," he said softly. "You know we can't do that."

"Why not?"

"Because Ty—"

"Why should Ty always come first?" She stood, her back to the balcony railing, and imagined pitching over the side and floating away. If only that would bring Grey to his senses.

"That's not fair," he said. "You read the contract. You signed it."

"I wish I hadn't."

"Well, I'm glad we did. Everything's on a professional footing. We know where we stand. Besides, the contract is an incentive—"

"I don't want incentives. I want…"

"What do you want, Penny? And don't tell me you want honesty."

"I want you, Grey."

"And I want you," he said, pulling her close, his warm breath on her neck awakening her desire. But she let the moment pass. "But what else, Penny? What will make you happy...and productive?"

She pulled away, stung by his cold, transactional words. Instead of whispering tender endearments, he only wanted her to perform, like a circus animal. Did he fancy himself her trainer? No, she wouldn't go that far. She would banish such cruel thoughts. He was kind and attentive. He'd proven his love over and over.

But something had shifted, whether in her, or between them, she wasn't sure.

****

Over the next few days, they led nearly separate lives, perched high in their luxury cocoon. He spent hours in his office, staring at shifting lines on graphs, tracking money, talking to investors, including their neighbor, Chip Hendrix. Grey pleaded with her to meet with him and Chip to discuss their portfolio. Each time, she declined.

"I don't know anything about finance," she protested. "Numbers are so abstract. I prefer real things—things I can touch and hold. You know that."

"Do you trust me, then, to make decisions for us? You'll have to sign more papers."

"Sure. Whatever you think is best."

"It's your money too, Penny."

"I know, but we already have more than I know what to do with."

"Suit yourself."

Three times he came to find her in the middle of the day, as she sat staring out the window. He was checking up on her, obviously, to see if she'd found a new dig.

"What are you doing?" he asked. "Your thousand-yard stare is creeping me out, Pen. Like you're under a spell, or something."

"I'm thinking."

"And? Anything you'd like to share?"

"Not yet." She shook herself from a stupor and smiled. "Working on it, though."

"Okay. Well, any time. The market's hot now, but you never know how long that will last. And besides, we're not the only ones looking."

"No pressure, or anything." She smiled again, as if to say she understood perfectly well what he meant.

"No more than usual," he responded.

She *was* thinking. And also listening to the souls of objects regaling her with their stories, trials, and tribulations. The Mayan pot filled with charcoal that fueled torches at night spoke about the shadows the flickering flames cast on dried mud walls.

Ancient benches that supported hard-working backsides during the day, while doubling as sleeping platforms at night, boasted of their round-the-clock utility.

And the Nebra Sky Disk, an Iron Age marvel made of bronze, its blue-green patina inlaid with gold symbols of the sun, the moon, and clusters of stars. An ancient work of science and art, beautiful in form and function. The Nebra Sky Disk called out: *I too passed this way. Remember me.*

Such knowledge vouchsafed to her was equally a

burden and a curse. What should she do with such gifts?

In addition to thinking and listening, she was, above all, waiting. Bette had promised to let her know when she heard something about the Hemphill investigation on Nevis. Grey had no idea how often she checked her phone for the expected message. Finally, after nearly a week, Bette texted.

INTERPOL involved, she wrote. *Massive international antiquities crime ring. Person of interest identified. Will let you know if I learn more. Stay out of trouble, Marsh. If you can.*

She stared at the phone, hoping for more details to materialize. Who could this person of interest be, if not Tyrone Lake?

Pauline hovered in the doorway to Grey's office as he clicked away on his keyboard, two monitors sending numbers and graphs crawling across their screens like nervous worms. She loved his back: the way the muscles on his shoulders moved beneath his shirt, the way his curly hair grazed his collar. Approaching him in silence, she wrapped her arms around his neck, catching him off-guard.

"Take me to bed," she whispered. "Right now."

He turned around. "You mean, this minute?"

There was a time when he would not have hesitated. She grabbed his cock and began to massage it. He released a groan, then stood, picked her up, and carried her across to the bedroom. Before she could make a move, he ripped her shirt open and buttons popped off, pinging to the floor. Pushing her onto her back, he jerked her pants down and flung them to the floor. Then he grabbed her arms and twisted them until she flipped onto her stomach. A slap on the buttocks and she rose on all fours so he could ride her hard, bucking, thrusting, until they both came, breathing hard.

Less than a minute after, Grey was already zipping his pants. Without a word, he returned to the office, leaving Pauline flat on her back in bed.

The lovemaking had a last-time feel to it, like sex fueled by memory—the memory of shared love itself, perhaps. Did he feel this, too? Did he give it a moment's thought?

She dressed and went downstairs, putting together a platter of odds and ends from the refrigerator. She opened a bottle of rosé from Provence, then carried everything out to the table on the balcony. She brought out the good dishes and cloth napkins. She called to Grey to join her. A summer breeze ruffled the table linens.

"Now what, Pen?" He surveyed the formal spread. "What's all this?" Then he produced the crooked grin. "Oh, I know. You found it, didn't you? A whopper. Where? What is it? Do you think we can double our capital? Ty will want to know right away."

He began pulling out his phone, but she stopped him.

"No," she said. "Sit down."

"Well, if it's not...Look, I'm in the middle of some trades and I should get back—"

"Grey, please. Sit."

He complied, clearly unhappy. "If we lose money today, it's on you."

"You'd never let that happen."

"You're right. Not if I can help it. What's this

about? Oh, my God. You're not—"

"Pregnant. No."

Grey was visibly relieved. Children were the last thing on either of their minds, though perhaps for different reasons.

"I don't know how else to say this, Grey, so I'll just say it. Tyrone Lake is in trouble. Serious trouble."

"Who says?"

"I can't tell you."

"What do you mean you can't— Penny, you don't know what you're talking about."

Grey's usually sunny countenance took on a menacing cast. She remembered how he'd looked the day he came close to threatening their obnoxious fellow graduate student Dan Finland at Dean Nojes's house. Grey had clenched his fists, ready for combat. He looked ready to fight now.

"He might be wanted by INTERPOL. Do you have any idea why?"

She gambled that he wouldn't see how she was testing him, giving him one last chance to come clean about Nevis—and tell her everything he knew that would put Tyrone Lake in a bad light. Maybe, if he did that, the two of them could start over. Give up nighthawking, for good. Spend time and money preserving and celebrating legitimately recovered artifacts.

Maybe they still had a future together.

Maybe they should escape to that fancy hotel in New York. They'd been so happy there.

Grey poured them each a large glass of wine, the liquid sloshing over the sides of the glasses as he poured carelessly. He took a gulp.

"I never said Ty was perfect," he said. "But he's smart. Too smart to get caught with his hand in the cookie jar."

"What does that even mean?" She watched him closely, his blue-gray eyes flashing in the sunlight.

"You'd be the first to admit he's not a saint."

"And?"

"And nothing," he said. "I don't know what you expect me to say. I don't think this affects our arrangement, in any way."

"Unless he's caught. And if he is, what happens to us?"

Grey smiled, but it wasn't a nice smile. It was almost wicked.

"I wouldn't worry about it, Penny. Just do your job, and everything will be fine. More than fine, probably."

With a shaking hand, she topped off her wine. They hadn't touched the food.

"Grey, I'm going to ask you, just once. Did Ty have the Hemphills killed so that we could get into their house to dig up the doubloon?"

He let out a long, slow breath. "You're already convinced he did."

"That's not an answer."

Grey leaned across the table and put her hand between his, which were calm and steady. "There's no evidence to prove what you're suggesting."

"That's still not an answer." She withdrew her hand.

"Then I don't know what to tell you." He leaned back, smiling. "You can be sure *I* didn't kill them."

"No, I know."

"Then stop worrying. Look, I've got more work to do before the markets close." He stood. "We good?"

"Sure." She looked out over the balcony. Suddenly sick of the view, she followed Grey back into the apartment.

They both stopped short.

Without so much as a knock, Tyrone Lake stood in the open doorway, dressed in a charcoal suit, his thin mustache a straight line above his tightly set mouth.

"Speak of the devil!" Grey rushed to embrace the man as if they'd just raised a glass to his good health.

Ty sat on the leather couch as if he'd been expected. He was obviously avoiding eye contact with Pauline, who put space between them, her back to one of the large windows.

"What's going on, Ty?" Grey asked. "If you're impatient about our next dig, believe me, I've been riding Penny pretty hard about it. She's working on it." Grey threw a quick glance her way.

Ty couldn't possibly have come here to confess his crimes—and clear Grey of any wrongdoing. Yet, if only he would, she and Grey might still have a chance.

"I have bad news, Greyson," Ty said.

Grey perched on a hassock opposite the couch. A glimmer of hope. Perhaps the man had a conscience, after all.

"Your father was found dead in his cell last night," Ty said. "Natural causes, most likely. Probably a heart attack."

Grey shot to his feet like a rocket lifting off.

"Grey?" Pauline's voice from across the room seemed to startle both men. "Your father?" She wanted to comfort him, but he didn't look like he wanted to be comforted.

"Didn't my nephew tell you?" Ty asked. "I know he hates talking about his father—my younger brother—but I assumed he'd at least tell *you*, Pauline. You're the love of his life, aren't you?"

Ty looked expectantly at each of them in turn. "Well, every marriage has its secrets, I guess," he added. "I wouldn't know, personally."

"My father was a loser!" Grey growled. "He deserved to die alone, in prison. He meant nothing to me, Penny. I'm nothing like him. I even took my mother's maiden name, to be rid of him. I didn't want you to think—"

"But *this* man is also your flesh and blood, Grey," she said. "I didn't want to believe you looked alike because I couldn't believe you'd keep something like that from me. You lied, Grey. All this time, you've been lying."

Pauline's heart raced as her body shook. She sank into a chair, unable to trust her legs.

"Now, children," Ty said.

A sudden upwelling of rage restored her strength. "Shut up!" Raising her voice to this man brought an instant of relief, which quickly evaporated.

"Penny, I didn't tell you because I'm ashamed of my family. Ashamed of my father, who didn't have the brains or the guts to steal without getting caught. I told you I'd never be like him, and I'm not. Look around. Look at how far we've come, already." Grey strode over and gripped her arms. "You trust me, don't you? Nothing bad will happen to us. I won't let it. And Ty won't, either."

"You shouldn't put your faith in him, Grey," she

said, as if Ty weren't in the room.

"You don't understand," Grey said, stepping away. "After my mother died, I'd have lived on the street, if it weren't for Ty. He was all I had. Who do you think paid for college? And Carthage? He taught me how to be a man. How to stand on my own two feet. I owe him, Penny."

"But you hid your connection." She could not keep her voice level. "You told me he was some kind of middleman. Just a guy you were doing business with. Why didn't you tell me he was your uncle?"

The room rang with Grey's silence. He looked to Ty for a cue.

"I'm leaving the country for a while," Ty said. "Grey, I expect you're coming with me. Pauline can decide for herself. If we have to manage without her gifts, we will. But if she comes, we'll make it worth her while, won't we?"

As if they could buy me off!

She faced Ty. "You killed that poor couple in Nevis, or had them killed, didn't you, Ty? That's why you have to get out."

Ty gave her a bemused smile and nothing more.

"Or are they after you for something else?" she continued. "Stolen shark fins? Rare birds? Ivory? Art? Jewelry? I'm sure the list goes on."

"Your hands are hardly clean," Ty said calmly.

"Is that a threat?" She was yelling now. "Bring it on."

"It's really none of your fucking business, Penny," Grey said in a quiet, even voice she'd never heard before, a voice that sounded all too much like his uncle's.

"Do you *want* me to come with you, Grey?"

Grey took her in his arms and kissed her with passion. She longed for the sweet, rich flavor of his kisses, but all she tasted was ash.

"I need you," he whispered. "I need you both."

She pushed him away. "Choose, Grey. It's him or me."

Grey again fell silent. Ty looked at his watch and moved toward the door.

Chaitanya appeared just over Grey's shoulder, his dark eyes pleading with her. *You have no choice.* His words echoed loudly in her head, reaching across a great distance like the voices of the Shigir totem.

"Grey." Her voice was full of sorrow. "We chose each other, all those months ago, in the little room in Dean Nojes's house. You said fate brought us together. You promised you'd never leave. Remember?"

The Hellers pulling out of the driveway, leaving her behind for a whole day and night. The memory poked her with the sharp, familiar sting of abandonment.

"I have no choice," Grey said, his words sending a shiver down her spine. He looked at Ty in the doorway before looking back at her. "I never expected to fall in love with you. Not really. I had everything worked out—except for that. The effect you had on me."

"Come on, Greyson," Ty said. "The plane is on the tarmac."

"I *did* choose you, Penny," Grey continued, edging toward the door. "I watched you. Sensed what you might be capable of. How we might pool our talents. And it all worked out better than I hoped."

"But you didn't want to love me." She rose slowly,

but did not advance toward her husband.

Grey lingered a moment in the doorway. Ty impatiently called to him from the elevator.

"This doesn't have to be the end of us," Grey said. "Not like this. We're good together—better together. Find me when you're ready."

And then he was gone. Was he pleading for them as a couple, or simply trying to hold onto his cash cow? Had he chosen greed over love? The uncertainty was sickening.

Her greatest fear had come true. He did not love her *enough*. He promised never to leave, but now he had left.

She closed her eyes, for how long, she couldn't have said. When she opened them, she was not alone. Chaitanya wrapped her in strong arms and carried her up, out, and away into the clear blue sky. She was sobbing now, tears falling away into thin air, never to reach the ground. She didn't know if he was returning them to the Thread Continuum. She didn't care. The life she thought she wanted, the life she had fought for, was over.

I have lost yet another family.

A *whoosh* and suddenly they were back on solid ground, in a place Pauline did not recognize. She'd stopped crying, but her chest ached as if her heart was in a vise. They stood on a modern city sidewalk next to a row of stores.

Chaitanya pointed to a modest-looking hardware store. "Your parents are in there."

"My parents?"

"Your real parents. The ones who gave you birth."

She stared at him briefly, waiting for him to say

295

more, or to stop her before she crossed the street on shaky legs and entered the store. Inside was dry and musty and lined with floor-to-ceiling shelves crammed with tools, paint, and all kinds of household supplies. A man and woman in their late fifties, wearing dirty green aprons, were both behind the counter, helping customers. They looked nothing like the parents who appeared in her dream. Yet she saw right away that she had her mother's eyes and her father's dimpled chin. They looked busy, happy, energetic. The Marshes, hard at work, in their element. It was clear they were in charge. This must be their store. She might have grown up here, learning how to work the cash register and stock the shelves. Perhaps she'd never have given any thought to archaeology. Or heard the souls of objects calling through the tunnels of time.

I might have been happy, just like them, given the chance.

"Chris!" her father called. A young man appeared, a bit younger than she. He had a dimpled chin, too. *This must my brother. The child who came along after I disappeared—and was allowed to stay.* She hated him for a brief instant, but this wasn't his fault. Father gave out instructions, and her brother disappeared toward the back of the store.

Pauline approached the counter slowly, as if in a dream. She tried coming up with a question to ask them—to hold their attention, if only for a moment. A daughter conversing with the parents she never knew.

"Can I help you?" Mother's tone was friendly but impersonal.

"Um. I'm looking for a...crowbar."

"Aisle fifteen. All the way in the back. You'll see

all the heavy tools back there."

She lingered. The encounter was over too briefly. "Do you..." she began. "Do I..."

"Yes?" Mother's gaze flickered past her to other customers waiting in line.

"You want me to show you, hon?" Father asked, stepping out from behind the counter. His gaze wandered as well. Others needed his attention. Others, far more important than she.

The truth assailed her like the voice of an impatient artifact. Her parents did not know her. They did not know she existed. Chris was their only child. Dean Nojes couldn't bear to tell her. Or she didn't know. But Chaitanya did. He'd said her parents had been empowered to forget her. She had not wanted to believe him. In some tucked away corner, she'd always held out hope that one day, she would be reunited with her original family.

She burst back out to the sidewalk, fury supplanting self-pity. Chaitanya cut her off before she could lay into him.

"Pauline, you're genetically encoded to be an Elected. Your identity was set in motion the instant you were conceived. In the process of transferring you for incubation in this world, you were taken from your birth parents, who were gifted with forgetting. There is kindness in our method. The looser your attachments here, the easier the transition becomes."

She thought again of the misery and loneliness that Bex, Cheyenne, and Helena endured on Earth, and wondered how the price they all paid could possibly be justified. Chaitanya followed her thoughts.

"You will have your answer once you are fully

docked."

"And what about my attachment to Grey—my husband? How did that figure into your plans?"

Either he did not answer or she could not hear him, for with her next breath, she was once again immersed in the shimmering yellow light of the Thread Continuum.

Chapter 30

Pauline was clothed in the same black unitard as her family in the Thread Continuum. She could not say when her earthly fabrics vanished, just as she could not say exactly why she ever thought she belonged anywhere but here.

Her blue eyes took on the deep, dark cast of her Thread Continuum family as her consciousness expanded and the world, with all its connected eras, became her forever home.

Pauline and Chaitanya breathed as one. Even when apart, they were still together, their consciousness united, their intentions in harmony. They danced together often, their twinned energies igniting a deep exchange of sensual pleasure beyond the power of words to describe, as it far exceeded the boundaries of the five earthly senses.

She could never have imagined such unalloyed joy in her previous life. Love, community, and the gentle but reassuring hum of a chord deep within her were constant reminders that she belonged and would never face abandonment again.

Still, there was more to do before her docking would be complete. Emissaries formed a circle of support, with Pauline at the center. Bex, Helena, and Cheyenne, the friends of her first flowering in the Thread Continuum, radiated silent encouragement.

Pauline flicked her wrist and conjured a flashing golden ball. A swarm of objects materialized in the pulsating light, all of them stolen by Tyrone Lake—with an assist from Greyson Henley, born Greyson Lake. Pauline sought out the rightful heirs of the stolen treasures—the Egyptian earrings, cuneiform tablets, silk purses, onyx bulls, glass beads, and so much else that had been hoarded, hidden, or sold to the highest bidder.

Every artifact had its own life—many lives, in fact, as its function changed from day to night, season to season, generation to generation. Those lives deserved honor and respect across the thresholds of time.

Pauline posed the key questions, seeking to learn who secretly yearned to care for the souls of these objects. Whose flagging spirits needed to be restored? Whose purpose would be bolstered by meaningful possession?

She sent objects flying through space at speeds that exceeded time itself. The Peruvian toymaker clapped with excitement as he took possession of the Incan funeral mask. A graduate student studying philosophy in India cradled the militiaman's sword in her arms. And the Susquehannock face pot, the first object she and Grey had found together, made its way into the hands of a retired auto mechanic in Scranton, Pennsylvania, whose heart skipped a beat when he discovered the treasure sitting on his kitchen table.

These acts of reparation enabled Pauline to atone for past transgressions and restore a measure of balance among the objects of the world. Justice on behalf of the souls of objects unable to rise to their own defense— that was at the heart of her work, all of their work, in the Thread Continuum.

As for justice on Earth, Pauline knew that Bette French and others who valued restitution would see to that.

Another task remained.

Pauline returned to Dean India Nojes's house near the campus of Carthage University, where the dean lay dying in bed. The dean's eyes flickered open when a light breeze swept across her face, heralding Pauline's arrival at her bedside.

"I hoped you would come." The dean's weakened voice bore no trace of her booming alto from the lecture hall. "I wasn't sure."

"I have something for you." Pauline held a jewel-encrusted brooch in the palm of her hand. "Touch it." The dean put a withered hand on the artifact and, as she did so, Pauline enclosed the dean's hand in hers. "What do you see?"

The dean's watery eyes lit up with happiness.

"Ahh. A noblewoman in Ravenna, the brooch pinned to her royal blue gown, as she parades down a wide boulevard with her consort. The crowds cheer them on." The dean smiled and sighed. "Thank you, Pauline. Thank you."

Pauline departed, and the dean closed her eyes one last time.

Her docking was complete, now. Chaitanya's refrain, *you are more,* had been fully realized. The pain of betrayal and abandonment fell away like a distant memory. Her family encircled her again, for the final ceremony marking her transition. A new name, to signal her rebirth.

Pauline chose Ameya, which meant "boundless."

Ameya, Chaitanya called. Her name, in his voice,

bore the warmth of the sun. *It suits you.*

****

Near the end of the twenty-first century, Ameya appeared on Earth before a young woman, aged twenty-four, who was destined since birth to join the Thread Continuum. The young woman was alone and unhappy, feeling friendless and disconnected. Worse, the strange spells that overcame her at regular intervals, the whispered voices, the random knowledge she possessed, had convinced her she was a weirdo and a freak.

Ameya faced her in a crowded hallway in the high school where the young woman taught history and geography to students not much younger than she. The young woman's gaze alighted on Ameya, a black-clad stranger who clearly did not belong there. Confusion, surprise, and fear registered on her face, feelings that Ameya dimly remembered from long, long ago.

Ameya gave the woman a moment to realize that no one else could see this apparition. The visit was for her eyes only. Ameya placed a hand on the young woman's arm.

"You are more," she said.

The young woman's eyes widened in disbelief. She shook her head and walked on by without a word.

Soon enough, she would learn that this was her forever beginning.

A word about the author...

Amy L. Bernstein writes for the page, the stage, and forms in between. Her literary preoccupations include rooting for the underdog and putting ordinary people in difficult situations to see how they wriggle out. Amy is an award-winning journalist and speechwriter as well as a playwright. When she's not writing about romance or dystopian futures, she loves listening to jazz and classical music, drinking wine with friends, and prowling around Baltimore's glorious waterfront neighborhoods.

http://amywrites.live

Author's Note

Archaeology is, to me, an artful science and a scientific art. In a future life, I'd like to return as an intrepid archaeologist. For now, I must content myself with admiring the extraordinary skill, dedication, patience, and courage required to practice the profession. Some of the archaeological finds in the novel are real; some are a mixture of fact and fantasy; and some are completely invented. I mean no disrespect to all the hard-working scientists in the field and the labs. As for nighthawking: it's pure treachery. Don't do it.